ROSEMARY AND THE WITCHES OF PENDLE HILL

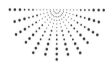

SAMANTHA GILES

AGORA BOOKS

ABOUT THE AUTHOR

Samantha Giles is probably better known as an actress. She played comedy character Bernice Blackstock in Emmerdale for over seven years, leaving late last year to pursue other creative projects. She has also been a regular character in three series of *Where The Heart Is* and *Hollyoaks*, as well as lead guest roles in many other well known TV programmes.

She started writing about three years ago, inspired by a dream she had about the four witch characters that feature in her debut, *Rosemary and the Witches of Pendle Hill*. Other than acting and writing, she also tutors for Act4TV in Liverpool, has her own Facebook Spell page called Samanthas Spells and is a big country music fan.

ROSEMARY AND THE WITCHES OF PENDLE HILL

SAMANTHA GILES

First published in Great Britain in 2020 by Agora Books

Agora Books is a division of Peters Fraser + Dunlop Ltd

55 New Oxford Street, London WC1A 1BS

ISBN 978-1-913099-65-7

For Evelyn and Olivia
who make everything magical

1

MEET THE FAMILY

My mum is a witch. I know this to be a fact, as does my little sister Lois, though Lois just takes everything in her stride as she's only five. If you told her Mum was a member of MI5 she'd just shrug nonchalantly and ask for another digestive biscuit.

The reason I know my mum is a witch is because:

a) She has a broomstick by the front door.

I remember asking her whether she was able to fly it, and she just laughed and ruffled my hair, saying, "What do you think?"

I think I wouldn't have asked her if I knew the answer to that. The truth is I've never seen her fly on it, but I've never seen Edith (my cousin) do a backwards roll, and yet she's got badges in Gymnastics, so I guess anything is possible.

b) She does spells sometimes.

She does the spells in "Dad's office" (the box room next

5

to the garage that Mum wanted to be a downstairs loo), and he gets furious as he's forever having to vacuum up her tiny pieces of glitter or snippets of paper. I don't exactly know what her spells do, but I know they are good spells and lots of people are always asking my mum to help them if they are sad or want to find a new boyfriend. Mum often makes us all go out and collect weird stuff that she needs for them, like oak leaves or elderberries.

c) There are four other witches who sort of "live" with us that me, Mum, and Lois see, but no one else seems to, including my dad.

Ever since I can remember, Mr Foggerty has been coming and going from our house. He is a very tall untidy-looking man with lots of wiry grey hair that is very frizzy. He has huge feet and smells funny, a bit like the chaise longue in Miss Ulwin's office (our headmistress). He doesn't have much time for children and is always in a desperate hurry.

Now I know he "lives" with us because if I ask Mum where Mr Foggerty is, she always says, "He's in his room." Yet we live in a modest three-bedroom house. My room, Lois', and my parents'. There ARE no other bedrooms, so where is he hiding?

I know Dad never sees him. Dad likes to vet all our house guests after Mum put up her friend's friend for one night and he was sick all over the bathroom floor. So, I know Dad would have something to say about Mr Foggerty. Well, he would smell him first.

We have an unspoken rule never to talk about any of our visitors when Dad is around, and funnily enough they never seem to come and go when Dad is here.

Mr Foggerty isn't the only one. We have Frances and Phyllis, the two elderly "Aunts" who always seem to be together, finishing each other's sentences. (They aren't really our aunts, but we refer to them as this.) Frances loves to watch me dance; she tries to copy it, her short pudgy frame swaying and shimmering like a fabulous glitter ball. She is as short and fat as Phyllis is tall and thin. They look like they should be a comedy act on *Britain's Got Talent*, except I'm not sure they have any talent. Phyllis likes to sing. Badly. You can often hear her before you see her, and this always indicates what sort of mood she is in. "One Banana, Two Banana, Three Banana, Four" for a good mood, but beware if you hear "How Much Is That Doggy in the Window?".

Then there is Uncle Vic, a small stout man with crossed eyes so you never quite know where to look. I had to clamp my hands over Lois' mouth when she first saw him as she shouted out, "Rosie, that man's got his eyes the wrong way round."

These are four people who we just accept as part of our "family". We don't really question their comings and goings. It is just normal to us, or it was, until **THINGS STARTED HAPPENING**.

2
MUM AND DAD

Before I tell you about the things that happened, let me give you a bit more of an idea of my life.

As well as our mum being a "witch" she was also an actress, mostly out of work though. Dad used to joke about it and say there was enough drama in his job (he worked behind the scenes in the theatre) without Mum having any too. I think he said this to try and make her feel better when she wasn't working.

Mum gets quite sad about not getting much work. She says that her talent is wasted and she should be in Hollywood doing films. This year Mum has had only a couple of jobs. One was wearing a chicken costume to promote a supermarket's new "Hot 'n' Spicy" chicken nuggets range but the costume got muddled in the factory and she ended up with the head of a parrot. For the other, she had to dress up as Elsa from *Frozen* for a children's party at Jungle Jaunts, a kids' indoor-play area. That one didn't go so well, as they didn't tell Mum that she was supposed to be able to sing. If I tell you she's not quite as good as Phyllis, you'll know how badly that job went. I don't think either of those things have made her feel like an actress. It's a bit like selling lots of chocolate and not being able to eat any yourself.

Mum is always having lots of ideas about how she could get more acting work. But mostly she writes lots of letters to famous directors.

No one has replied.

Yet.

Mum can't really understand it because, years ago, she met an actress at a radio-play recording. This lady was a BIG NAME in the 70s and 80s, and she told Mum that the key to success in "the business" was having a man's name as your first name and surname.

Famous people who have this:
Ray Charles (singer)
Bob Dylan (singer/songwriter/poet)
Terry Scott (actor)
Jamie Lee Curtis (actress)

Mum was very impressed with this piece of advice. She was halfway there with her first name, Rae (spelt Ray for a man), and so she just made up a surname and became Rae Anthony.

It all sounds highly illegal to me, but apparently if you are an actor you can call yourself ANYTHING! Imagine that? Even so, I still don't want to be an actor. Personally, I think that's WHY Mum doesn't get much work, people don't know if a man or a woman's going to turn up. I prefer it when Mum is known as her family name, i.e., the same surname as us, Rae Pellow.

Dad doesn't seem to be that happy with what he is doing either. I think he might be a bit sad, and he can be quite grumpy, too. He's always moaning about the awful train journey to work and how his "to do" list keeps getting longer.

I notice when Dad's sad and when he's happy. When he's happy, he laughs and jokes and really looks at us when he talks to us. He has this greeny-blue light that sparkles and fizzes all around him. When he's sad, he has this grey mist that circles his entire body and finishes with a little tiny cloud above his head. Sometimes I even see rain coming down from the cloud, but the funny thing is his hair never seems to get wet. His eyes look dark and tired, and he sort of seems to walk slower. He bats Mum away when she tries to cuddle him, and then her purply colour around her seems to dull and shrink.

I've always been able to see colours around people. I thought everyone could until I asked Lois what colours she saw around me and she wrinkled up her face and said, "If I say pink can I have a biscuit?" I haven't ever told anyone, even though I think my mum would understand. I'm scared if I tell her then it might go away.

Sometimes when Dad is sad I press our Scottish Bagpipe fridge magnet to try to cheer him up. (In our house, when anyone presses the Scottish bagpipe magnet it plays a tune, and whatever you are doing you have to stop, get up, and all do Scottish dancing in the kitchen.)

Dad doesn't really join in properly, even when me and Mum and Lois are all shouting, "Come on, Daddy, watch us."

All he says is, "That looks more like Irish dancing."

"Come on, John, join in, it's the rules," Mum says.

"Hasn't that bloody battery worn out yet?" Dad replies. "We've had the damn thing for three years."

But it never seems to. I think it's magic.

Lois doesn't really notice any of this. She is only a baby,

even though we all have to pretend she's a big girl and placate her by telling her that it's okay she's not the baby of the family, Maggie and Bob are (they are four and a half years old).

In case you're wondering, Bob and Maggie are our cats. Mum calls Bob her "familiar", which is what witches have as a kind of helper. This cannot be right. Bob has never helped anyone do anything. In fact, he does the opposite. He's very lazy, likes being cuddled A LOT, and quite often wees on the floor. He's epileptic, so he does have a medical reason for this. Try telling yourself that though when you accidentally walk through a wee patch. Boy, cat wee really stinks!

Lois may be oblivious to what goes on, but I notice everything.

3
ME

Can you see I have quite a lot to contend with at home? A crazy Mum who's desperate to work, a Dad who often has a raincloud above his head, a house full of bonkers witches and wizards who come and go like it's normal, and an annoying little sister who should go in the *Guinness Book of Records* for her wind.

I love school. It's my solace really. Don't get me wrong, I do love being at home too, but since Dad started his new job we see so much less of him. He doesn't get home till about 8 o'clock, when Lois is usually asleep and I'm upstairs reading.

He looks all stressed and we have a quick chat, but that's it until the weekend. Sometimes I wonder how different it would have been if my parents hadn't had me and Lois. Then they wouldn't always be so worried about working and earning money and all that.

Maybe I could find a way of earning some money, too. I think about what I'm good at and suddenly a plan forms in my head.

So, I write to the BBC.

Rosemary Pellow
21 Arkansas Road
Liverpool
L15 7LY

September 14th, 2020

Dear Sir or Madam,

I love watching Dancing Divas! I think it would be great to have a version with kids in it. I am working on my Grade 2 ballet and my Grade 3 modern at the moment, so I think I could be one of your contestants. My mum says I'm pretty, so I would look okay in the costumes.

Also, it would be a way of earning some money for my family. I don't need to earn loads, but a few pounds would be good.

I'm good at making dances up too, although I can't yet do the splits even though I do practise a lot. You see, it hurts a bit.

Thank you for reading my letter and please reply.

Yours sincerely,
    Rosemary Pellow, aged 9

I decide to have a rootle through my mum's spell boxes to see if I can find any spells that might get us more money. I do think about speaking to Phyllis or Frances about spells but decide Mum might be cross if I tell them our business.

It's quite interesting what I find in Mum's boxes:

Some dried lavender
Two dead spiders (Yuk!)
Dried mistletoe
Dried comfrey
Dried elderberries (they stink)
Different coloured candles
Silk bags in a variety of vibrant colours
Acorns
Some old chewing gum
Lots of pretty-coloured crystals
A paper star with Mum's handwriting on it.

I'd only got through one box when I came across the star. It was quite big, I suppose the size of a grownup's hand, and it was green. There was a big circle in the middle with the words "Wish List" and coming off of the circle like little spikes were lines attached to other words: *security, self-esteem, confidence, independence, freedom.*

It was the last two words that frightened me. I wasn't sure what "self-esteem" meant, but I knew what "independence" and "freedom" meant. It sounded like she was wishing to be on her own, free from all of us. How could this be?

I kept very still for a few moments trying to take in what I had found, trying not to panic or breathe too quickly in my anxiety. I felt scared, and I felt angry that I had snooped.

It's true what they say, that if you are looking for things you won't necessarily like what you find. Was our mum so unhappy that she wanted to be free to be on her own without me Lois and Dad? I scanned over the last few months quickly in my head. She was fed up with not working, yes, and she seemed exasperated with Dad. But she was always fine with me and Lois. She'd pick us up from school full of smiles. Sometimes we'd walk home and have a laugh as we went past the "bottom tree". We'd stick our bums out to match the funny shape of the tree and she'd take a photo. She helped me with my homework and listened to me when I read to her at night. She didn't seem to be preoccupied with wishing she had another life.

Then I thought back to Sarah Jane, one of the girls in my class. Her mum always collected her from school most days and never looked sad or unhappy with her life. Then, last Christmas, she got rushed to hospital. She hadn't broken any bones or anything, so none of us were really sure what had happened.

I remember at school we all made a card for Sarah Jane with sunshines and rainbows on and it said, *We hope your mum gets well soon.*

Mr Bobbin, the religious studies teacher, patiently explained to us that sometimes people get poorly not on the outside, but on the inside, so you can't always see their illness. Thankfully, her mum did get better in a way. She came out of hospital and still collects Sarah Jane and her little sister, Sasha, but she looks very thin and fragile, as if she might break if she's not careful. She also has this little black dog which seems to follow her around. It waits for her outside the school gates, but it's not always there, so perhaps sometimes they leave it at home. All these thoughts are whirling round my head. Does my mum want out? *Okay, I can handle stuff,* I thought, taking a deep breath and trying to ignore the pain in my tummy. But what about Lois? She's like Mum's shadow, always wanting huggles and kisses, and if Mum ever goes away for a night to see her sister in London, Lois is inconsolable. She does the "I'm being such a brave girl" act with Dad, but with me she's mega needy, and I can't cope with the responsibility of having to look after her. I do love her, she's my little sister, but she can be a royal pain in the bum sometimes.

No, I'm sure Mum wouldn't want to run away and leave us all. I felt loved by my mum, she was a warm cuddly Mum who always had time to talk to us. I decided I had to keep a very close eye on her from now on to see if I could spot any strange signs that perhaps I had missed before.

I quickly replaced all the things in the box, gingerly kicking the dead spiders to the corner of the room with my shoe.

4

A SHOCK DISCOVERY

Whilst we were having our tea that night, I watched Mum with an eagle eye.

She was humming whilst spooning rice pudding into a bowl for Lois.

She certainly looked okay.

I decided to strike out. "Mum, do you like living here?" I asked boldly.

Mum looked a bit surprised. "That's a funny question, Rosemary. Of course I do, it's my home."

I ploughed on. "Would you rather live somewhere else, say, if you could?"

"No," Mum said frowning slightly. "What are you getting at, darling?"

"Nothing. Just wondered if you could choose somewhere else to live where you'd go?"

"Well, I choose to live here, which is all pretty good right now as, believe it or not, I've got an audition tomorrow at twelve noon. So you girls try to think of me then whilst you're having your lunch and think some happy good luck thoughts to me."

My heart sort of sank, and I felt a little rock in my tummy — of dread, I think it was.

"What's the job for then, Mum?"

"Well, it's a play, a wonderful play called *Who's Afraid of Virginia Woolf?*, and I'm going up for the role of Martha. It's a fabulous part."

"I'll help you with the script after tea if you like, Mum," I say, desperate to spend some time with her to try to find out what's going on.

"Alright, darling, thank you. I've got a little spell to put together first, so you can be my special helper with that once we've put Lois to bed."

"I want to be a special helper, too," whined Lois with rice pudding dripping from her chin.

"You can get the coloured bags out, okay?" Mum said briskly whilst she gathered up our dirty plates.

Later that evening, once Lois was in bed (she had forgotten all about the coloured bags, thankfully), Mum and I sat in at the kitchen table with all her boxes.

"Now put some comfrey in this little bag, Rosie, and some mistletoe in this one."

"What do they do then?"

"Well, the comfrey is to attract money and the mistletoe helps to purify and breaks hexes."

"What's a hex?"

"It's a bad thought that someone has put out there on to someone else. I'm not sure I really believe in hexes, but Frances and Phyllis do, and so I'm bowing to their superior, if somewhat old fashioned, knowledge."

It was somehow quite therapeutic opening little clear bags with the dried herbs in and sprinkling a few fingerfuls into the tiny brightly coloured organza bags that Mum gave me. Then I had the job of assembling all the ingredients and putting them carefully into bigger bags with candles and unusual stones, and finally I was allowed to cut the ribbon for Mum to tie around the spell scroll, which was the instructions. They were written in all fancy handwriting with swirls and loops and looked so important and precious.

Suddenly, my concentration was broken by a frantic banging on our front door.

Mum rushed out of the kitchen to the hallway and, just as we got to the door, Uncle Vic burst in almost carrying Frances, who was wailing uncontrollably.

"What are we going to do Vic? I can't bear it. Where do we start looking?" Her already chubby face had ballooned and looked red and blotchy. She had snot running down her nose. Uncle Vic looked embarrassed, worried, and slightly annoyed. Actually, it was difficult to tell, as when your eyes are looking in different directions you constantly look confused. I think it was safe to say he was worried, as he kept patting her pudgy arm in a comforting sort of way.

"Now, now, Frances, let's not overreact. Let's get you lying down with a chamomile tea. Rae, have you any valerian root? I might need to add a thimbleful of that too in this instance."

Mum was about to dash off when a little voice from the top of the stairs floated down.

"Is that the internet shopping?"

At least, I think that's what she said. It's difficult to tell when Lois has her dummy in. She could have been asking for the time in Hong Kong for we all we knew.

"No, darling, get back to bed, please. It's PE tomorrow, so you need your sleep," Mum placated whilst grabbing the chair in the hall for Frances.

Frances sank into it like a brick being thrown into the ocean and pulled a large mauve handkerchief out from her handbag and blew her nose noisily. In fact, it was so loud I thought a ship had come into port. I had to stifle a giggle as Frances' skirt had risen up, showing two flesh-coloured pop socks, one of which was halfway down her calf making her look extremely comical.

"Rosie, go and get Frances a glass of water please, darling." Mum motioned to me as she took Uncle Vic to one side.

I went back into the kitchen and hurriedly got a glass down from the cupboard to fill with tap water. I came back into the hall just as the tail end of Mum and Uncle Vic were disappearing through the wall.

I nearly dropped the glass.

Was I seeing things?

I looked at Frances to see if she was looking aghast like me, but no, she was still sniffling and rummaging about up her nose with her handkerchief.

"Thank you, Rosie, my love," she stuttered, her soft Scottish accent sounding at odds with her obvious distress. "Could you pass me my handbag down there so I can check my face?"

It was all I could do to stop my mouth opening and closing like a goldfish. I located her glittery silver handbag down by her chubby ankles and passed it to her.

"I think I'll just pop up and use your lavvy if that's alright, dear. I fear my face might need a little wash."

"Are you alright, Frances?" I managed to whisper.

"Oh yes, just a little bit of bad news, that's all my dear, but your Uncle Vic and Mr Foggerty will take care of everything. There's nothing to worry about, nothing at all to worry about."

She wore her soothing expression like a mask, and I could see underneath she was not convinced at all. I couldn't wait for her to lumber up the stairs, so I could investigate the wall.

I nonchalantly leaned against it, watching Frances huff and puff up our stairs. It felt pretty firm. No squidgy bits, no cracks that I could see. I felt it over with my hands to see if I had missed a secret doorway or handle or anything. But how could there be? The radiator was right in front of it, so even if there was a secret doorway how on earth would you be able to open it?

I ran into our sitting room, which is where you would find yourself if you had walked through the wall. I really expected to see Mum and Uncle Vic sitting on the settee deep in conversation, but there was nothing. Just a very sleepy Maggie showing her fat, fluffy tummy. She meowed at me languidly and rolled to her other side.

"Did you see Mum and Uncle Vic, Mags?" I asked her.

She meowed again and how I wished I understood cat language. Mind you, knowing Mags, she was probably saying *bog off and leave me alone*.

Mum had disappeared, leaving me and Lois home alone with two cats and a dappy old lady who hadn't seemed to notice a thing. Was I scared? Yes, a little bit.

All my life I had accepted our extended family's comings and goings, never questioning where they suddenly appeared from on those occasions when they didn't use the front door. I was used to my mum's herbal remedies and charms that she made, but this was something way out of my comfort zone.

Uncle Vic had gone through the wall. With my mum. It was like having a really weird dream that you can't wake yourself up from.

Clearly, I was not going to be able to push myself through the hall wall. It wasn't even worth trying.

Just at that moment, my thoughts were interrupted by the sound of a key in the lock and in walked my dad.

"Dad?" I exclaimed. I must have sounded deranged but was trying to disguise the panic in my voice. "You're early..."

"Not really, Rosemary, it's twenty to eight. You should be in bed by now. Where's Mum?"

He hung his coat at the bottom of the stairs and saw me glance nervously upstairs. He might not be able to see Frances, but what if he heard her? Suddenly my face fell. There, hovering above his head looking grey and threatening, was his cloud. It was back.

He started to go up the stairs.

"She's upstairs, is she? That's where you motioned to when I just asked you."

"No, no, no," I interjected and pushed past him. "I mean, yes, she might be."

"Steady on, there's no rush. Anyway, I need a wee first."

I made it to the bathroom just before him and thanked God we didn't have a lock on our door. So, though it was shut, I knew I could sneak in.

"Sorry, Dad, desperate. Won't be a mo," I said as I pushed the door open a crack and slid my slim body around it.

The bathroom was empty. She had gone.

"Hellooooo. John, are you up there?"

I heard the slightly breathless voice of my mother coming from the bottom of the stairs. Then her footsteps on the stair carpet. Relief flooded me. At least I wouldn't have to explain Mum's absence.

"Rosie, it's bedtime now, darling." She looked exactly the same, no bruises evident, no dishevelled clothing, just two tiny pink dots in the middle of her cheeks giving her an air of being a bit flushed, like she'd been rushing.

I eyed her suspiciously as she strolled out of their bedroom after having given my dad a quick peck on the cheek.

"Go on into bed, Rosemary. I'll come back up and say goodnight once I've got our dinner on. Quick now, please, it's getting late."

"Where have you been, Mum?" I asked her quietly.

"I've finally found that play on our bookshelf so I can swot up ready for my audition tomorrow. Darling, it's too late for you to help me with the lines now." She hadn't answered my question.

Then I saw it. A five-pointed star attached to the heel of her shoe as if by static. As she descended down the staircase, a gust of warm air seemed to rise up from the hall, twirl itself around my mother and swoop down again towards the front door, taking with it the silver and black star, which fluttered precariously.

I could see the thin material it was made from as it plunged forth; its finale was a steep dive downwards, and then the star disintegrated into glitter that scattered every which way across the hall-floor tiles. It was like a rocket torpedoing to earth and smashing into tiny particles when it hit the ground.

Whatever it had been, it had gone.

It was time to tell Adi.

5

ADI THE MATHS GENIUS

The next morning at breakfast, you could be forgiven for thinking everything seemed much as it always had been. Dad showered, hugged us all, and left. His raincloud though was still very much in evidence, and I wondered what I could do to help. Phyllis, who always had a solution to every problem, hadn't yet appeared, which was strange. She was often around when the others weren't, as, unlike them, she never seemed to leave the house. Well, never by the front door anyway. Mum was surrounded by bright purple with little sparks flying off at all angles, so I could tell she was excited.

Then I remembered: The Audition. We had just gone out the front door and were trying to get into the car when out came Frances, Uncle Vic, and Mr Foggerty — all together, which was most unusual. Mr Foggerty looked his normal, untidy self, though I noticed his shoes looked clean and he was wearing the addition of a yellow-spotted tie. Mmm, perhaps he was going somewhere important?

Frances looked brighter today and was wearing her best bottle-green velvet dress. It made her look like a bauble from a Christmas tree. I did feel a bit sorry for her though after yesterday. Uncle Vic had his suit on. I was worried that his crossed eyes made it difficult for him to see, as it now had a scattering of stains on it. It looked like egg yolk on his jacket lapel, chocolate on the neck of his shirt, and dried custard on his knees.

I was so busy staring at Uncle Vic's stains that I didn't realise Frances was speaking to me.

"Thank you, Rosie, for all your help yesterday. You are a little treasure." I went to open my mouth to ask her where she had disappeared to so suddenly last night, when I remembered I still hadn't seen Phyllis. As I watched them walk briskly up the road, I was struck again by the fact that none of them had colours around them. I looked at Mum's white sparks shooting out from the purple surrounding her. I saw Lois with orange and yellow pulsating gently all around her. I remembered how Adi's changed from electric blue to bright white when he got a maths problem right or the teacher praised him. (I couldn't see my own.) Our houseguests lack of colour had been something I had never really questioned, yet in the light of yesterday's strange goings-on, I realised how different from us they really were.

"Come on, Rosemary, get in the car. We're going to be late," Mum called.

"Mum, where's Phyllis?" I asked, still puzzled as to why she hadn't appeared this morning.

Silence.

"Mum, where's Phyllis?"

"Yes, I did hear you darling, I'm just concentrating on driving."

The tell-tale sign of brown smoke radiating from Mum's lips told me that this was a lie. Mum never concentrated on driving. She would chat pretty much constantly, looking at us in the rear-view mirror and then suddenly break or swerve to avoid cars or animals or pavements.

"She's gone on her holidays for a while." More brown smoke.

"On her own, Mum? I've never seen her go anywhere."

"Mmmm, well sometimes people do need time alone... Don't worry, she'll be back. They'll find her — erm, I mean, they'll pick her up from the station when she returns. Now who's going to wish me luck for my audition today?"

"Me, me, me!" Lois shouted excitedly.

Bless her, she probably didn't even know what an audition was.

"Can I come with you to your medition, Mum, please?" Lois pleaded.

"It's 'audition', Lois, you dufus, not 'medition', and you're at school."

"I don't want to go to school. I want a weekend," she replied sulkily.

"That's enough please, both of you. Firstly, Lois, no you can't come. Mummy has to do this on her own. It's like a chat where they decide whether or not to give you a job. And secondly, Rosie, stop winding her up."

"I don't want you to get a job," Lois mumbled.

First sensible thing she's said all year, I thought.

"If — and it's a big IF — I were to get this job, my love, you would still see Mummy every day. I don't have to go away, and I'd still be able to take you to school. And once the show is up and running, I'd be able to pick you up, too."

"Who would pick us up when you weren't able to then?" I questioned nervously.

"Well, Frances or Uncle Vic, I suppose."

My heart sank. I know it sounds horrible, but I so did not want either of them to collect us from school. Usually it was only "believers" (in magic) who could see them, Frances once told me. But occasionally, they had to allow themselves to be visible to grown-ups in order to collect us from school, for example. How embarrassing would it be to have a cross-eyed, chubby man with a dirty-looking suit pick us up? People would think we had fleas or lived in a home for down and outs, and it would be just as bad if Frances came, especially if it was one of those days when she was wearing a short skirt that didn't meet her knee-high pop socks. I'd much rather Dad collect us, but he worked long hours and always left the arrangements to Mum. He always got home after her, so we were never faced with having to explain what we were doing "home alone".

We got into the school playground and Mum hung around until the bell went, so I didn't really have a chance to corner my friend Adi and warn him that we needed a "big chat".

"Hi, Rosemary," he greeted me in that deadpan way of his.

He was the only one of my friends who called me by my full name. Everyone else called me Rosie. We were an unlikely friendship in many ways, as Adi didn't like dancing or dressing up or playing dolls or creating new worlds on the computer. He was simply a maths genius and a *Star Wars* fanatic. If the teacher had a question about maths, Adi was always the first to put his hand up. He could calculate complicated sums in his head without writing them down or doing column addition or long division. He's the maths equivalent of what JoJo Siwa is to girls' hair accessories.

Adi was smaller than me, which I guess wasn't that unusual as I am very tall for my age. He had lovely brown skin the colour of milk chocolate and unruly black hair. He wore large black-rimmed glasses that made him look a bit like an owl, and he was always having to push them up on his nose as they slipped down all the time.

Adi was a bit quirky in lots of ways. If he was asked by Miss to do something he didn't want to, or if Miss told him off, he would put his hands over his ears and screw up his face whilst making a grunting noise rather like this: "uhhhh-hhhhhhhh".

At first, we were all a bit concerned that we might have another Spencer in our class, who was what the teachers might call "disruptive". He would flip out for no reason and lose his temper over the slightest thing. He bit Miss Ulwin, our headmistress, on the arm. At least, I think he said arm. She hasn't got much flesh on her, so I bet that really hurt.

But all Adi did was his hands-on ears trick. Apart from that he was very earnest and actually very kind. I was put next to him for Maths and I thought it was going to be really annoying sitting next to a boy and not next to my friends Mae and Gloria, but Adi helped explain how to do fractions, which I was really struggling to understand.

Adi always seemed to be solving some sort of puzzle or another. He also told me that on September 31st, 2025, all Maths geniuses would be called up to test drive a new rocket to the moon. Mum said Adi had been watching too many episodes of *Star Trek*. I was going to correct her, as it's *Star Wars* he likes not *Star Trek*, but I thought she wouldn't know the difference. Adi would be furious, so I've never mentioned it to him. He always says to me, "Rosemary, may the force be with you," and then waits for me to reply with an expectant look on his face.

I don't like to tell him I haven't a clue what he means.

It's lunch when I get any time alone with him. Unlike me, Adi had hot dinners, so the whole time I ate my sandwiches in the packed-lunch area of the hall, I kept a firm eye on how quickly Adi was eating his dinner. It looked like he had a meat pie with mash and veg. Yes, he was alone. Yes, he was eating a bit faster now I'd caught his eye and glared at him. I zipped up my lunchbox and took my biscuits with me to have outside on the bench furthest from the classrooms. I'd only been sitting as long as it took to eat three mini Maryland's when Adi joined me.

"What's the big news then, Rosemary?" he asked whilst scuffing his shoes back and forth on the playground.

"Adi," I whispered, "you have to promise not to tell anyone what I'm about to tell you."

"Yeah, yeah, okay, just tell me." Adi got a bit more intrigued. I could feel it.

I don't know why I felt that I had to tell him, but I just had a feeling he would understand and not judge me.

I took a deep breath and blurted it out.

"My mum is a witch and we have other witches and wizards living with us, only we don't know where in the house they go as we never see their rooms or anything, and last night I saw Mum disappear through the wall with one of them. When I questioned her about it, she avoided answering me. But I saw her. I definitely saw her go through the wall."

"Whoa, whoa, slow down, Rosemary. Your mum went through the wall?"

"Yes, but listen, Adi. Phyllis, one of the Aunts, has disappeared and everyone seems to be pretending she's just gone on her holidays, but I know something bad has happened to her. I can just feel it."

Adi stared at me, his face unreadable.

"Mum's not a witch like they are — I mean she can't disappear or make herself invisible. She's more of a modern-day witch. She calls herself a 'wiccan', I think. She just does spells for people using herbs and things. Only good spells. She's not a bad witch. None of them are."

"Yes, I've heard of wiccans. Interestingly, not all of them call themselves witches, but those that do believe in using the power of nature to create 'spells'. And as for doing bad spells, well they would only come back on you times three," Adi muttered wisely.

I nodded. I was impressed he knew all this.

"Right, okay." Adi tilted his head upwards and his eyes went from left to right, then he screwed them tightly shut. "Anything else I need to know?"

I pondered momentarily whether to tell him about Dad's cloud reappearing last night, which seemed to coincide with Phyllis' disappearance, and all the colours I could see around people, but decided some things were better kept secret.

"My dad doesn't see them. Well, no one can really see them unless they choose to show themselves, or unless you are a believer."

Adi looked incredulous. "A believer in what?"

"In magic," I replied, as if it should be obvious.

"But how can they live with you and your dad not know?"

"They are never there when Dad's home. They just come and go, and it's just always been like that. The other night Frances was up in the bathroom when Dad got home and when I dashed upstairs to warn her, she had gone, so I know she probably just made herself invisible. I've never really questioned any of it until now." I paused. "So you don't think it's bad then, my mum being a witch?" I added in a small voice.

"No," Adi turned toward me. My face must have looked dismayed. "No, it's COOL, Rosemary. But what does worry me," he continued, "is your mum disappearing through the wall and your aunt missing. I'm guessing this isn't the first time your mum's gone through the wall, so something serious must be going on to make her take the risk of being seen by you and your sister. It can only mean one thing."

I looked at him with my mouth ajar, waiting for the worst to come.

"What?" I prodded him.

"Whatever is on the other side of the wall must be to do with where Phyllis and the other witches go to when they're not at your house. Maybe it's their headquarters? Whatever it is might give us some clues as to where your aunt has disappeared to."

"What are we going to do, Adi?"

Adi looked out ahead of him at all the boys and girls shouting and playing and skipping and chasing each other in the playground. Spencer was swinging his jumper around his head like a lasso and hitting unsuspecting girls with it randomly. They were dropping like dominoes and running off crying to the dinner lady.

Finally, after what seemed an age, he spoke. "We go through the wall, too."

6

OUR PLAN

Adi had said he would have a think about how to get through the wall and get back to me. I figured it would be difficult for him to come up with a plan unless he had actually examined our wall to see if I had missed something. So I suggested to him that he call round to our house later that evening on the pretext of dropping off some Maths homework or something.

My mind was so full of questions like, *How will we get through the wall?* and *What will we find on the other side?* that I realised I'd forgotten to ask Mum how her audition had gone when she met us from school. I needn't have worried, she was on it.

"How was school, Rosie?" And before she could pause for breath for me to answer, she said, "I've got some very good news! I've got a job! I actually got the job today, isn't that great?"

"Wow that's amazing, Mum," I said with as much enthusiasm as I could muster up.

To be truthful, I was afraid of her doing this job. It had been so long since our mum had had a "proper" job, if you like, whereby she had to go to work EVERY DAY for ALL DAY, that I was just worried about what it would mean for us. I wasn't sure I was happy about the possibility of us all being neglected.

Lois' approach was much more no-nonsense, and I wish I could have had the same simplistic reaction. "Does that mean we can have a McDonalds for dinner, Mum?"

"It most certainly does, my little crazy girl. You can both have a Maccy D tonight as a celebration of my good fortune."

"When does the job start, Mum?" I asked tentatively.

"On Monday, my love, but it's only a few weeks of disruption and then before you know it the job will be over and we'll be back to normal. And listen to this," Mum continued excitedly, "the part I'm playing is called Martha!"

"Martha as in a big fluffy sheep?" Lois questioned, screwing up her face in disgust. It's a family joke that when we think of the name Martha, it conjures up the image of a big fluffy sheep.

Mum laughed. "That's right, Lois, but she's not really a sheep. Are you pleased for me, girls?"

I paused and looked at my mum's lovely face, her auburn hair curling softly around her face, her big blue eyes gazing at me imploringly, willing me to share the absolute joy that someone had thought Rae Anthony was good enough to be given a proper acting job.

"I'm over the moon, Mum, it's brilliant. And I know you'll be brilliant, won't she, Lois?"

"Yeah. Can I have chicken nuggets instead of a burger this time, please?" As we walked to the car a little thought popped into my head. If Mum was going to be working and therefore busy and out of the house a lot more, it would be easier for me and Adi to find a way to get through the wall!

We were eating our McDonald's at the kitchen table when the doorbell rang, and I rushed up to see if it was Adi. Before I had even left my chair, Mum motioned me to stay seated.

"I'll get it, young lady. You're eating your dinner."

Lois was engrossed in *Scooby Doo* on the TV whilst dunking her chicken nuggets into the barmeque (as she called it) sauce, so I snuck out of my seat and held myself like a ninja behind the door, holding my breath so I could listen to what was going on at the front door.

I tried to peek my head round the frame, so I could see who she was talking to, but she was holding the door only slightly open, and I couldn't see a thing. I could tell she was talking to a stranger as she had her posh voice on. I managed to hear the following snippets of conversation:

Mum: "...authorised...identification pentagrams..."

Stranger: "Phyllis... BIWIT... BUTBUM aw..."

Mum: "BUTBUM!"

Stranger: "AW"

Mum: "children...away...temporary, Pendle?"

Stranger: "No-Laws...disruption, Phyllis...hiding"

With that, I had to do my swiftest ninja moves back to my table, as I just about managed to see Mum opening the door wider to let in THE STRANGER. All I managed to catch was the fact that they seemed to be wearing a pure-white trouser suit with a white Indiana Jones-style hat that covered their eyes and half their face. I really didn't have any more time to look, as I was terrified Mum would catch me ear wigging, and to be honest I was a bit scared of THE STRANGER.

I'd just popped the last of my burger into my mouth when Mum re-entered the kitchen ALONE. I tried to act all nonchalant.

"Was that Adi?"

"No, Rosemary, it wasn't. Have you finished, Lois?"

I was about to ask who it was, or even admit to my mum that I'd seen her usher in THE STRANGER, when the phone rang. It was Dad. As Mum was telling him her job news, I made the decision not to ask any more about THE STRANGER. I knew they had come into the house. I knew that, as they didn't come into the kitchen, there was only one other place they'd gone: through the wall.

I knew Mum wasn't going to tell me anything. It felt weird, her lying to me. I didn't like it, but I guess she was trying to protect us, and I understood that, but I knew I was old enough to find out the truth myself.

I went over the snippets of conversation that I had heard. I knew a pentagram was the star which symbolised Witchcraft, like the star that had been attached to Mum's heel and disintegrated. What was BIWIT and BUTBUM and AW? What did Pendle have to do with it? I knew Pendle Hill was a place in Lancashire. And who were the No-Laws? I had to write these things down and quick before I forgot them.

Mum hung up the phone, and I could see her eyes were all watery. "Mum, what's wrong?" This time she didn't lie, and her voice was flat and sad.

"It's just your dad, Rosemary. He didn't seem very excited for me about this job. He knows how much I need to work, and he was too busy going to his next meeting to really show any real interest."

I put my arms around my mum and tried to comfort her as much as I could. "Don't cry, Mum, I'm sure Dad is happy for you. I expect he'll talk to you properly tonight. Please don't be sad."

Mum hugged me back and kissed the top of my head.

"Don't take any notice of silly old me, darling, I'm just a bit over emotional. It's been a big day. Finish your dinner, I'm going to run a bath for you both."

As Mum went upstairs dabbing her eyes with her hanky, I took myself into the hall and tried not to think about my dad making my mum sad. It seemed a regular occurrence lately.

I needed to get his cloud to go and give him back his greeny-blue colour that surrounded him when he was happy. Was it a coincidence that Frances and Uncle Vic had turned up distressed (clearly by Phyllis' disappearance) at the same time Dad's cloud returned? Perhaps if Phyllis came back Dad's cloud would disappear?

For now though, I continued to search the floor and wall for clues. As I was on my hands and knees I felt a shadow at the front door. It was Adi, finally!

I opened the door before he could press the bell. I really didn't want Mum coming downstairs and preventing him from helping me examine the wall.

"Come in, Adi," I whispered. "Mum's upstairs running a bath for me and Lois. This is the wall they disappeared through. You'll have to look quickly before Mum comes downstairs or Lois comes out and we give the game away."

Adi's eyes looked huge in his oversized glasses and he glanced up the stairs. "Right, we are going to try to find out the entrance to this 'other place'. In other words, the portal."

He very carefully brought out an ordinary looking stone from his pocket. In fact, it might have been one from our driveway. It was small and brown and pebble looking.

"Adi," I said patiently, for I was really not able to see how a stone was going to help. "I think you might need something a bit more technical than a stone, and also what on earth is a portal when it's at home?"

"A portal is a door which leads you into another world or dimension," he replied, looking at me as if I was thick. "Just watch, Rosemary."

Adi took his pebble and walked up and down the hallway, holding it in the air and dropping it occasionally. I followed him earnestly. Honestly, we must have looked daft. He took the chair by the sideboard and stood on it and held his stone higher and did the same dropping thing up and down the hall.

"Adi," I sighed, "nothing is happening, and we need to hurry."

"Just hang on one more minute."

I watched him as he held the pebble about a centimetre away from the mirror. Nothing. He moved the pebble around the base of the mirror and once again let it go.

Well, if I tell you the most amazing thing happened, would you believe me?

The pebble didn't drop. It floated. Yes, it floated in mid-air around the base of the mirror.

"That, Rosemary, is the portal." Adi looked at me with a grin. "Gravity is very weak in that area, hence the pebble floating. Gravity is strong everywhere else where the pebble drops. A rapid change in gravity always indicates that another dimension exists."

"Is that Adi I can hear?" my mum called from upstairs. It made us jump, and the pebble dropped.

Then Lois appeared peering round the kitchen door, covered in food, as usual, all down her T-shirt. "Hi, Adi, what was that noise? What's that in your hand? Can I play with it?"

Ding dong.

"It's Frances. Adi, go in the kitchen quick."

"Rosemary," Adi whispered, "I can see her through the

glass."

Of course! Adi was a believer, which meant he could see our houseguests. As I opened the front door, Mum came rushing down the stairs.

"Hello, Rosie. Did I see a nice, young man through the glass just a minute ago?" Frances asked.

"Yes," Mum agreed, "where's Adi gone, Rosie? Don't you think you should offer him a drink instead of loitering in the hallway throwing balls or whatever you were making all that noise with on the floor tiles?"

I didn't contradict her, even though I was slightly annoyed that we'd been interrupted.

"Come through, Frances," Mum said as she ushered her into the kitchen where Adi was trying his best to under-stand Lois' attempt to explain why Scooby Doo on the TV had been violently sick. "Now who on earth is that?" Mum exclaimed as the doorbell rang AGAIN. "Rosemary, please just get that will you."

I rushed into the hallway and opened the door to Mr Foggerty and Uncle Vic both looking extremely solemn.

Uncle Vic attempted a smile, though it did look more like a grimace. "Now, young lady, is your mother in the kitchen?"

"Yes, come through, Vic," called Mum.

I led the way into our kitchen, which was getting more crowded by the minute. I looked to Adi to try to introduce him to everyone, but he was fiddling with something on our fridge. His long, slender fingers reached out to press a button on a certain fridge magnet.

"Noooooooooooo, don't press it, Adi!" I shouted. But it was too late.

Out chimed the sound of the Scottish bagpipes and there was no time to be embarrassed. Mum, Lois, Mr

Foggerty, Uncle Vic, Frances, and I lifted our skirts and trousers and started Scottish dancing with vigour. There were no discussions, no sighs, and no attempts to avoid the unavoidable. It was what we HAD to do. Poor Adi stared in shock and disbelief; but, to be fair to him, after a few seconds he did try to join in. (Badly.)

At last it was over, and everyone just carried on with their business. I was about to usher Adi out and suggest that he returned when things were a bit quieter, when all of a sudden Mum dropped the teaspoon and took a deep intake of breath.

"Oh no, the bloody bath!" she said and rushed out of the kitchen.

No one except me took a blind bit of notice of her. Frances was deep in conversation with Uncle Vic whilst simultaneously fishing tea bags out of steaming mugs. She managed to drop every single tea bag on to Uncle Vic's shoes, which she would slowly retrieve one by one.

I was vaguely aware of Lois droning on in the background for some rice pudding, but no one appeared to be taking any notice of her, either.

Mr Foggerty took out his yellow handkerchief from his suit pocket and absentmindedly dabbed the bald patch on top of his head.

"Is it raining, dear?" Frances questioned, looking up to the ceiling.

Uh oh, I thought. There was a hastening of droplets from the ceiling, then my mum's voice shrieked from above. "I need help up here, Rosemary. There's water EVERYWHERE!"

The bath had overflowed again. Our poor kitchen ceiling. Would it really take another battering? How long before the entire ceiling collapsed? The drip, drip, drips were pretty steady. Uncle Vic had taken a saucepan from the cupboard and placed it strategically on the floor to catch the water. Frances was struggling with the tin opener for Lois' rice pudding. Adi sidled towards the hallway.

"I'd better go, Rosemary," he said. "See you tomorrow."

I gave him a look that I hoped conveyed my frustration with the situation. "I'd better go and help my mum," I said. "She'll need towels, and lots of them."

The bathroom floor was soaked and Mum was emptying bath water down the plughole whilst trying to mop up great puddles from the floor.

"Dad will go mad," I said peeling off my already sodden socks and trying to ignore the sound of Lois' wails which I knew would reach a crescendo in the next few minutes.

"Yes, well, we won't tell him, Rosie. Once the kitchen ceiling dries out, I'm sure it will be fine, and I can always patch it up with a bit of Polyfilla."

Mum had a habit of "patching things up". The problem was she would become engrossed in whatever task she was doing and inadvertently "forget" the cake in the oven, the bath she was running, or the coffee she was making.

"I think we've got the worst of it, Rose." Mum exhaled, her cheeks pink with the exertion. "I'd better get Madam up here for a bath. You too, young lady."

"Lois," I shouted. "Bath's ready."

"Oh no, what's she crying about now?" Mum looked frazzled, so I offered to go and fetch Lois and see what all the boo-hooing was about. I reached the kitchen and she was standing in the doorway wailing. Tears were cascading down her face, tiredness etched under her eyes, Bea (her cuddly bunny) in her arms.

"Come on Lois what's wrong?"

"I want my rice pudding."

"Well, wasn't Frances doing it for you?"

"She was," she stuttered, "and she put it into the microwave, but then they all rushed into the hall and disappeared, and I can't reach the microwave."

My heart sank. "Where did they go, Lois? Did you see them?"

"They left me without my rice pudding."

"Yes, alright, I'll do your rice pudding, here."

I skidded over to the microwave and summoned it to life.

"Sit down, and I'll bring it over."

They must have gone through the wall, they must have. Could Lois have seen something? I had to prise the information out of her in such a way that didn't get her into a strop. How I wished Adi had been here just a few moments earlier. He would have found a way of seeing where they'd gone. Why did they vanish so quickly? As if by magic, my question was immediately answered by the sound of a key in the lock.

DAD.

I guess they fled because they knew he was about to come home. I handed Lois her rice pudding, which she attacked with gusto.

"Hey, Dad," I called as he started for the stairs.

Then I could hear the muffled voices of my parents. They didn't argue very often. Dad said he didn't "do rows" and that Mum often ended up fighting with herself. This was definitely a row though.

"What's happened up here, Rae? The floor's soaked!"

"The bath overflowed."

"For Christ's sake, that's not the first time. Can't you be a bit more careful? We can't afford for the ceiling to come down in the kitchen."

"What would you know? You're never here," Mum said.

"What's that supposed to mean?"

"Exactly what it says. You're never here. When you are here, you might as well be at work. You hardly speak to me. You never even look at me. I could be walking around in a fig leaf for all you care. You can't even muster up any enthusiasm to congratulate me on my job."

"That's a bit unfair. I was going into a meeting when you rang," Dad explained.

"You're always JUST doing something, and I'm sick of it! I do everything in this house, and I just need a little bit of appreciation from you. Actually, I'd just like to be noticed. That's all."

"I'm doing my best here. I'm working long hours. I'm exhausted."

"So am I, John. So am I. Look just forget it. I need to get the kids bathed. Lois, Rosemary!" she screamed.

I hated hearing my parents fight. I could see their anger and sadness and disappointment in a physical way. Dad would be surrounded by grey. His raincloud might have thunder cracking around it or it might just be black, depending on whether he was feeling angry or just resigned to it all. Mum would have dark purple with fiery red around her, which would then fade to smudgy grey. It was distressing to see.

I was so caught up in my thoughts, I barely heard Lois say as we started to climb the stairs, "The lady in the mirror looked so cross, because she was having her tea."

"Hang on, what did you say, Lois?"

"Actually," (this was currently her favourite word and she used it ALL the time), "I said the lady in the mirror was cross."

I held my breath and grabbed her halfway up the stairs.

We could see the aforementioned mirror over the bannisters.

"Was the lady in that mirror?" I said, pointing to the big mirror hanging over the radiator in the hall.

"Actually, yes. I saw Frances and Mr Foggerty and Uncle Vic talk to her and then they walked through the wall."

"How did they get the lady in the mirror to appear? What did they do?"

"You're hurting me, Rose. Let go of my arm."

"Listen, Lois, if you tell me, you can have my Build-A-Bear to cuddle tonight, and I'll let you use the purple tablet to play on. Just, please, try to remember."

"Can I play with your LOL doll, too?"

I sighed. My sister drove a hard bargain.

"Yes, okay."

Lois paused for effect, I think. She was good at being a drama queen.

"Mr Foggerty just pressed something underneath the mirror and said ARADIA three times."

"Are you sure, Lois? Sounds like a word that you just made up."

Lois shrugged me off. "Actually, yes, and I want my bath. Muuuum!"

I let her go into the steaming bathroom with its shiny, wet floor. My mother was sitting on the closed seat of the loo. Her arms were outstretched toward Lois. She looked defeated.

All I could do was mutter the word over and over again under my breath:

Aradia.

Aradia.

Aradia.

7

THE PORTAL

That night I lay awake in bed, my brain going over the events of the day. I couldn't stop thinking about THE STRANGER. What on earth did they want? Where had Phyllis disappeared to? What was through the wall? And why was there such a sense of urgency to everything that Mr Foggerty, Uncle Vic, and Frances did? I could feel the unrest in the house.

Lois had needed so many huggles, partly because she was tired and partly because she had been left waiting so long for her rice pudding. Dad had gone to bed early having barely spoken to anyone. Mum had stayed up late reading lines from her play. I could hear her practising her American accent.

Eventually, she'd crept up to bed, and through the moonlight shining into my bedroom I could just make out the time on my clock: 11:51pm. I was suddenly gripped by curiosity. I replayed the moment when Adi had dropped the pebble right by the bottom of the mirror and how it had floated so effortlessly. I wondered if it would do the same for me. Perhaps if I muttered the word "Aradia" something might happen?

Before I'd had a chance to really think through the consequences of my actions, I was out of bed and creeping softly downstairs. I didn't want to go in the kitchen and disturb the cats, so I found a pen by the telephone in the hall that I thought would suffice nicely in lieu of a pebble.

I stood in front of the mirror, my ghostly reflection looking back at me. I was pale. My thick, blonde hair was ruffled and sat unruly in big curls just above my shoulders. I could see the dark shadows underneath my eyes. My dad had the same when he was tired, and so did Lois. The three of us took on a sort of unworldly, gaunt, wide-eyed look when we were weary. I also had my dad to thank for the size of my eyes, though. Like him, Lois and I had huge round pools; mine green, hers grey blue like Mum's.

I felt a little fizz of excitement in my tummy as I held the pen aloft just above the centre of the mirror and let go.

Clatter.

It fell to the floor.

What was I doing wrong? I wondered. I passed my fingertips along the base of the mirror. I don't know if I was searching for a button or just seeing if I could "feel" the atmosphere change. Again, I felt nothing and heard nothing, except for the faint meow of Bob or Maggie beyond the kitchen door, probably sensing my presence.

Come on, Rosemary, I willed myself on. *Just keep trying.*

I moved the pen slightly to the left and down so it was completely parallel to the base of the mirror. As I let go, I whispered the word:

"Aradia. Aradia. Aradia"

The pen hovered and flicked its ends one way and the

other, like a paper aeroplane. I gasped. The reflection in the mirror was changing. There was a rushing sound in the background, a bit like the buzz as the tube trains rush towards you on the London Underground, and there before my eyes appeared the face of a beautiful lady with flowing, jet-black hair. It tumbled below her shoulders, though I could just make out the form of a large raven sitting on her shoulder, partially covered by her hair. Her amber-coloured eyes surveyed me critically, and her full, red lips curled up slightly. I don't know if this was in derision or amusement. I was speechless at her beauty.

When she spoke to me, she had a strong Italian accent, and the bird's mouth opened in unison with hers as if he, too, were saying:

"This is Aradia. Name and Pentagram Identification."

"I... I... I'm Rosemary," I stuttered, "and I'm sorry, but I don't have any pentagrams on me. I have a Build-A-Bear Certificate which has my name and address on it."

The Lady stared at me. Her long, slim nose crinkled, and she scrunched her eyebrows together.

"No, no, no, no, no," she said, her accent sounding like one of the waitresses in Luigi's pizzeria. "You can only enter our kingdom if you can do magic. You lady, you no magical. You child. You have no Pentagram ID, so I say to you, *arrivederci*." With that, her image careered backwards away from me as if hurtling into a tunnel. The whooshing sound came again, and suddenly there I was staring back at my own pinched face.

Had this just really happened? I glanced at the digital display on the phone handset and, yes, it was now 12:05pm, so only about fifteen minutes after I had crept from my bed. I couldn't possibly have been dreaming. I gently opened the kitchen door, wanting to feel something solid and comforting, and felt the warm fur of one of our cats zig-zag in and out of my legs. I crouched down and picked up the soft bundle.

How on earth was I going to get into the world beyond the mirror without being "magical"? I was no more magical than a pair of pants. I couldn't even do a simple card trick! Mind you, I think the lady in the mirror, Aradia, as she called herself, was looking for something slightly more spectacular than that.

I wondered whether I could ask Frances for help, but something told me they would deny the existence of Aradia. They would put it all down to a party trick. I would have to sleep on it and hope that Adi had a good plan tomorrow.

That night I slept fitfully. My dreams were full of beautiful ladies called Aradia with long, flowing hair but evil tiger-coloured eyes that looked right through me. I woke with a start, sticky with sweat. I must have looked a little rough, for Mum took one look at me and immediately put her hand to my brow.

"Rosie, are you feeling okay? You're very flushed looking. Let me take your temperature..."

"I'm fine, Mum, honestly. Just had a few bad dreams that's all."

I did feel okay, just a bit tired, and you know that feeling when you wake up and the dream was so vivid you sort of feel you are still living it, or that it somehow really DID happen? Well that. Plus, I had to see Adi to tell him what had happened last night.

Once dressed, I scampered down the stairs and, just I

was walking into the kitchen, I heard Mum shout, "Mind as you go in, Bob's had a fit just inside the door."

I lifted my feet up, grimacing at their sticky wetness, and sighed with the knowledge that I had just stepped in his wee. It was going to be one of those days.

"Thanks for warning me, Lois." I scowled at my little sister who was already in the rocking chair munching her way through a warm angry pig, as we call them in our house. (I always used to pronounce croissant phonetically, and Lois thought I was saying "cross oink", so we altered it to the more user friendly "angry pig".)

"Actually, I didn't know what you were doing," she whinged with her mouth full.

Mum followed closely behind me. She must have known, as she was holding a flannel. "Sit down, Rosemary, and let me just wipe your feet, and then perhaps I can clean up this mess, if I ever manage to get time."

Suddenly, Dad's lanky figure appeared in the doorway.

"Watch where you're walking," Mum and I chimed just as Dad also stepped straight in Bob's wee.

I could tell Dad was not happy. He didn't actually say anything, he just did a big sigh and peeled his socks off his feet, threw them in the direction of the washing machine, and turned to go back upstairs.

I didn't see Frances or any of the other house guests this morning, as Dad was taking us to school, which was a bit of a treat really, as usually he was gone by 8 o'clock to get his train. I could see his cloud clearly above his head, still dark grey, and the colours surrounding him were maroon and dull mauve, almost like a bruise. The colours seemed to throb and pulsate like they do in the cartoons when someone bangs their head. If that was indicative of how he was feeling, I felt sorry for him.

Mum, still in her dressing gown, tried to pull him towards her for a kiss before we left the house. He didn't push her away, as such, but he moved his face to the side so that her lips met his cheekbone rather than his mouth.

"Are we alright now?" I heard her whisper to him.

"Yeah, yeah, yeah," Dad replied dismissively and then turned his attention to us.

He ruffled my hair and put his arm around me. "Come on, Rosie-posie, let's get you and the wind beneath my wings to school."

He was smiling and trying to be jokey, but his face looked tight, as if he was finding it physically difficult to smile.

As we gathered our bags and coats, I stole a look back at my mum who was watching us leave, her arms crossed, the belt of her pink-and-blue, spotty dressing gown trailing on the floor. She looked kind of small and thin today. The colours around her were muted and hazy. I hoped by the time next week came she would be sparkling and bright.

I saw Adi in the playground and told him what had happened last night. He listened intently with his mouth slightly open, as if at any moment he was going to add something, but he didn't.

"Well, Adi, how can we convince them that we can do magic?"

For a moment, I thought Adi had been enchanted, for he stood so still. I couldn't even see his breath in the cold, October air. I shook his arm gently.

"Adi, have you heard what I've been telling you?"

At last, he brought his gaze back to me and took a deep

intake of breath. "Right, I have an idea, Rosemary, but I'll need to work on it over the weekend."

"What sort of an idea?"

"Just wait and see, but it does definitely involve magic."

"Adi, you're a genius," I grinned.

8

THE BUS INCIDENT

Mum picked us up from school looking a bit brighter. She said she'd sold three Love Spells and a Sell Your House Spell today, so she had about £40 in her purse, and she was feeling really rich. "Let's go to Smyths and get you both a little treat, shall we?"

Lois and I were delighted, even though the more-grown-up side of me wanted to tell Mum to spend her money on herself. She could do with some new clothes. I was sick of seeing her in the same holey jeans and charity-shop jumper.

"Right, you can have an LOL Doll each, girls," said Mum jubilantly.

"Mum, they are £10 each, so that means you'll spend half your money on us and only have £20 left," I explained to her in a worried tone.

"Rosemary, your maths is brilliant," Mum said. I pulled a face. "Now go on, stop worrying and choose your doll. I will get myself a new mascara or something," she soothed.

After a grapple with the dolls, we paid for our purchases and headed off to Boots for Mum. We passed the Sony store and the shop front was dazzling with all its televisions advertising the latest flat-screen bargain in huge Technicolor.

I suddenly did a double take.

There on every TV screen in the window was our very own Mr Foggerty at the wheel of a bus.

"Mum, look," I shouted almost in disbelief. "It's Mr Foggerty on the telly, look!"

We couldn't hear what was being said, but the news headline underneath said;

Mystery Man Leads Passengers To Safety

"Oh my God," my mother said, her hand covering her mouth. "We need to get back."

She grabbed Lois' hand and half-dragged her back towards the car, much to my little sister's protestations.

I scurried along behind. "What does all that mean, Mum? What's Mr Foggerty done? Is it something bad?"

"No, no, Rosemary, he's helped people. It's nothing to worry about. Let's just get home and find out what's going on."

At home we found Uncle Vic and Frances in the lounge watching the TV news headlines with the sound up very loud. Dad would have gone mad. For once, Mum seemed not to worry that me and Lois were there and could hear EVERYTHING that was being said. It was great!

Mum was trying to figure out what was going on. "Rosie saw him on the TV screens in the Sony shop. We couldn't believe it. What's happened?"

"Shhhhhhhhhhhh!" Frances and Uncle Vic said in unison.

Without taking his eyes off the screen, Uncle Vic pointed. "There's witness reports!"

An elderly gentleman with a comb over and a large nose was being interviewed by a lady in a grey coat.

"Mr Toon, you were on the bus. Tell us what happened."

"Right, well I was on my way to see my daughter. And the bus was quite busy downstairs with mostly pensioners or young Mums, you know what with all the kids being at school and the like."

"Mmhm, mmhm."

"All of sudden this person all dressed in black with a bally clava thing on ran down the stairs of the bus and demanded the bus driver take them to Strawberry Fields, or else."

"It must have been terrifying."

"Well, there was pandemonium, as you can imagine. The bus driver passed out. I was worried about the cheese in my bag I'd got for my daughter. You know how cheese gets if it's too warm, especially soft cheese…"

"Mmhm."

"All of sudden, this fella gets up from the front. I'd not noticed him before, a funny looking lanky chap with mad hair."

Me and Mum giggled. Had HE not looked in the mirror lately?

"And he dragged the bus driver out of his seat, jumped into the driving seat, and stopped us all from careering into the pavement. Then he did some sort of funny karate move with his hand and the lunatic all in black slumped on the ground."

"Mr Toon," said the lady in the grey coat, "do carry on."

"Well that's it, really. The chap with the mad hair dropped us all off at our destinations and kicked out the loony at the 'cop shop'. The funny thing was, traffic in town is horrendous most of the time, but that Mayor must have sorted out all those bus lanes or something, as we seemed to fly round. And before I knew it, I was eating a brie and bacon sarnie with my daughter and complaining of heart burn."

There were a few more clips from "eyewitnesses", many who claimed they never saw the man described by Mr Toon, but most confirmed seeing the number 261 bus zooming round at speeds of over 60 miles an hour; but funnily enough, no speed cameras recorded it.

Our attention went back to the screens as a Photofit picture of Mr Foggerty came up. Mum explained that this is a picture an artist has drawn from how eye witnesses have described him. Underneath was the caption:

Wanted In Connection With Thwarted Attack

The newsreader continued:

"Whilst police are questioning the agitator, who handed themselves in to headquarters, they also are anxious to find the man pictured, even though many of the passengers denied seeing him on the bus. Whether this man did or didn't intervene in this incident still remains a mystery to police, but passengers are grateful that they were delivered safely home."

An elderly lady then appeared with a plastic rain hat on and a heavily lined face with red lipstick drawn well over her natural lip line.

"I just want to say thank you for getting me home in time for *The Chase*, I've never missed an episode."

Uncle Vic started to raise himself up from the settee. "Well, there we go, another example of BUTBUM AW. I think we all know who is behind this."

I remembered THE STRANGER using that expression during the conversation they had with my mum at the front door. I seized my chance whilst I could.

"Uncle Vic, what does BUTBUM AW mean again?"

"Britain Under Threat by Unsavoury Men, open brackets, and Women, close brackets." He reeled off very quickly. "BUTBUM (AW)."

I did a little fist pump very subtly. I'm sure no one saw it.

"Ar," said Uncle Vic, and he looked from Mum to Frances for help.

Neither said a word.

"Actually, I don't call my bottom a butt or a bum. It's rude. It's a bottom, and here," Lois pointed to just below her tummy, "is my front bottom."

"Alright. Thank you, Lois, we don't need to know all about your bottoms," Mum interjected, "all we need to know is that they are clean and wind free."

Lois giggled. "I'm hungry."

"Alright, one moment and I'll start your dinner. Go and lay the table in the kitchen, both of you."

We both left the room, but I hovered in the hallway, determined to listen in to what Mum was saying to Frances and Uncle Vic.

Mum was trying to talk quietly, but I could still make out what she was saying.

"The thing is, Vic, I start this job on Monday. I really cannot get involved with this. I'm going to just have to let you get on with it. I will of course try to be at the energy raising events, but I have to focus on earning some money for the family."

Frances was cooing. "Oh my dear, you've done enough for all of us by being the Guardian of the Portal and providing us with this safe house for Phyllis to lie low in. You concentrate on your lovely wee job and leave the No-Laws to us. The Pendle Trials were so long ago, it should all have been buried. Foggy knows what he's doing. We will find Phyllis. Don't you be worrying."

"Yes, yes, don't worry, Rae, Foggy will be back soon. We have everything in hand. Hecate is on board now, so before you know it order will be restored. Come along, Frances, let's leave Rae to get on with things."

I dashed into the kitchen to help Lois lay the table before they all came out of the lounge.

Who were the No-Laws and what were the Pendle Trials from long ago? Who was Hecate, I wondered? This certainly confirmed to me that Phyllis really was missing. Who had taken her and who was she hiding from? Was it the No-Laws that Uncle Vic was referring to? Was the person in black that tried to ambush the bus one of these No-Laws?

I couldn't picture Phyllis being sad or scared. She wasn't

quite as bonkers as Frances, but she was quirky in her own way. She was my friend. She always listened very carefully to anything you had to say and was full of helpful advice. Sometimes, however, she took things too literally. Mum told me and Lois to be very careful what we said in front of Phyllis, for example do not say: "I'm starving" (you will get force fed A LOT of food and then be up all night throwing up) or "I wish it would snow" (she once caused a pile up on the M62 with sudden, freak snow showers).

The thought of Phyllis being lost, misunderstood, or in trouble was quite scary. I couldn't help thinking that her disappearance and Dad's cloud reappearing were somehow linked, which made it even more important that Adi and I worked out how to get through the wall to find out what was REALLY happening. If finding Phyllis meant Dad would get better too, then we HAD to do this.

The weekend seemed to go soooooo slowly. Mum was incredibly jumpy and seemed to find it difficult to eat anything. I think she was just nervous about her job starting. Dad was brilliant on Saturday and took us swimming, which took my mind off the fact that Phyllis was missing.

Sunday was a different matter. Dad spent most of the day at his computer. He moaned that Mum had left bits of green paper on the floor and he didn't say much other than "yes, please" and "no, thanks". It was a strange day. I asked Mum if there was a full moon, as apparently full moons can make people moody, but she said no and not to worry. Dad was just tired. So I stopped thinking about it and concentrated on what Adi and I were going to do.

Just before bedtime on Sunday, I noticed a little note that had come through the front door in an envelope that just said *Rosemary* on the front. It was from Adi, and in his scrawling, crazy handwriting it said:

Telegram:
Good news stop Magic at the ready stop
Hold on to your hat stop Adi stop

I didn't have a hat, but who cares! We were on!

9

MAGICAL MATHS

I woke early and could hear movement downstairs already, even though the time on my clock said 6:30am. Of course! It was Mum's first day in her new job. As I hauled myself out of bed, I realised excitedly that I had almost forgotten about Adi's note last night.

I crept into the kitchen and, as I thought, Mum was pottering downstairs in her dressing gown, her face already made up, complete with "eight-hour cream" on the lips, which smelt awful. She only wore it now when she was in a mood with Dad, as he always refused to kiss her when she was wearing it cos he said it smelt "like sick".

"Who's picking us up from school today, Mum?" I was dreading the answer really.

"Frances, my love, today and tomorrow, and then Uncle Vic is doing the rest of the week, I think."

I finished my croissant with a tickly butterfly feeling in my tummy. I was nervous about the day ahead. Anxious for what Adi and I were going to attempt to do later and anxious for my mum whose colours were bright, pulsating, and making little zippy noises, like mini rockets going off.

I began to try to work out a plan for how and when Adi and I would be able to try getting through the portal. It would be tricky after school with Frances here fussing about. Also, Lois would want to play with us and there was NO WAY I was taking my little sister through with me.

I could hear movement from upstairs. Lois was trundling down the stairs followed by Dad, who had dark shadows under his eyes and looked exhausted. Lois on the other hand was full of energy, still frantically sucking her dummy, which Dad was trying to prise off her.

"Come on, take that plug out your mouth, madam. You know it's supposed to be left upstairs."

Mum appeared at the kitchen doorway looking like she'd really made an effort.

Even Dad said, "You look nice, love." I could tell he meant it because white air came out of his mouth as he exhaled.

He even patted her on the arm as he went upstairs to get ready. "Good luck today, love, you'll be fine I'm sure."

He leaned in for a little kiss, which I knew Mum would appreciate. "Urghhh, you've got that horrible stuff on your lips again." And he leaned out again before she got her kiss.

Mum just rolled her eyes in an exasperated fashion and told us to hurry up and get ready for school.

"Good luck today, Mum," I said as I hugged her and kissed her cheek. "You'll be great."

She gave me a tight smile. "I'll be glad when this first day is over. The first day is always the worst, isn't it, darling…?"

After she dropped us off at school, I watched Mum thread her way through the scores of parents, her big black bag full of notepad, script, sandwiches, and coffee flask flung over her shoulder, obliviously hitting unsuspecting latecomers as they rushed past her.

I barely saw Adi all day apart from to warn him we were being collected by the dreaded Frances, so to keep an eye out. I would give him the thumbs up if it was okay to come to ours straight after school and the thumbs down if it was clear we weren't going to be able to distract her.

Once the bell had gone, I could see Adi out the corner of my eye loitering. He had special permission to walk home, as he only lived across the road from the school, so he was lucky he didn't have to wait for anyone to collect him. His parents worked long hours, so he had his own key. Mum said I can only have my own key once I'm in high school, so seeing as I'm only in Year 5 I've got a while to wait yet.

Adi kept his front-door key on a piece of blue nylon string attached to his loops on his trousers. Murray and his friend Dan, who we called Daredevil Dan cos nothing was too big a dare for him, were always trying to find a way to pinch Adi's key off of his trousers during PE. They would pretend to be really slow at getting changed and then Mr Ross, the PE teacher, would find them in the boys' toilets trying to flush it down the loo. All they did was constantly block up the toilet and poor Adi had to take wringing wet trousers home so he could get in his front door. Adi just ignored their antics. He was dead brave. I think I would have burst into tears.

So, there I was waiting for Frances, thinking to myself that she would be longer than usual as she would be collecting Lois first. Then I saw my little sister dawdling toward me with her friend Daisy and her mum.

"I've brought Lois over to you, Rosemary, as she said your mum was getting you from the office today."

I opened my mouth, about to correct her, when

suddenly a plan formed in my head. I flipped Adi the thumbs up, and he nodded briefly and nonchalantly walked out of the playground.

"Yes, that's right," I said smoothly in my most grown up voice. "Mum told me to go to the office to wait for her. Thanks for bringing Lois over, Mrs Davies."

I grabbed Lois' hand. "Right, come on, we're being big girls. We're walking home on our own today."

I smiled vaguely at Mr Bobbin and pointed in the direction of lots of parents to indicate the person picking us up had arrived, and we shot out of the playground on to the street.

Whatever had held Frances up was going to play to my advantage! I couldn't wait to get home and try to get through the portal with Adi. A flicker of conscience passed through my brain — what if Frances turned up and was worried about where we were? I guiltily brushed it aside and focused on what we had to do.

Lois was already moaning. "Where's my crisps, Rosie? Mum always brings me crisps or biscuits."

"Don't worry, Lois, the sooner we get home the sooner you can have whatever you want. Let's try to walk faster, and then we'll be home quicker."

I dragged a very reluctant little sister around the streets, until 15 minutes later we arrived home. There was Adi waiting for us, sitting on the step reading a comic.

I knew Mum kept a spare front-door key under the plant pot. Once we'd got indoors, I replaced it, just in case we needed it again. Then I gave Lois crisps AND biscuits (I had to give her enough food to keep going) and set her up on the computer. Adi and I were ready!

"Are you going to tell me what magic you've come up with then, Adi?" I asked nervously.

"Wait and see, Rosemary. It might not work, but we'll give it our best shot." Adi rolled up the sleeves of his blue school jumper, repositioned his glasses on his nose, and took a deep breath.

He took a coin out of his pocket and a pen and paper. We both stood looking into the mirror. I bit my lip. Adi did a little wink at me and then we began the ritual of holding and dropping the coin in front of the mirror. I was about to suggest that I took over when, *bingo*, the coin unsteadily at first floated, then seemed to settle into a hovering position.

"Aradia. Aradia. Aradia," we said in unison.

Whooooooosh, that rushing sound came again, and this time I felt slightly nauseous watching a faraway object in the mirror come towards me. A bit like travel sickness, I suppose. Suddenly there she was again in the mirror, the beautiful raven-haired lady.

"This is Aradia. Name and Pentagram Identification."

"Adi Adani and Rosemary Pellow. We have no current pentagrams."

Aradia sighed. "I'm sorry, but you cannot come through unless you can do maaagic. Goodbye."

"But we can do magic!" Adi shouted desperately.

Aradia paused and studied us both with her piercing amber eyes. She smirked.

"Well, you I have sin before," she pointed at me. "But not the boy. I will love to see this magic. So, impress me."

I could tell Adi was nervous, because he kept going from one leg to the other, like a flamingo resting a leg in water and then swapping to the other one. I dug my nails into his side by way of reminding him to take charge here.

"Yes, right," Adi said in a high pitched but loud voice. "This is my assistant," he pointed at me to my surprise, "and we are going to use magic to tell you your shoe size and your age."

I looked at him aghast. "Mum said you should never ask a lady her age," I whispered to him.

"I'm not asking her age," he growled. "I'm *telling* her. There's a difference."

Aradia paused to stroke the raven's chest, which was again perched on her shoulder. It seemed to turn its beak and whisper in her ear.

"Alright," she said. "But I promise you, leetle boy, you will never be able to guess my age, but you can have your leetle try. Why not?"

"Have you got a pen and paper?" Adi asked boldly.

"Yes, I have. Let's get on with this maaagic." She elongated the word and flounced her hands around the air as if it was a big joke to her.

This was not going to go down well with Adi. He hated anyone dissing him, especially BEFORE he had had a chance to prove his worth.

"Right, you will need to keep up with me," he said briskly, "and don't show me your workings out, just your final figure at the end. Multiply your age by one fifth of 100, add today's date, i.e., 15 as it's the 15th of October, times this by 20% of 25, add your shoe size, then finally subtract 5 x todays date i.e. 5 x 15. Now let me see your FINAL figure."

Aradia's fingers had been working ninety to the dozen, and I know most of the sums she did using a calculator. She turned the page round to us to show us this figure:

70,405

Adi looked puzzled and seemed to say nothing for ages.

"Well?" I whispered to him from the corner of my mouth. "Tell her how old she is and her shoe size."

I thought Adi was going to hyperventilate, he was breathing so fast and hard.

He looked directly at Aradia and said, "You are 704 years old and you take a size five shoe."

I couldn't believe it. I thought I was going to have to kill him.

"704?" I gasped. "Adi, have you gone mad? She's about 35, even I know that. You've totally blown it this time."

I felt like crying. Our one chance. I had really trusted Adi. How could I have been so daft!? He must have got muddled with his nerves or something. It was all over. How were we going to find out what was on the other side now?

I was waiting for the swooshing noise to come and Aradia's world to catapult away from us, but she was still there staring.

I looked to Adi, who was mute and in shock, I think. I looked at her. She looked furious. She slowly reached down beneath her and resurfaced holding the highest stiletto shoe I had ever seen. It was red and black with glitter and the heel was like a long black spike. As she thrust it towards us in the mirror, I closed my eyes and cowered. It was over. She was going to kill us with a stiletto spike.

The stabbing sensation never came, so I reopened one eye and saw more clearly that she was actually showing us the bottom of her shoe, and neatly printed in black was the number "5".

"I am impressed, leeetle boy. How did you know I was born in 1313, huh? Maybe I nid better face cream," she cackled. "You can come through."

"And my assistant," Adi bravely stated.

Aradia gave me a steely look and sighed reluctantly. "And your assistant."

At that moment, the mirror seemed to expand and open into the wall like a pair of wardrobe doors parting to allow you entry. We started to walk towards the desk where Aradia was seated. The floor and walls were all wooden, a panelled, walnut-coloured wood, and Aradia's desk was a curved high-topped area rather like you would see at a hotel reception. I turned to look behind me, to see if I could see our hallway, but all that was visible was more panelled, walnut wood from floor to ceiling. Our house and the entrance to it had totally disappeared. As we got within a foot or so of her desk, the raven flew off her shoulder toward us. I gave a small cry of fear.

"Paloma is just going to search you. Stand with your legs apart and arms in the air."

Paloma the bird made little cawing noises as she ducked and dived in-between our legs, through our arms, and round our heads. It was almost like a circus act, and also the weirdest thing I have ever encountered.

When the search was over, Aradia beckoned us and gave us each a silver pentagram. It was identical to the one that had been attached to Mum's shoe, the time when she had gone through the wall and then denied it. I remembered seeing it float down the stairs and disintegrate into tiny sparkles. The stars were made of the most flimsy, thin material, a bit like silk, I suppose. They felt so fragile and yet strong, too, like a spider's web. Aradia motioned to us to put the pentagrams on to our chests like a badge.

I hesitated. How on earth was this going to stick to my top? But of course, one pat with my hand and it had stuck like glue; in fact, I tried to remove it and re-stick it further down, but it wouldn't budge.

"You may go through." Aradia gestured toward a long corridor, and Paloma fluttered off ahead of us, presumably showing us the way. We followed her graceful flight down the corridor, which had doors leading off.

Every door had a brightly coloured number on it. We seemed to be walking very quickly, and I noticed a dazzling orange number "57", a fuchsia pink "21", a green sparkly "15", and a sunshine yellow number "13". The numbers were totally random, and I wondered whether they had any relevance as to what was behind that particular door.

Eventually, Paloma stopped outside a shiny gold number "3", which was the smallest number I had seen. She tapped her beak against the door and then flew off. I was feeling anxious, and I stole a glance at Adi, who seemed to be taking everything in his stride.

"What happens now, Adi?" I whispered frantically.

"I don't know, Rosemary, but I think I might need some clean underpants."

Despite myself, I giggled.

The door creaked open and together we stepped forwards to enter the room.

My stomach met my mouth as our feet made contact with not floor but air, and, before we knew what was happening, we were tumbling downwards at an incredible rate.

10

THREE FALLING

I had never been so scared in my life. I didn't know if I was still screaming or if it was Adi's screams I could hear ringing in my ears.

It was pitch black, and I thought, *this is the end*. But then suddenly it wasn't.

We landed on something soft and bouncy, which if I could have guessed, I would have said it must have been a cloud, for it seemed to literally catch us and hold us like a giant, squidgy hand. Adi said there was no way you could fall that far for that long and survive by just landing on something soft, so anti-gravity must have been in effect and stopped us from being killed. In other words, before we hit the ground we must have started to go back upwards slowly to adjust our speed, so that we landed safely. It didn't quite make sense to me, but I had more important things to worry about.

"Adi, are you there?" I asked once I'd got my breath back.

"Yeah are you okay, Rosemary? I don't know if this was such a good idea, you know. How are we gonna get back?"

"Back? You've only just arrived," came a faraway voice.

"Adi, grab my hand. I'm scared," I whispered.

"Me too," he replied.

"Who's there?" I finally plucked up courage to ask.

Let me tell you, I'm not that keen on the dark anyway, so to have fallen goodness knows how far in the dark and have landed in the dark and be spoken to by something you can't see cos its DARK isn't much fun!

They might as well have read my mind, for suddenly the lights came on and, boy, were they dazzling!

"That's better. Now I can see you both," grinned the face behind the voice.

I blinked a few times, as I seemed to be having a conversation with a gigantic tawny owl. He was about five-foot-tall, with shiny plumage and an incredibly polished beak. His claws were huge, and the talons creamy white at the tips, so it looked like he'd had a French polish on his toes. I couldn't stop staring.

"Are you staring at my French manicure or my apron?" the owl said to me. His apron was pink and frilly with *I Know I'm Wise, Tell Me I'm Sexy* written on it. So to be fair, yes, I probably was staring at both.

"Er, erm, both really," I said boldly.

He laughed. "Yes, well, I'm a modern owl. There's nothing wrong with a manicure, and it's good to be in touch with one's feminine side, though if I'm honest, they muddled the colour up in the factory. I did actually order a pale-blue apron, but never mind. Now you're both here, what can I do for you?"

Adi and I both looked at each other blankly. What *were* we doing in this huge room with stone flooring (even more of a miracle that we landed so safely)? The room was a large banqueting hall with trestle tables piled up in one corner, large ornate looking lights sprouting out from stone walls, and heavy, plush, dark-red velvet curtains at each corner.

"I haven't got long," continued the owl. "I've got to set this room up for a large banquet tonight. By the way, why on earth did you pick Room 3 to start with? You could have got here by coming down the stairs in Number 55. You know what they say: avoid the dive, pick 55. Didn't you realise room three only means one thing? Free falling! Well, we call it three falling here." He chuckled and wiped his eyes with a surprisingly dextrous finger hidden away under a shock of feathers.

I realised the door numbers did have a system of sorts, but I guess you had to know what each number stood for in order to know what was going to greet you behind it.

I glanced at Adi, who I think was still flabbergasted. I'd had a lifetime to get used to strange goings on, so I wasn't going to let a giant, talking owl phase me.

"We came through to look for our Aunty Phyllis who disappeared recently in strange circumstances. We didn't choose this door to come through. Aradia's raven brought us to it."

"Ar," the owl said very slowly and with a great deal of feeling. "Ar. Yes, yes, Paloma. I wouldn't have much faith in her, personally," he continued. "Very pleasing on the eye, but totally unreliable. She, my young pumpernickels, has led you up the garden path, and Hecate won't be pleased when she hears about this."

"Who's Hecate?" I asked tentatively.

"She's my boss. In fact, she's everyone's boss right now, and she's been brought in from Headquarters to our North West branch here to try to get to the bottom of dear Phyllis' disappearance. I think if you come again, you really ought to go straight to Room 21 and meet her."

"Now, young man, what are you doing over there?"

I looked to where the owl was addressing Adi, who was holding his ear to the wall and concentrating.

"Adi, what is it?" I joined him at the stone wall.

"I can hear crying, Rosemary. It's really weird. It sounds far away, and it sounds a bit like your sister. You don't think she followed us through the wall, do you?"

Before I could reply, the owl interjected with, "No, not possible to follow you through, unless she was actually standing with you when the Gates of Aradne opened. What you are hearing, young man, are the cries of the child from the other world, not this one. The veil is very thin, so you will hear if anyone is in distress from whence you came."

Then I heard it too. The distinct cries of Lois. It made me feel sick. "We have to get back Adi, now. I can't leave Lois all alone. What if something happens to her? ... Can we get back through this stone wall, owl?"

"Please, call me Jonathan," bowed the owl, I mean Jonathan. "I'm afraid you cannot get back through the wall this way. We shall have to go back the way you came, so lucky for you I'm here. Hop aboard. I can drop you off and still get these blessed tables ready, but we must be quick."

"Thank you, thank you so much, Jonathan." I said gratefully.

"Grasp on to my feathers, boy, that's it." Jonathan fussed around us, pushing us up on to his back with his feathered wings. "Ready for the off? Hold on tight."

What a contrast! As much as I hated the "three falling", I absolutely loved this ascension into the sky. There didn't seem to be any roof on the banqueting hall, as we just flew up, away from the cold stone floor and magnificent wall lights, up into a dark sky with so many twinkling stars. The air didn't feel cold. It felt warm and comforting. My plaits were flying in the wind behind me, and I snuggled into Jonathan's warm, soft plumage. We'd only been flying for a few moments, it felt, when Jonathan shouted, "This next bit is going to feel weird. Just go with it, and remember for next time, it's 21, the key to the door."

With that, he did a sort of big swoop, and Adi and I were sucked off of his back into what I can only describe as a vacuum, a swirling wind, like the eye of a tornado.

Adi later said he felt like he was the water being swirled down the plughole.

It was most unpleasant, like all the air had gone out of me, and I was being folded and bent in peculiar ways.

Suddenly, it was over, as Adi and I gently floated down on to my very own hall floor, as if we had been placed there by divine intervention.

And there she was, my dear little sister, crying her heart out standing in the doorway to the kitchen. Although, to be fair, she did stop once she'd seen us. I think she was gob smacked.

"Lois," I ran to her, and we took her into the kitchen to get her a drink and a biscuit. "Are you okay? Is Frances here yet?"

"I'm here, girls, I'm here. Just give me a minute," came the Scottish burr, albeit a panting one, from the hallway behind us.

Adi and I glanced at one another. "Lois," I said giving her a cuddle, "we're here now, so don't worry, and Frances is here, too. She will do our dinner, and I promise I will never leave you on your own again, okay?"

I wasn't 100% sure that I could keep that promise, but I did really mean it at the time of saying it. She looked so forlorn. I had been almost sick with fear that me and Adi were about to get trapped in that place, that at the time I would have said anything just out of pure relief to be home.

"Adi, I think you'd better go quickly before Frances sees you and gets suspicious," I whispered. "Go out the back way."

Poor Adi looked a bit pale, if that was possible, and to my amusement, his glasses were cock eyed, making him look quite cute and very vulnerable. He seemed to gather himself together quickly. He re-adjusted his glasses and, with a raise of his hand, slid out the back door.

"How long have you been waiting for me and Adi to get back, Lois?" I tentatively asked my sister.

"Ages and ages," she said, wiping her nose on the face of Bea (her rabbit). I didn't say anything. Mum goes mad when she sees her do that, but I thought it best not to bring it up under the circumstances.

I could hear Frances' heavy footsteps coming towards us from the hall. I wondered what was taking her so long.

"Next time you go through the wall with Adi, me and Bea are definitely coming with you," Lois added with a smile.

The little moo, she knew exactly what she was doing as she fell into Frances' arms and turned her head back to me for effect, knowing I couldn't argue with her in our present company.

"Now girls, I'm sorry about all this," puffed Frances, her arm around Lois as she attempted to adjust her skirt. "For goodness' sake, please don't tell your mother I forgot yous today. She'll have my guts for garters, so she will. Now let's sort your dinner out, shall we? How did you get in?"

"Mum keeps a key under the plant pot out the front."

"Oh my god, thank the lordy for that. It won't happen again, girls."

"It's okay, Frances, we were fine, and don't worry, we won't tell Mum."

Frances looked a little embarrassed. "I'm not one to ask for secrets to be kept, but I think in this instance it might be as well to keep schtum. Your mother has enough on her wee plate at the moment."

"Why did you forget to pick us up though, Frances?" Lois asked beseechingly.

Frances looked slightly baffled, as if she hadn't thought she might be asked this. I could sense she was toying with the idea of telling us the truth or not, so I fixed her a beady stare.

"If truth be told, I was in the middle of having a chat with Foggy, erm Mr Foggerty. Remember we saw him on the TV the other night?" she added nervously, as if trying to get us on side.

Me and Lois nodded silently.

"Well, we were having a wee chat about what he'd been up to and the time just ran away with us. Suddenly I thought, 'Oh my God, those bairns. I've forgotten them.' So now I'm here, let's forget all about it and get you some yummy tea." She gave Lois a squeeze.

So, Mr Foggerty was back.

I decided to take my chances.

"How did Mr Foggerty know that there was going to be an incident on that bus, Frances? And please don't fob us off. We've both seen THINGS."

Frances looked cornered. "You've both seen us go through the wall then, I take it?"

We nodded again silently.

She paused, looked up to the ceiling, then down to the floor, and pulled her wrinkled pop socks back up to meet her knees.

"Oh dear, this is a muddle. I will have to talk to Mr Foggerty and Uncle Vic about all this you know, dears. And in answer to your question, yes, Mr Foggerty *and* Phyllis knew there was going to be a troublemaker on that bus. We've been aware of this group for some time, their leader, Mal Vine, has been otherwise engaged, so to speak, and has recently re-emerged."

Frances gave a shudder at his name. I opened my mouth to ask a question, but she stopped me with a raise of her hand. "Let's just say, we all go back a long way. We are part of a team whose job it is to intercept these people and stop them from causing trouble to innocent folk."

Frances paused as if replaying everything she had told us.

"And is this group the No-Laws? And do they have something to do with Pendle Hill?" I asked bravely, repeating what I had overheard Uncle Vic saying.

Frances looked slightly pained. "Aye, the Pendle Hill Witches. You do know we're witches, don't you, girls?"

I nodded.

Lois giggled. "Good witches though, Frances, aren't you?"

"Of course, my love."

"So where's your broomstick then?"

Frances looked at Lois fondly. "We don't always travel on a broomstick now. We have much more sophisticated means of travel, which is why dear Phyllis became unstuck. Broomsticks are for fun, like motorbikes are."

"I'd like a motorbike. Actually, no, can I have a short-bread biscuit instead?"

Frances heaved herself out of the rocking chair and made for the biscuit tin in the cupboard.

"Phyllis *is* missing then?" I asked.

"I've probably said far too much, girls. Yes, she is, but we will find her. We're not members of BIWIT for nothing! British Institute for Witches in Trouble," she added, glancing at our puzzled faces.

At that moment, we heard a key going in the front door, and my mother's perfume filled the hallway like sunshine in a dark room. I felt a rush of relief and love for her. She'd only been working one day, but it seemed so much had happened!

"Mum!" Lois and I shouted and ran out to hug and kiss her.

"Hello, girls. As it's our first day, we finished a bit earlier, which is just great!"

"Did you have a good day, Mum? Are the people nice?"

"I had a fabulous day, darling. Nikolai the director is just lovely, and the cast are great. Marcus Polo is playing George. He's quite famous, you know, and absolutely charming."

Mum swept through into the kitchen, where Frances had just turned on the oven for our dinner.

"Why don't you sit yourself down, Rae, and I'll do the bairns' food while you tell us all about your day." Frances fussed round Mum a little nervously, I thought. "Let me make you a nice cup of tea."

"Well, that would be absolutely lovely. Thank you, Frances."

Mum chattered away, asking us about our day, peppered with little anecdotes about hers. Apparently, Marcus, who was playing opposite Mum, was "a gentle-man", as well as totally "charming". All the while she was talking, I had several things going round in my head: No-Laws, Mal Vine, and Pendle Hill Witches.

What was the link between them and what did they have to do with Phyllis' disappearance?

11

ADI'S WOBBLE

A di is avoiding me.

I'd got to school the day after our visit and he wasn't in.

The following day he did come in, but every time I approached him in the playground he'd put his hands over his ears and do that "uhhhhhhhhhhhh" noise really loudly.

I couldn't shout over it. I didn't want the whole school to know what was going on. It was incredibly frustrating. The more I tried to catch Adi's eyes, the more he would avoid me.

I decided to leave him alone for a few days. Surely his curiosity would get the better of him, and he'd calm down and want to go through the wall again. He was scared, and no one, least of all Adi, wants to have that pointed out to them. Yet, telling him in no uncertain terms that he was a coward was the only thing I felt I had left to do that might make him talk to me again. After all, there was no one else I could talk to about what was happening, and I badly needed to tell him what Frances had told me.

Who was this Mal Vine she had mentioned, apart from

being the leader of the No-Laws? Where had he been "otherwise engaged" and why had he re-emerged now? His name had been whirling around in my brain once I'd got into bed, and I had the most peculiar dream about him that unnerved me.

In the dream, I was wandering in a dark cave calling out for Phyllis. There was a light I could see in the distance, and as I approached it, my legs shaking all the way, the light became the face of a man. Without being told, I knew it was Mal Vine. He looked weather-beaten, as if he had been at sea all his life. His skin was brown and lined, his hair was greying and flopped around his face, as if it needed cutting. He had a sharp chin and small brown eyes, but his most distinguishing feature was the scratch marks down his cheek. He smiled at me as I approached him, and as he smiled his eyes completely disappeared into crinkles of skin, which made him look like he was wearing some kind of strange Halloween mask.

"I can help you find Phyllis, Rosie. Why don't you let me help you?" His voice was hypnotic and deep and echoed all around the cave.

"I... I already have my friend Adi helping me. Phyllis would want me to help her, not a stranger."

"Oh, but I'm not a stranger, Rosie. Far from it."

His eyes hardened slightly, but he smiled again, and as his image faded I remembered him tipping his fingers to his forehead in a friendly salute to me. I felt anxious when I woke, as the dream had seemed so real, and I felt even more alone with no one to share my experiences with. Mae and Gloria were good friends, but they weren't Adi.

. . .

It was the following week when I finally managed to corner Adi. I'd had enough of him avoiding me. It was a Monday, and Mum had literally skipped off to rehearsal, glowing with a golden colour surrounding her. It was fuzzy and warm looking and made her appear younger and more alive somehow.

Dad was vibrating dark browns tinged with green. I didn't know what the colours meant, but it was clear he couldn't seem to make a decision. He came downstairs twice in different shirts before finally changing back into what he'd had on in the first place: a black hoodie. (To be fair all his outfits were variations on black.)

Mum in contrast was today wearing a NEW (okay, charity shop new, but new nonetheless) dress. It was a sort of 70's style (so she said), with lots of different colours on it — orange and pink and black and yellow — with a big bow at the neck. She had on bright-pink, opaque tights and her retro black shoes that she wore every day on this job. Normally, Mum only wore those shoes if she and Dad were going out or if she had an audition.

"John, are you going to be home at a decent hour tonight?" she asked Dad as he was putting his coat on.

"Er, not sure, why?"

"I've invited Marcus and Nikolai over for a drink after rehearsals." She lifted her head up from doing up her shoes and added, almost as an afterthought, "It would be lovely if you could meet them, too."

Dad adopted a pained look on his face. "It's Monday, Rae. Do you have to have people over on a Monday? Why not a Thursday or a Friday?"

"Would it make any difference really, John?"

"I just don't really want to socialise on a Monday, that's all."

I saw Mum chew her lip and hesitate. "It's just a drink, John, that's all. This job is important to me. These people make me feel like something, and I want to share that with you."

"You are something, Rae. You don't need a load of turns to make you feel special or talented, do you?"

"Yes, sometimes I do, actually."

Dad turned away and let himself out of the door.

"Will me and Lois get to meet Marcus and Nikolai then, Mum?" I asked, partly as a way of distracting her, but, also, I wanted to meet this famous actor and director that Mum talked about in such an animated way.

"Yes, probably, Rosie, briefly. Come on, let's get going now. Lois, have you finished cleaning your teeth?"

I could hear Lois upstairs talking to Bea and had heard no sign of her electric toothbrush having been on.

"Coming, Mum," shouted Lois.

"Yes, but have you cleaned your teeth, young lady?" Mum asked again. We both knew she would have to end up going up and standing over Lois whilst she cleaned her teeth. Sometimes my sister just managed to orchestrate the whole world to run around after her at her pace.

Believe it or not, we were early arriving at school and once Mum had dashed off to rehearsals, I kept my beady eye out for Adi. I soon spied him walking down into the playground, his rucksack on his back, his Spiderman comic in his right hand. He was weaving in and out of children whilst still giving the impression of being totally transfixed on his magazine. I took a run up, grabbed his comic, and fled over towards the pirate ship where there was a little bit of privacy.

"Oy! Rosemary, give it back!" Adi shouted indignantly at me.

I waved it in the air. "Come and get it, Adi, or are you a coward?"

I raced towards the ship and tucked myself into the little round tunnel bit where you could just about squeeze three of you at a push. Adi followed and breathlessly launched himself into the tunnel next to me.

"Where is it? Give it back, Rosemary. That's so mean of you."

"As mean as you have been in ignoring me, Adi..."

"Where is it, Rosemary? Are you sitting on it?"

"No." (I was, actually.)

"Then give it back now or I'll tell the teacher."

"Are you gonna tell the teacher what a coward you are, too, Adi? Not wanting to talk to me about our visit to Aradne and what happened there? Why don't you want to go back, Adi? I can't talk to anyone else about it. You're the only person, and it's not fair. I need to find Phyllis, and I can't do it without you."

Adi was silent.

He pushed his glasses further back on to his nose. They did have a habit of sliding down — his face wasn't quite big enough for them, I guess.

"Rosemary, I'm really scared. What if we go again and we don't come back? Mum says we are going to India for Christmas holidays, and I really, really, want to go. What if I can't? I won't see my cousins or Grandparents."

"Adi," I said gently. "Nothing bad is going to happen to us. I promised Lois she could come next time, and do you really think I'd take my baby sister if it was dangerous?"

I was sort of crossing my fingers whilst saying this, as I didn't really know if it could be dangerous or not.

The truth was, I really needed Adi. He was a logical thinker. He knew about physics and maths and stuff like that, which I knew would be useful if we were going into another dimension. We would never have found the entrance to the portal in the first place if it hadn't been for his knowledge of the facts about gravity.

"Adi, please, we need you, and if you conquer this fear and we go back and you prove how courageous you are, I know you'll be so pleased with yourself. You'll be dead proud."

I reached underneath for his comic that I was sat on. It was a bit soggy from rainwater that had collected within the tunnel. I felt bad giving it back like that to him.

"Sorry about your comic."

"It's okay, Rosemary. It will dry if I put it on the radiator."

I got out of the tunnel just as the bell was going for the start of school. We had reached an impasse. I didn't know if Adi was going to come with us again or not. Sometimes you just have to leave people to mull things over, and hope they make the right decision, Mum always says. This was one of those moments. I just knew time was ticking by, and I had to go back to the other world.

With or without Adi.

12

MARCUS

Frances was extremely agitated when she picked us up from school. She kept looking around every few moments as if she was expecting to see someone. We had to almost run to keep up with her, she was striding out so fast.

"Frances," I asked breathlessly, "why are we in such a hurry and why do you keep looking around?"

"Just want to get back, Rosie." She flicked her eyes from left to right again and then seemed to relax as she focused on something or someone in the distance.

I could just make out a rotund figure in mostly brown coming towards us at quite a pace. It had to be Uncle Vic. As we got closer, I could see the shininess of his bald head, and he raised a hand in quick recognition of us. Lois was moaning all the way. Our only solace was the short time she took to munch away on her digestive biscuits that Frances had brought for her.

At last we reached Uncle Vic, and once he'd got his "Hello, girls, how was school?" out the way, he sidled next to Frances and began trying to secretively speak to her. I was too tired to try to listen in to what they were saying. I had Lois begging me for a piggyback. I was trying to carry my water bottle, my empty lunch box, and my book bag, and all I wanted to do was get home and play a mindless computer game.

Frances was like a cat on a hot tin roof when we got home. She was jumpy and forgetful, whilst Uncle Vic was overcompensating by trying to smile at us and offer us biscuits and extended computer time. It was most suspicious.

A message popped up on my Roblox game from StormtrooperA1:

```
Sorry Rosemary. I won't let you down
again. Ready when you are.
```

Adi's message somehow buoyed me up, and I went back into the kitchen to confront Uncle Vic and Frances. They were sitting at the kitchen table, mugs in hand, deep in discussion. I launched in:

"What's happened, Uncle Vic? Is there any news on Phyllis?"

Uncle Vic looked up at me. At least, I think he was looking at me. He might have had one eye on Bob who was fast asleep on the rocking chair.

"Now, now, young lady, this is nothing for you to concern yourself with."

"Actually, Vic," interrupted Frances, "it is only fair we keep Rosie in the loop. After all, she does know about the portal. She knows what we are and what Foggy is doing. She's a big girl now. We can't keep treating her like a mushroom."

"A mushroom?" I queried.

"Keeping you in the dark, darling," Frances added.

Uncle Vic sighed, took a sip of his tea, and patted the seat next to him, motioning for me to sit down.

"Mr Foggerty is on another mission right now. In order to do this, he has to try to move forwards through time, so he can see what the No-Laws are planning and then prevent it before it goes too far."

I nodded. "But who are the No-Laws? Have they taken Phyllis?"

Uncle Vic glanced at Frances, who shrugged.

"They are a nasty bunch led by a man called Mal Vine."

I shivered at the mention of his name. "Who is Mal Vine?" I asked, anxious to know more about the man I had seen in my dreams.

Frances glanced nervously at Uncle Vic. "He's a very unhappy, bitter man who wants to destroy any kind of love in the world. We believe Phyllis was lured out of hiding by Mal starting up his campaign of chaos so close to her home..." Frances tailed off and glanced once more at Uncle Vic.

"Phyllis has been in hiding?" I exclaimed, realising this was why I never saw her leave the house.

"Well, yes, let's just say she has been trying to keep out of harm's way. It's one thing Mal Vine causing mayhem in London, but when it's on her doorstep, it's another matter." Frances smiled nervously.

"But we are all safe," I added, confused. "We weren't on the bus."

"Mal doesn't just use physical methods to hurt people. Sometimes he just tries to destroy love or things that we love. In London he's already been responsible for the recent burpee cold, with thousands of workers having to stay at home until their foul-smelling burps have run their course, as well as the cloak of sadness he threw over the East End."

I immediately thought of my dad and the way his cloud seemed to be threatening my parents' happiness together. Was this Mal Vine's work too?

"We think that Phyllis' disappearance was an accident. She went forward in time, which was part of her and Mr Foggerty's plans to thwart the No-Law's bus incident, but unfortunately she became stuck in a wormhole."

"What's a wormhole?" I'd never heard of such a strange term, and I was sure they weren't talking about a hole in the ground where earth worms live.

"It's a tricky thing to explain, Rosemary, but I'll do my best," Uncle Vic continued. "A wormhole is basically a shortcut through space and time. Think of time as a piece of paper. If you want to get from one end of the paper to the other, it's quite a journey. But if you were to fold the piece of paper in two, you could easily jump from the bottom to the top of the paper. This is effectively what a wormhole is. It's a jump or a bridge through time. Unfortunately, these wormholes are not terribly reliable and are prone to collapse, and that's what we think has happened to Phyllis, though we have no real way of knowing, as yet. Our boss, Hecate, is trying to work out how we can find a way to retrace her steps and possibly find her, if she's not already a goner."

"You mean she might be dead?" I asked aghast.

Frances gave Uncle Vic a long, hard stare. "I'm sure she's not dead, my love, just a bit lost," she said. "We're going to find her, don't you worry."

"Let's hope we do before someone else does," Uncle Vic added sombrely.

"What do you mean, Uncle Vic? Do you mean Mal Vine?" My mind went back to my dream and him offering to help me find her.

"I think that's enough for now, Vic. I'm just going to 'pop upstairs', as I think Rae will be back at any moment and she's got VI-SI-TORS." Frances sounded this last word out to Uncle Vic as if she was spelling out a tricky word.

He got up hastily, patted me on the arm, and rushed out of the kitchen. I picked up their mugs and put them in the dishwasher, a little frustrated I hadn't been able to ask any more questions. Two minutes later, I heard Mum's key in the lock.

"Hellooooo, girls. I'm home, and I've got someone with me."

"In the kitchen, Mum," I called. "Lois, Mum's home. Come and say hi."

Lois trundled out of Dad's office and wiped biscuit crumbs from her mouth with Bea's nose. I glared at her.

Mum sashayed into the kitchen looking bright eyed and rosy cheeked. Following her was a very tall man with black slicked-back hair, green hooded eyes, and the biggest nose I've ever seen in my life. He was wearing a black roll-necked jumper that was TUCKED into jeans, and POLISHED DRESS SHOES. He had a dark blue circle around his body with fat little balls of green that would get to a certain size and, *poof*, would somehow explode in exuberance. It was very strange to watch.

"This is Marcus," Mum said with the kind of delight you would have if you'd just found a pound coin.

I surveyed Marcus with steely eyes.

My dad never wears shoes with jeans. He wears trainers or boots, but not DRESS SHOES. My dad never tucks jumpers into jeans. My dad's hair is unruly and curly and cool, not greasy looking with stray pieces that escape and float over his eyes. There was something, I don't know, untrustworthy about Marcus. He was smiling like a crocodile, all teeth and cold eyes. He flicked his gaze from me to Lois and obviously thought she'd be the pushover as she was the youngest.

"Hello, girls," he said in a deep, gravelly, faux-American voice. "How lovely to meet you both. I've heard so much about you. And who's this cute teddy you're holding?"

"She's a rabbit and she's called Bea," stated Lois, who then unceremoniously wiped her mouth with Bea's nose again.

"Lois!" Mum scolded. "How many times have I told you not to use Bea as a handkerchief or napkin? Go and get some tissue if you need to wipe your mouth, please."

She turned back to Marcus and sort of fluttered her eyelashes and flicked her hair back. "Sorry, Marcus, what must you think of my daughters!? Can I get you a cup of tea or a beer or something?"

Marcus laughed and rubbed Mum's arm. "Don't worry, Rae. Remember I've got dogs." (What was THAT supposed to mean? Even Mum looked slightly puzzled.) "I'd love a cup of tea, and then I'll move on to the hard stuff," he said.

Mum bustled about in the kitchen, making tea and heating up baked beans and hot dog sausages for a quick dinner for Lois and me, whilst Marcus sat at the kitchen table trying to engage with us.

"So girls, tell me about yourselves," he stated.

Lois just stared at him, and I did my best not to be too rude, even though I wanted to ask him all sorts of questions like: *Do you have to put sun cream on your nose?* and *Do you have to blow it more cos it's so big?* and *Does it get in the way?* and *Have you ever shut it in a lift door?* and *How big are your bogeys?*

Instead I just said: "I'm Rosemary, and I love cats."

"We don't like dogs," Lois added.

Marcus looked slightly dismayed.

"Don't like dogs, dear, dear," he flicked a look back to Mum, but she was carefully squeezing out teabags from the mugs.

"We prefer cats," I said hastily.

"I've always been a bit suspicious of cats," Marcus said, grimacing slightly as he caught sight of Bob who was still fast asleep on the rocking chair.

"Oh, Bob's lovely," I said in defence of our sleeping ginger cat.

"Yes, but be careful he doesn't wee on you," added Lois very seriously.

"He doesn't wee on purpose, Lois." I said.

"I didn't say on purpose, Rosie," Lois chimed. "And Maggie likes to scratch you," she added with relish.

Marcus looked a little nervous now.

"Don't take any notice of Lois, Marcus." I was trying to give him the benefit of the doubt. "She's exaggerating. Our cats are friendly and wouldn't hurt a fly."

At that moment, Maggie appeared in the kitchen retching and coughing and generally sounding as if she was being strangled.

Marcus looked terrified and stood up quickly, trying to back himself up against the kitchen wall. Suddenly, Maggie wheezed and spluttered and there appeared on the tiles a long black mass of hair mixed with grass and food.

Mum bent down to stroke her, but she shot out of the cat flap. Marcus looked disgusted.

"It's okay, everyone. It's only a fur ball! Nothing to worry about!" Mum looked at Marcus, who was looking like he might cough one up, too. She giggled.

"Don't worry, Marcus, she won't hurt you. It's just normal for cats to cough them up every now and then. It's the fur from all the washing themselves they do. In fact, it shows what a clean cat she is." She giggled again. "Your face is a picture!" She tapped his arm in playful way. "Go and sit in the lounge, and I'll join you in a minute."

Marcus hurriedly made his way into the lounge whilst Mum dished our dinner up to us.

"Marcus is playing George, who is my character's husband in the play. He's actually quite famous," she whispered.

"Famous?" questioned Lois.

"Yes, darling, he's been in lots of things over the years, so people know who he is and sometimes they even ask for his autograph."

"What's he been in?" I asked.

"He was in a series of films called *The Camelot Days*. He played Cyrano de Bergerac on Broadway and he did a series of adverts for, erm, Olbas Oil. But maybe don't mention that one to him."

"Olbas Oil?"

"Yes, Lois, you know it's the stuff you put up your nose when you've got a cold and can't breathe properly."

"'Cept Marcus probably needed the whole bottle." I had to hold my giggle in.

"Rosemary!" Mum berated me and held her finger to her mouth. It sounded to me like lots of Marcus' jobs had been due to his large nose.

We ate our dinner peppered by the sounds of Mum's laughter coming from the lounge. Marcus was doing an awful lot of talking.

A bit later on, Mum popped back into the kitchen to get a beer for him and a gin and tonic for herself and told us to go and get ourselves washed and ready for bed once we'd finished our food.

Suddenly, a thought occurred to me.

"Mum, where's Nikolai, the famous director who was coming here, too?"

"Oh, poor Nikolai couldn't come, darling. He had too much work to do. I do hope Daddy gets home soon so he can meet Marcus."

She scurried back into the lounge, and me and Lois made our way upstairs.

As we passed the lounge, it wasn't difficult to hear what Marcus was talking about: himself.

"Now," he continued with gusto, "let me finish telling you about the movie I did with Dwayne 'The Rock' Johnson."

We got ourselves washed and in our jim jams in record time. I don't know why, but Lois insisted on wearing her very old Pinocchio nightie, which was too short and had a brown felt-tip pen mark right on her bum, so it looked like she'd either sat in something or pooed herself. We were coming down the stairs when, *hallelujah!*, Dad arrived home. Mum was just coming out the lounge with an empty bottle and glass.

"Hello, darling, I'm glad you're home. You must meet Marcus. What do you want to drink?"

Dad looked a bit harassed. "I need the loo," he said in hushed tones, "and then I'll have a G&T."

He took the stairs two at a time, meanwhile me and Lois gave each other a mutual look of solidarity and headed off into the lounge.

Lois leant against the fireplace, and I sat down in front of Marcus and gave him my biggest smile. He looked very at home on our sofa, reclining with a slightly sweaty forehead.

Neither of us spoke. I heard a very faint noise, like a balloon being very gently let down, and thought nothing of it until moments later the smell hit me. Lois had struck again. It was a combination of baked beans and hot dog sausages mixed with Cheesy Puffs, and it was an A-star quality. As Dad would sometimes say: "I'd be proud of that, if I'd done it."

Lois was nonchalantly humming to herself, oblivious to the carnage she was about to cause. Marcus looked smug until the smell had clearly hit him. He subtly moved his nostrils to and fro, as if checking they weren't playing some awful joke on him, and then he looked slightly wide eyed and pale as if he was going to be sick. Finally, he glared at me. I wanted to laugh and say, "don't look at me. It was Lois, the cute little one."

At that moment, Mum returned with drinks, swiftly followed by Dad.

"Good god, what is that smell?" Dad said without any hesitation. Mum looked embarrassed. "Is that you Lois?" Dad continued.

"Is it me what, Daddy?" she answered innocently.

"Have you farted?" Dad asked more crossly now.

"No, it wasn't me," she said benignly. "I think it might have been Marcus."

Marcus looked like he was going to burst a blood vessel.

"I doubt that very much darling," Mum said hastily. "Now go and stick your bottom out the back door or something, please."

Lois left the room sulkily and then returned moments later.

"Marcus, this is John. John, Marcus. Sorry about that, she's had baked beans tonight. I think we'll have to ban them for another week."

Marcus clearly had no idea what Mum was on about re: the baked beans. He obviously hadn't lived.

"Lovely to meet you, John," sneered Marcus silkily.

"Yup, you too," my Dad replied shortly.

"Thank you for lending me your wife, John, for this play. She's a wonderful co-star. I hope you enjoy what we've done with it when we open."

"Yes, I'm looking forward to seeing it," Dad replied tightly.

Mum looked very fidgety, as if she didn't quite know what to say.

Then there was silence.

I wondered what to do that might break the ice. Then it came to me. "I'm just going to the loo," I said to no one in particular.

"Me too," copied Lois, following me.

"How's it all going then?" I heard my dad say.

"Wonderful. Your Rae is really making the part her own. Have you been helping her, John, with her lines, etc.?"

"No, I like to leave that to Rae. She knows what she's doing."

"Of course, of course, John. Anyway, that's what I'm here for, to guide her, to give her extra help whenever she needs it."

"I think you'll find she's perfectly capable of managing on her own," my dad responded sharply.

Thank god for the fridge magnet. I stood on tiptoes and pressed it with Lois at my side. We both thought it was a great idea. The music started and, to my surprise, Dad was the first one in the kitchen,

"Come on, Rae, Marcus. The bagpipes wait for no one."

Mum quickly followed and half-heartedly started Scottish dancing. My dad, for the FIRST time ever, was doing it with gusto. Marcus stood in the doorway aghast. The four of us made a circle and flicked our legs up, dancing round with laughter tickling our lungs. As the music ended Marcus muttered, "Wow, yeah, lovely to meet you all. I'd better go. Don't see me out, Rae. I'll see you tomorrow."

"See you again, Marcus." My dad shook his hand as Mum hastily followed Marcus into the hall and shut the front door after him.

Dad downed the rest of his drink, winked at me, and turned the oven on.

13

THE PENDLE WITCHES

The next morning when I woke, I could already hear the TV was on in the kitchen. I pulled my dressing gown on, thinking it was strange that Lois was up before me and made my way downstairs with Maggie weaving in and out my legs. Dad was sitting in the rocking chair with a cup of tea, glued to the news. He glanced up at me and placed his fingers to his lips in the "shush" gesture and then pointed to my croissant on the side.

I had just taken a bite of my lovely, still-warm croissant, when I saw the unmistakeable image of Mr Foggerty appear once again on the television news, along with the caption:

Wanted In Connection With Attempted Attack in Manchester

My stomach did a sort of loop-the-loop as the presenter recapped what had happened.

"Last night, once again, we believe a potential attack may have been thwarted by the mysterious, bearded elderly man seen in the image below. What we know is that a hooded person entered the busy bar and restaurant Charlie Brown's in central Manchester around 10pm last night. They were seen to be carrying a large black bag. Before panic set in, before the busy punters were even aware of the potential danger, some eyewitnesses recalled seeing a bearded man carrying a large besom broomstick sweep into the crowded restaurant, drag the hooded person out with force, and simply disappear into the night. In the early hours of this morning, police were called to Pendle Hill, Lancashire, after locales reported a suspected meteorite explosion. The suspect was found tied up to the white stone on the hill's summit with a tag tied to his ankle that read 'Harm Ye None'. Some 200 yards away were the charred remains of the black bag, which had contained a huge amount of black dahlias."

I was still trying to take in what I had just seen, when I realised Dad was speaking to me.

"Sorry?"

"I said, isn't it strange that some people saw that funny looking man and others didn't?"

"Mmmm," I replied, distracted by the eyewitness reports.

A 20-something man with a long fringe and a strong Manchester accent was very casually retelling the events from his perspective.

"It was proper weird, man. Out comes this old fella with a broomstick and a black bag. I didn't see no other person in a hoodie, then the old fella disappeared. I

looked down to get me phone out me pocket, and when
I looked up, he'd gone. In a puff of smoke."

"Well, I wouldn't rely on what he had to say, looks like
he'd had one too many sherbets," said Dad getting up from
the chair. "You can put your programme on now, Rosie. I'm
off in a sec."

I suppose I should have noticed that Dad seemed a little
brighter than he had been for ages. Whether it was the
verbal sparring he'd had with Marcus the night before, I
didn't know, and didn't really have time to ponder. But as he
left the room I noticed his cloud was white with a hint of
gold around the edges, as if the sun was trying to break
through.

As I ate the rest of my croissant, I went over the events
in my head. It made sense now why Frances had been so
jittery yesterday when she collected us from school. She
and Uncle Vic must have known that Mr Foggerty was
imminently putting himself in danger with this mission.
Suddenly, I was glad they hadn't told me much about it. I
was relieved to know it was over. Was this the work of the
No-Laws? If so, I really wasn't sure I wanted to get mixed
up with them. And the black bag had been safely
despatched to the top of Pendle Hill — there it was again,
Pendle Hill. I had to find out what the link was. This was
the third time I'd heard it mentioned.

I presumed that if he had managed to get the person all
the way to Pendle Hill from central Manchester, that Mr
Foggerty MUST be okay. He was going to have to keep a
low profile from now on, though, as the television news
people seemed to know he was the same man who had
intercepted the Liverpool bus, so there must have been a
few believers who had seen him.

Mum appeared in the kitchen wearing a familiar-looking, bottle-green velvet dress. I stared at it puzzled, until she said:

"Yes, darling, this is Frances' dress. She said I could have it, as it's a little too long for her, and she kept on tripping over it."

I have to say it did look spectacular on Mum, though I silently wondered why she was getting so dressed up for rehearsals. "Daddy said there's been another one of those strange attacks."

"Well, kind of," I replied. "Someone went into a restaurant in Manchester with a bag of black dahlias." I lowered my voice to a whisper. "Someone we know stopped them and tied them up on some hill in the countryside."

Mum paled. "Foggy," she whispered. "They should have kept me in the loop. Pendle Hill."

She sat down at the table and put her hand to her mouth.

"When is this going to end, Rosemary?" she said to me, but I got the feeling it wasn't really a question.

"What's so special about Pendle Hill, Mum?" I asked. "Why did he take them there and what are the flowers about?"

She looked off into the distance. "Black Dahlias symbolise betrayal and dishonesty in magic. There was a lot of dishonesty during The Witch Trials and many people felt betrayed by loved ones."

"Eh?" I asked, feeling a little fizz of apprehension.

Mum sighed. "I haven't got much time to go into it all this morning, Rosie, but in a nutshell: in 1612, some women and men from Pendle Hill were hanged for witchcraft. There was a big trial where they were accused of being witches and having murdered children and adults, and they were found guilty and hanged. Foggy is a direct descendant of Elizabeth Device, one of the accused, and Phyllis, Frances, and Uncle Vic are related to some of the others; so that place is very special to them. To all involved, actually. It doesn't surprise me that Mr Foggerty went there..."

At that moment, Lois appeared at the entrance to the kitchen, clutching Bea and looking sleepy but smiley. There were so many questions I wanted to ask Mum. This knowledge had opened up a whole array of other avenues I wanted to explore. Who were these people that our house-guests were related to from years gone by? Why would Mr Foggerty have taken that person to Pendle Hill just because he had some relatives who had lived there years ago? It didn't make sense. There had to be more to it than that. How was any of this leading to discovering Phyllis' where-abouts? I didn't know much about wormholes, so I knew Adi would have some answers, and I couldn't wait to see him so we could arrange when we were going back through the portal.

I didn't get my chance to see him until break time at school.

"Got your message, Ads," I said to him out the corner of my mouth, as I nonchalantly passed by him in the playground.

"Don't call me Ads, Rosemary. I hate it."

"Soz."

"I can't come round until Thursday, if that's okay. It's Jar Jar's birthday tomorrow, so I can't disappear." (Jar Jar was Adi's nickname for his little brother.) "Can you wait till then?" He looked at me anxiously, his big brown eyes full of a mixture of excitement and nerves — trepidation, I guess you'd call it.

"Yeah, okay, come round straight after school. I'll find a way to distract Frances."

I bent down and pretended to re-do my shoelaces, then straightened myself up and carried on walking as if our conversation had never happened.

That night I frantically googled The Pendle Witch Trials.

I discovered that, in 1612, Elizabeth Device's daughter, Alizon, had been accused of causing a pedlar named John Law to become lame because he wouldn't sell her these pins. John Law said she struck him down with a curse that caused him to have a stroke, and she confessed to this when questioned by the Justice of the Peace for the area (a kind of chief of police type person), who was a man called Roger Nowell.

Another family that had been the Device's rivals were the Whittles, and they were also accused of witchcraft along with several other people. Roger Nowell made it his mission to put many local people on trial for witchcraft, and as a result of this, ten people, all from the Pendle Hill area, were found guilty and hanged on Gallows Hill in Lancaster. There was nothing about Mal Vine though.

I closed the Google window down as Mum called me to have my dinner. I still couldn't work out what would make Mr Foggerty take that person to Pendle Hill, other than the fact it was in the middle of nowhere and therefore a good place to safely explode a bag of black dahlias.

I hadn't had a chance to ask Frances anything about Mr Foggerty and his mission and whether he was safe, and now that Mum had arrived, Frances had gone again. There was no sign of Uncle Vic either.

"What did you think of Marcus?" Mum's question broke my thoughts.

"Yeah he was okay," I said non-committedly whilst shovelling Spaghetti Bolognese in my mouth.

"What do you mean by okay?" Mum's eyes narrowed slightly and she tilted her head to one side.

"A bit creepy, and he doesn't like cats either," I replied, my gaze firmly fixed on the TV.

"You're just not used to meeting theatre people, darling, that's all." She picked some white flick off her velvet dress.

"He thought you were all rather fabulous, even Lois with her wind, the little monkey. Now, Thursday night I shall be late home, darling, as I'm rehearsing in the evening, too; so Uncle Vic will be looking after you until I'm home, as Frances can't do Thursday."

"Oh no, does that mean Uncle Vic is meeting us from school, Mum?" I groaned, imagining him turning up full of stains. "Can't you have a word and ask him to put some clean clothes on?"

"Rosie, really, don't be horrible. His clothes ARE clean. I just think he's messy eater and misses his mouth from time to time."

"I'm not surprised. He probably can't see his food properly."

"Now, don't be rude. Just because you're slightly cross eyed doesn't mean you can't see properly. He's a very busy man, and he has lots to think about, and I'm sure the odd stain on his clothes is the least of his worries. I will see if I can dig out some other clothes and sneakily offer them to him as a gift or something. I'm sure Dad's got some stuff that he doesn't wear anymore. Leave it with me."

"Any news from Mr Foggerty, Mum?"

She looked down as if avoiding my gaze.

"No, darling, not as yet. I haven't had a chance to speak

to Frances, really. I'm as much in the dark as you. I shall watch the news later and see what they say."

I knew then we couldn't wait for news on Mr Foggerty. We had to head back through the portal to get some answers from Hecate before anymore incidences occurred. Phyllis' life could be depending on it.

14

HECATE

At last, Thursday arrived and I woke with butterflies in my tummy knowing that this was the day for Adi and me to return to the other dimension and seek out Hecate as Jonathan had instructed us to do.

The school day seemed to drag by, but finally the bell went, and I found myself outside watching the rotund figure of Uncle Vic striding across the playground toward me with Lois tagging behind. He had actually remembered to bring her some crisps, which would make our walk home a bit easier.

I had to do a double take because he was wearing trousers that were far too long! They trailed on the floor behind him. His jacket was oversized, too, but his shirt seemed to be straining around his stomach. Then I realised what was going on. He was wearing some of Dad's old clothes. Mum had obviously been true to her word and given him some of Dad's cast offs and not thought that they wouldn't actually fit him! I could have cried.

Let's get out of here before anyone notices him, I thought. I already had a plan. I was going to tell him that I'd arranged with Mum for Adi to come over for tea, so we could work on homework in the lounge. Undisturbed. This way he wouldn't wonder where we were when we went through the wall.

Trust our luck, as we were walking home, Murray and Dan suddenly appeared tagging along behind us

"Who's your mate, Rosie?" Murray shouted whilst I could hear Dan stifling giggles. I ignored him. "Oi, Oi," he repeated. "I said who's your mate who needs to grow into his clothes?"

Uncle Vic was busy eating another packet of crisps, the ones that Lois had rejected, so he was oblivious to the childish abuse I was getting from behind us. As for Lois, nothing and no one would ever disturb her when she was eating. So I knew I would have to deal with these two clowns myself. I turned round to face them and rather snootily said:

"He's our Uncle, if you must know. And where he comes from, it's fashionable to wear clothes that are too big for you."

"Ooooooooooohhhhhhh," the two boys sneered.

"Where's he from then? Boggy Bottom?" Dan laughed.

"Winkle Street?" Dan was breathless with laughter, so Murray continued.

"Scratchy Bottom? What's he gonna do then, this Uncle of yours? Lasso us with his oversized trousers?" Murray said.

At this moment, they both raced ahead of us so they could turn and face Uncle Vic and Lois whilst walking backwards. "Oi, Uncle," they shouted in unison. "Can you even see us!? Oh yeah, look, one eye is looking at me and the other eye is looking at you, Dan." They both had hysterics.

I have never seen Uncle Vic lose his temper, or say much at all really, other than perfunctory statements, like

"How are you girls?" Even now, he didn't actually SAY much. He stopped, suddenly very still. Lois stopped, too, but didn't take her eyes off her crisp packet. I was far enough behind to pause and view what unfolded at a safe distance.

He raised a finger on one of his hands to the boys as if to say, "Watch this a minute", took his empty crisp packet, and blew into it, like you do at home when you're mucking about. It was full of air. He then banged it against his other hand so it made a loud popping sound. Only this wasn't the popping sound of a bag of air. It sounded more like a firework going off. Murray and Dan seemed to jump in the air and, as they landed, they ended up back to back with their arms wrapped around each other, so they couldn't move. They lay flailing on the ground, and as we walked past them, Uncle Vic said, "I *choose* to be different boys. It's much more fun. Come along, girls, nothing to see here." And on we trotted.

I still had to convince Uncle Vic to keep Lois entertained while Adi and I went through the wall, somehow. Luckily for us, I didn't have to think too hard. We got home, and who was sitting at the kitchen table? Mr Foggerty! I have to say I was pleased to see him, not just so we could make our journey safely, but also to see that he was unscathed after his tussle with the agitator.

"Mr Foggerty!" I exclaimed. "Are you okay?" Lois looked at him with curious intent.

"Yes, I'm fine, Rosemary. Thank you for asking."

He twitched a bit impatiently in his seat and scratched his beard. "Right. Can I interest you in some fudge or something? Uncle Vic and I have got a bit of grown up catching up to do."

Lois screwed up her nose. "Is that cuddling and kissing?"

Mr Foggerty and Uncle Vic looked confused.

"It's what Mum says when she wants to give Dad a cuddle and a kiss," I hastily added before Lois said anything else inappropriate.

"I like shortbread, though, and digestive biscuits." Hurray, she had gone back to her favourite subject: food.

"It's okay, I'll get Lois a biscuit and set up her game on the computer in Dad's office."

They both looked relieved and Uncle Vic put the kettle on to make tea whilst I hurriedly got Lois changed and settled on the computer with biscuits, just in time to intercept Adi at the front door before he ding-donged.

"Get in quick, Adi, we haven't much time," I whispered to him.

"Okay, okay," he replied. "I've got the same jumper on as I had before, so maybe my pentagram will still be on it?"

"Good thinking," I said. "I've done the same with my school blouse. I'd hidden it at the bottom of my wardrobe, so Mum wouldn't wash it. You know, just in case. You'd better do the same with your jumper, Adi."

"It's okay, my mum refuses to get washing out my room. She says if I don't put it in the wash bag, then it won't get washed."

Adi took out a pebble from his pocket and began the ritual of dropping it around the mirror area. We were getting good at this. As soon as it hovered, we both stood side by side looking into the mirror and said in unison:

"Aradia. Aradia. Aradia."

That whooshing sound came again. I closed my eyes and grabbed Adi's hand, and he squeezed my fingers so tightly I thought he was going to take my hand off. All of a sudden, it was quiet, and I opened my eyes and there was Aradia, this time wearing some reading glasses that made her eyes look even browner and larger than before.

"Ummm," she said in a slightly sneery way. "I didn't expect to see you two again."

She waved her portable bleeper towards our pentagrams, which had magically appeared on our tops, and I quickly opened my legs and drew my arms out and nudged Adi to do the same as Paloma squawked and flew in and out of limbs, frisking us once more.

Before Paloma could fly off down the corridor, I commanded, "Take us to Door 21, please."

Paloma turned her head. I swear she gave me an evil look and then took flight down the corridor.

We ran after her, breathless with nerves, anticipation, and excitement. Then suddenly, we couldn't see her.

"Adi, I thought I saw her stop in the distance," I was panicking now. "Where has she gone?"

"I don't know, Rosemary. My glasses keep slipping off my nose."

"They are too big for you, Adi," I scolded.

We ran up and down several times, until I suddenly heard this faint cawing, almost like a chuckle.

"Shush, Adi, I can hear something."

I scanned doors immediately near to us and there, resting on the round knob of a black door with a fuchsia pink 21 on its front, camouflaged by the colour of the door, was Paloma. She was preening herself and making this little gentle caw sound. In fact, I would go as far as to say she was laughing at us.

I regained my composure, looked Adi in the eye and said, "are you ready?" In that moment he must have been my kindred spirit, as he nodded serenely, smiled, and patted my arm in a gesture of controlled calmness.

"Let's go, Rosemary."

"Paloma, you may knock."

As soon as she had tapped on the door with her beak, she took flight again, kindly dropping a little poop on my left shoulder as she ascended. I was fuming. *Horrid, nasty bird*, I thought, trying my best to wipe the creamy, semi-liquid bird poo off my cardigan.

"This is disgusting, Adi. She's horrible that bird. It's all over my hand now."

"Shhhh," Adi whispered. "Try the handle."

I wiped my hand on my skirt and tentatively tried the doorknob. It opened.

As we stepped into the room, we were totally dazzled by the light inside. It was such a contrast to the blackness of the door itself. The door swung shut behind us, we were at a disadvantage now, for neither of us could see anything.

I grabbed Adi's hand (again! I hoped he wasn't going to get the wrong idea), and he spoke what I was thinking:

"Rosemary, it's so bright, I can't see anything."

The most beautiful serene voice came out of nowhere and half-sang, half-said, "Come along, children. Sit your-selves down on the cushions by the hearth. There's juice and all kinds of sweets to eat. Your eyes will adjust, and you will soon see your surroundings. There is nothing to fear."

As we walked forward, our arms shielding our eyes from the brightness of the light, my feet stumbled upon something metal on the floor. I bent down and picked up a large shiny black key. As I held it, it seemed to grow hot so I hastily popped it into my pocket. We took a few more steps, and then we could feel our feet hit against something soft. It must have been the cushions.

"Let's sit here, Rosemary."

We sat, and though the room was still dazzling and we couldn't see what we were sitting on, we could feel the warmth of a fire in front of us. It felt so cosy and comfortable. We waited in companionable silence.

A few moments later, the lights started to dim down gradually until we could see a fantastic marble fireplace in front of us with a blazing fire crackling away. On the black tiles of the wide hearth were white glasses filled with juice and a beautifully carved white wooden bowl with all kinds of brightly coloured sweets and chocolates inside. On looking closer, the bowl was carved in the shape of a hand. I stretched out to take a glossy pink wrapper, and as my fingers met the sweet, the fingers of the bowl came alive and unwrapped the sweet and handed it to me. It was delicious, a combination of strawberry and chocolate and something else that I couldn't put a name to, like a popping sensation in my mouth which melted into tiny fragments of caramel.

I was busy choosing another sweet and encouraging Adi to do the same with my mouth full of chocolate, when I noticed a grand armchair out of the corner of my eye. I looked round, startled, and gave a little shriek of surprise.

There, sitting in the biggest pale-pink fluffy chair I've ever seen, with a baby at her breast, was a lady in a white flowing gown. She had soft waves of blonde hair, which reached down to her waist. Her eyes were azure blue, her mouth like a crimson rosebud. Her skin was creamy but had the faintest hint of freckles over her shoulders and nose. She had another sleeping infant snuggled up to her in the chair, and she was stroking his or her flaxen hair with her long fingers. I noticed how short her fingernails were. They looked like the hands of a mother, gentle but practical. She smiled at us both and spoke softly.

"I am Hecate. I've been waiting to meet you both. Welcome."

"Th-th-thank you," I stuttered.

Now we were here in this cosy room, which looked like someone's very grand lounge, I didn't know what to say.

"Jonathan sent us," Adi said very confidently, I thought.

I was too busy being mesmerised by this lady. There was something about her that reminded me of my mum, but I couldn't tell you what. She didn't look like my mum or sound like her. It was more a feeling, if you know what I mean. She certainly didn't have any colours around her, but then most people who we seemed to come into contact with, in this dimension, had an absence of colour around them.

"Ah yes, Jonathan." She continued smiling at his name. "He told me to expect you. But there is someone missing I think. Another child should be here. There has to be three of you."

"My sister, do you mean?" I asked

"Yes. Lois. She will come next time, yes?"

"Erm, yes okay, I did promise her she could come, but it was a bit tricky this time."

"Well, bring her next week. On Halloween. We will need her then. She has some power we need."

I quietly wondered whether Hecate was referring to Lois' farts, but dismissed it.

"Do you know why you are here, children?" Hecate fixed us with her clear eyes and the kindness in her expression made you feel you could tell her anything.

I knew why we were there. Jonathan had told us Hecate might be able to tell us where Phyllis had disappeared to, but I wasn't sure how to verbalise this, and I did feel a little in awe of Hecate.

"Let me start by telling you what I am here for." Hecate

continued breaking the silence. "You've heard of BUTBUM (AW), I believe?"

We nodded. "As you know, dear Phyllis, along with her colleagues Francesca, Victorious, and Beowulf have been instrumental in intercepting and preventing further attacks on the people of Britain by the group who call themselves the No-Laws. Their leader is a man called Mal Vine. He's a descendant of John Law, the pedlar who started all this nonsense, so he formed the group partly to try to continue the feud that his Great Uncle John had with the so-called Pendle Witches, who he believed caused his misery. And partly because Mal had developed a particularly warped view of love, probably thanks to his parents' foolish actions in destroying everything *he* loved. So, it has become his mission to create misery and chaos where he can. Where there is love, Mal and his followers want to bring hate."

"What did his parents do to make him feel so much hatred?" I asked, puzzled.

"That is of no consequence to you right now," Hecate stated, lifting her hand to the side as if she were brushing away that question. "What you do need to know, is that during one of these missions, Phyllis disappeared. I am here simply to restore order. I am known as Hecate, the Goddess of the Crossroads. I have the power to see where you are from, where you are now, and where you are going to. Rose-mary, your mother is the Guardian of the Portal, so it is only right that you, having discovered it, must take on this task to find Phyllis. The power of three is very important in magic, which is why Adi and your sister must join you. The three of you will bring your different strengths together in order to complete this mission and restore balance. And all will be well again. Until the next time." She spoke the last bit under her breath.

I wasn't properly listening, as I was still getting my head round the fact that Frances was really Francesca and Uncle Vic was Victorious and Mr Foggerty's first name was Beowulf. No wonder he was called Foggy by the others.

"How can we complete this task, Hecate?" I looked to Adi as he spoke, for he seemed to be in a bit of a trance. His eyes were completely fixed on Hecate, and he looked so serious and earnest. I sort of wanted to laugh.

Suddenly the reality of the situation hit me. Finding Phyllis wasn't going to be a walk in the park. It could be dangerous if Mal Vine and his followers were still intent on causing chaos. Plus, if Phyllis was lost and unable to find her way back home, how on earth would we?

"Whoa, hang on a minute," I raised my hand. "This is all a bit fast. Adi and I aren't witches, you know. Nor is Lois. We don't have any special powers. Adi only got us in here cos he's a maths genius. We are just ordinary kids exploring. We'd love to help and all that, but I'm not sure we can do this on our own. Come on, Adi." I grabbed his arms and pulled him back around towards the door, when suddenly the lights went out.

"Stop right there," came a very croaky, deep voice from behind us. The lights came back on and we spun around. I wished we hadn't. Hecate had gone. The baby had gone. The sleeping infant had gone.

In their place was a bent old lady with an owl resting on her shoulder. She wore head to foot black, had a humped back, and she glanced up at us with tiny currant eyes that were the bluest shade of blue you'd ever seen. Her nose was hooked, and she had thin grey hair and warts galore on her face. I even saw hair protruding from the biggest wart, which was on her chin. Her gnarled fingers pointed at us both, and she beckoned us to come closer.

I so did not want to do this, a) in case she smelt, and b) cos I was scared. She made a little circle with her forefinger, the same one that had beckoned us, and then curled her hand and pulled it towards her, as if she was pulling us towards her on a rope, chuckling all the while. It was uncanny, as we started to drift towards her, even though every instinct in my body was trying to stop myself and turn to run away. But it was like one of those dreams you have when you are desperately trying to run, but you can't, and every pace feels like you are wading through treacle. By now I was terrified.

We got to about a foot from her. I have honestly never seen so many wrinkles on a person's face. She looked like the map of Britain and Ireland all in one.

"Not so fast, you two. Did you not hear a word I was telling you before? You have been chosen. It is an honour. You do not run away when an honour has been bestowed upon you."

Adi and I looked at each other.

"I'm sorry, Madam," I spoke quietly, as my nerves were in tatters and my heart was beating away like a drum in my chest.

"But Hecate was talking to us just a few moments ago, and now she's disappeared and you are here, so we don't mean to be rude or anything, but we've never seen you before in our lives."

A dry raspy laugh came from somewhere deep within her chest.

She coughed into her hand and then flung whatever she had regurgitated over her left shoulder, narrowly missing the owl's head.

"Can't you see it's me? Hecate. I am a Goddess, a trans-former. I am the Virgin, the Mother, and the Crone. Before you saw the Mother, now you see the Crone. You may not realise it, but you summoned me when you decided to find Phyllis. I will show you the way, so you do not have to re-trace your steps. I will see all three of you next Wednesday. Jonathan will take you home."

Hecate seemed to struggle to speak the last few sentences, and her eyes closed and her mouth dropped as if she had fallen into a deep slumber. The owl that had been sitting on her shoulder flew down, circled the room several times and seemed to disappear. A moment or two later, we heard the familiar voice of Jonathan.

"Seen enough for one visit have you, my friends?"

We turned with relief and there, standing resplendent in a new bluey-purple apron that read:

Only
Wears
Lilac

was Jonathan!

Adi and I ran to him and gave him a huge hug. It was rather lovely, actually, to be engulfed in his soft, silky feathers.

I turned my head back to look at Hecate in the chair. She was still in her old woman guise, slumped and sleeping, and a shiver went through me. How could she one minute be such a wonderful, soft, loving lady and then suddenly change into this old harridan? Jonathan must have read my mind.

"Maybe next time you'll see her as the young Virgin. It's all perfectly normal here, darlings, nothing to worry about. Just like you change your underwear, she changes her appearance. You'll get used to it. Right, come on. Jump on.

Home time, remember?" he said as we climbed on and he took flight. "Next Wednesday, Halloween, bring the key, bring the shoes, and bring your sister."

"What shoes do I need to bring, Jonathan?"

"Why, the ones on your feet, of course!" he laughed.

As we tumbled into the sinkhole and landed back into our hallway I glanced down, and there on my feet were a pair of beautiful gold Latin-dancing shoes. I didn't recognise my toes. They were painted bright red and looked like someone else's. As I gently unbuckled them and noticed my own trainers lying neatly by the stairs, his words sounded out in my head:

Key.

Shoes.

Sister.

15

DARKNESS EVERYWHERE

W hen we got back to the house, Lois was still on the computer in Dad's office, Uncle Vic and Mr Foggerty were still deep in conversation in the kitchen, and according to the phone in the hall, we'd only been gone 15 minutes. It was absurd.

"I'd better go, Rosemary. That way no one knows I've been here," Adi whispered.

"The only thing we didn't find out is who is THE STRANGER? Remember me telling you about them turning up at our house? Do you think we're getting in too deep here?"

I was starting to feel scared about this mission that Hecate wanted us to do. Plus, now I had promised to take my little sister with us. The only power Lois had, as far as I could see, was her lethal farts. We certainly never had any trouble getting a seat on a train or bus, in fact we often had the entire carriage to ourselves.

Then I silently reminded myself that we owed it to Phyllis to rescue her. Since she disappeared, everything had gone wrong. Dad's cloud had returned, my parents were rowing, and slimy Marcus was on the scene. Perhaps if we found her, everything would go back to normal. Dad's cloud might go and Mum might get more work. Besides, here was Adi, who hadn't even met Phyllis and he was willing to help find her. I knew Adi well enough to know that he didn't deal with trivial matters, he didn't do small talk, and he didn't waste his time on stuff he thought was unimportant. At that moment, I was so grateful that he was my friend.

"Adi, we must find out about wormholes. Mr Foggerty told me he thought that's where Phyllis was stuck."

Adi nodded earnestly. "Don't worry, Rosemary, it will all be fine. I've been doing a lot of thinking since we went through the first time, and I know we can do this! I will go through my *Star Wars* back log of comics and find the ones that focus on wormholes. If Hecate thinks we can do it, then of course we can."

I smiled half-heartedly. "Yes, my mum says if you believe, then anything is possible, so I suppose you're right."

Of course, I didn't actually believe that right then.

The next day at school, Adi and I exchanged knowing looks at each other. He looked very serious, as if he had been given the mission of a lifetime (which, to be fair, he probably had).

I was still nervous about what we were getting ourselves into. Meanwhile at home, there were so many other things going on. Mum was getting more anxious by the day, as she only had one week left of regular rehearsals before their technical rehearsal. This was where they practised the play on stage with all the lighting and sound cues, and then did a proper dress rehearsal with costumes and make up so they were ready for an audience.

Dad seemed to be lost within himself. He came home from work on Friday night looking grey. His cloud was almost black with mist swirling all about it.

Mum's colours had changed slightly, too. She was now greeny brown at the edges, which for some reason I didn't really like. It was as if she was hiding behind some fog or something. She was extra bright and a bit giddy. She kept starting a sentence and then forgetting where she was going with it.

"Right, girls, wash time. Now what am I doing with this banana, Rosie?"

"It's for Lois, Mum. You were going to chop it up and make her banana custard, remember?"

"Oh yes, of course. Now custard, custard."

She opened a custard and went to pop it in the microwave.

"Oh! There's already one in here!"

At other times, I would find her staring into the distance looking wistful. She had dark circles around her eyes, too, so between the pair of them, I don't think her or Dad were getting much sleep, and yet I was the one dealing with all the stress!

I was playing on my dad's tablet on Friday evening when I heard my parents arguing in the kitchen. Dad had only been at home a few minutes, yet it was gone half-past seven. I think, to be fair, Mum had forgotten about me as she was going over her lines in the kitchen, and I usually go to bed around 7pm. Lois was already fast asleep.

"Hello, John, I am here, you know? How was your day, Rae? Yes, good thanks, John. Getting a bit nervous, as we've only got a week to go. Thanks for asking…"

"There's no need for that, Rae. I've only just got in, and I'm just getting myself a drink."

"I don't really think you should be drinking. Alcohol is a depressant."

"Meaning?" my dad snapped.

"Marcus says alcohol makes you feel depressed, especially if you are prone to depression, and that you should avoid it."

"Tell Marcus to mind his own business for a start, and by the way, I am not depressed. I have a very busy job, lots of stress, train bloody travel that is always running late, and I'm exhausted."

There was silence for a few moments. I could tell Mum was giving Dad one of her assessing looks, the kind she gives you before she tells you a big-home truth.

"You are in denial. You walk around so bloody miserable all the time. You hardly speak, you don't join in, you ignore me, you sleep all the time or you say you're tired. You *have* to be ill, John. Either that, or you can't stand us all. Or perhaps it's just me you can't stand!"

Silence again. I could hear Dad opening the freezer, probably to get ice. There was the scrape of the kitchen chair on the floor as Mum must have been getting up to try one last time.

"Marcus' dad was quite ill with depression. He knows the signs. I really think you ought to seek help with this, John. It's nothing to be ashamed of. In fact, this play we're doing is all about mental illness, too. Martha and George behave in a certain way with each other so they don't have to face up to the truth of their situation."

Dad's voice was dangerously quiet now.

"I don't want to hear about Marcus. He's a pretentious idiot, who clearly thinks he can tell my wife what is wrong with me. I shall be furious, Rae, if you have been discussing me with that prat."

"No, of course I haven't. Don't be ridiculous. Marcus just notices things. He's an actor, so he studies people."

"Tell Marcus to study this!" my dad shouted.

Obviously, I couldn't see what was going on, but I have a feeling my dad might have been sticking one finger up in a rude gesture — something he liked to do when words failed him.

"I can't go on like this, John. The dark moods and the silence — it's not fair."

I heard Mum leave the kitchen and go upstairs. I sat quietly for a few moments wondering what to do. It made me feel scared, the fighting they were doing lately. Was my Dad ill? He didn't have flu or a sore throat or a broken arm, but then I guess some illnesses you can't see.

Sarah Jane's mum, for example. Mr Bobbin had told us that she was ill, and yet on the surface there was nothing wrong with her. It was an illness in her head. *How awful*, I thought, *to be ill in your head where no one can see the poorliness*. At least if you have broken your leg, you get grapes and cards and visitors. If you have an invisible illness, then no one can give you love and sympathy. One thing was for sure, Dad was right about Marcus. He was a PRAT. I didn't know why, but I knew I didn't like him.

In the end, I crept up to bed before Dad came into the lounge and before Mum remembered she had forgotten me. As I went past the kitchen door, I saw the dark shape of my dad scooping baked beans out of a tin, half slumped at the kitchen table with a large G&T.

My dreams were a mixture of Hecate and Mal Vine. One minute she was being nice, the next she was the scary old lady. The baby at her breast took on the face of Mal and saluted me. I kept shouting out, "How can I do this mission?" and all Mal Vine would reply in a whisper was, "You can't." I felt like I couldn't tell the difference between my dreams and my reality, as both were making me feel like I was out of my depth.

The next day, Mum was uber chirpy. We didn't see Dad until lunchtime, when he came downstairs wearing his jogging bottoms with a dark shadow following him. I don't know what the dark shadow was. It seemed to be attached to his body, like one's own shadow, yet it hovered at angles that your own shadow couldn't. It seemed to peer round his body when he was standing up, and when he sat it looked as if it had long fingers curling round his shoulders and arms, hooking into his legs and supporting his feet in a sinister kind of way. No one else seemed to see this shadow with Dad. His cloud still remained. It was completely black — you could barely see it, unless you were in a well-lit room; otherwise it folded itself under the black shadow. Lois wouldn't leave Dad alone. She kept trying to get on his lap, to which Mum would make light of.

Lois just gazed up at my Dad and snuggled into him. She didn't seem to mind that Dad wasn't up to talking today. He let his arms go limply around her and sipped his coffee in his own world. I wanted to get out of the house.

I felt uncomfortable and anxious, because I'd never seen Dad like this at all. Mum said if I got her purse from her handbag, we could walk down to the library. She had our library cards in there.

I didn't need asking twice. I ran upstairs into their bedroom, where she said her bag was, and rifled through to grab her purse. I saw the card straight away, even though it was folded in two and tucked into the inner pocket of her bag. I slid it out of its pocket, looking up and half-cocking my head to make sure no one was coming upstairs. It was the kind of card you'd get in somewhere posh like Paperchase, shiny with a fluffy, homemade-style sheep on the front with the caption: The Wonder of Ewe.

Inside it read:

Dearest Martha,

Ewe really aren't a fluffy sheep. You are a beautiful woman who shines like a star. Thank you for being my pretendy wife. I am loving being your pretend husband. I want you in my life always, darling girl.

Yours forever,
  George

I quickly stuffed it back into my mum's bag and grabbed her purse. I didn't need to think too hard to know that card was from Marcus. It had to be. Mum was playing Martha and I know she'd said Marcus was playing her husband, George, in the play.

I don't know why, but I felt so angry that he knew about our little family joke about the name Martha reminding us of a fluffy sheep. It made me feel like he was trying to wheedle his way into our family. I had to put a stop to this now. Dad thought Marcus was a waste of space, and so did Lois and I. If Mum was being fooled by him, we had to do something about it, and fast. What was the best way of doing this?

Magic of course.

16

MEDDLING IN MAGIC

Mum and I walked down to the library, and she sat patiently flicking through the magazines while I chose some new books.

We walked home silently. I was pondering what to say, if anything, about Marcus. In the end, I decided Mum didn't know what was good for her, and I had to just take the matter into my own hands. As a prequel, I brought up our houseguests instead, as I was really missing them this weekend.

"Seems quiet this weekend, doesn't it, Mum? No Frances or Uncle Vic or Mr Foggerty..."

"Well, we never see them on the weekend, do we, Rosie? They are busy people."

"Is Dad ill, do you think, Mum?"

"What makes you say that?" she replied sharply.

"He's just so grey looking," I paused, "and he seems quiet and sad and not joyous very often."

Mum's eyes filled with tears, and I felt terrible for bringing it up. Wasn't this proof enough that she loved him?

"I think Daddy gets sad sometimes, for no particular

reason, and there's nothing much we can do, Rosie, except be there for him."

"I don't agree, Mum," I said defiantly.

Mum looked up, surprised at my outburst.

"What do you mean?"

"I think we can do something. I don't know what yet. But isn't there any magic or anything you can do Mum?"

"Darling, magic isn't the solution to everything. You can't wave a wand, so to speak. People have to take responsibility for their own actions. Magic should only be used as a last resort, when all practical measures have been explored. We can't use it as a way of avoiding facing up to our own demons."

We had reached our front door. I didn't agree. Dad was being taken over by something dark. If Mum couldn't see that, then I really had to do something.

I would look in her *Book of Shadows* in Dad's office as soon as I could.

As it happened, it was Sunday morning when I managed to finally find what I was looking for. It was 8am. My sister was snoozing, and my parents were also still in bed. I crept downstairs, fed Bob and Maggie, and stole into the office. I knew where Mum's boxes of witch ingredients and books were and quickly found her *Book of Shadows*. All the spells were handwritten. I flicked through. "Charm to Ensure Good Luck", "Sell Your House Spell", "Protection Spell", "Spell to Manifest a New Job", but nothing about getting rid of an annoying Marcus.

Then, underneath all her books, I found a slim, very old-looking first edition of *Francesca's Finds, AKA Spells You Can't Normally Track Down*. It was rather damp, but on page 21, there it was waiting for me: "Spell to Disenchant a Lover". I read on eagerly.

Ingredients:

- Some fresh saliva (that of a scabby dog, or failing this, your own will do)
- A nail clipping of the person who wants to disenchant the lover
- A basil leaf
- A clove of garlic
- A tablespoon of apple cider vinegar
- A pinch of rosemary

This spell needs to be cast on a waning moon. Mix all of the above ingredients in your cauldron facing west. As the sun sets, put the mixture into the person's drink of their choice, be it tea/ coffee/ wine/ beer/ juice. As you stir their drink in a clockwise direction with the added ingredients, say the following:

> "A pinch of this, a pinch of that,
> A spit of this, a spit of that,
> Mix together with a nail,
> give it a shake, it will not fail
> Your victim will enjoy this drink
> and this lover will be banished
> quicker than you think."

Once your "lover" has drunk the potion, you need not fear their advances any longer.

I knew this was the spell I was going to have to use! All I needed to do was find out when Mum was going to see Marcus, get the mixture made on a waning moon (whenever that was), get him to drink it, and then *bingo!* We'd be sorted!

I quickly scanned the list of ingredients once more to check I could source them all. Mmmmm, scabby dog might be tricky; think I'd just use my own saliva. Now was I meant to use my nail clipping or that of Mum's? It wasn't quite clear. Well, I guess I was the one who wanted to get rid of Marcus. Mum didn't yet realise what a knoblet he was, so in that case it would have to be my nail clipping. Basil we'd got growing in a pot. Rosemary was outside in a plant pot, as Mum said it was lucky to grow it outside your house. Apple cider vinegar...mmmmm, not sure what that was, but I'm sure normal vinegar would be okay. We always had garlic. Yes!

All things had a big tick on them. I flicked through Mum's moon calendar to see if that would help me. Luckily, at the beginning of the calendar was written:

SPELL WEAVERS WANTING TO BRING THINGS TO THEM SHOULD ALWAYS CAST SPELLS ON A WAXING MOON WHICH IS AFTER A NEW MOON, BUT BEFORE A FULL MOON. A WAXING MOON IS WHEN THE MOON IS GROWING TOWARDS FULL. IF YOU WANT TO RID YOURSELF OF SOMETHING OR SOMEONE, THEN GO FOR A WANING MOON, WHICH IS JUST AFTER A FULL MOON, AS THE MOON SHIFTS AWAY FROM BEING FULL, BUT BEFORE IT BECOMES A NEW MOON.

Scanning the calendar, I could see the next new moon was 31st October, Halloween, i.e., in three days' time. It was now Sunday, so I had today, tomorrow, or Tuesday to get this done before Wednesday's new moon, which also coincided with us going back through the portal with Lois. I had to act fast!

I heard the pad of little feet coming into the kitchen, so I hastily shoved the spell book back underneath Mum's *Book of Shadows* and arrived in the kitchen just as Lois did, who incidentally still had her dummy in. Yes, I know, she's five and still has a doe at night. (We call it that in our house.)

"Lois, give me your doe," I said with my hand outstretched. She gave me one of her devilish grins and looked up at me sideways with cheeky eyes whilst plucking it from her mouth.

"Now, shall I get you some breakfast, seeing as Mum and Dad are still in bed?"

"I'm up, darling," came the voice of my mum from the hallway. "I'll pop the oven on, Rosie, and do your croissants."

"Muuuuum," I spoke slowly, elongating the word.

"Mmmmm?" she replied as she simultaneously flicked the switch down of the kettle and took out two mugs from the cupboard.

"Will you be seeing Marcus anytime this week before Wednesday?" Just as I was waiting for her to answer, Dad appeared in the doorway. His dark shadow was still behind him, hugging the black cloud above his head, but I noticed it wasn't quite as big as it had been. I still felt a bit dismayed that nothing had changed, but hopeful, too, as now I had the knowledge to get rid of Marcus, which should certainly make some difference. I had to find out when Mum was going to see Marcus, and now I couldn't really ask her because it might annoy Dad if I brought his name up again. I sidled over to Mum who was making coffee for both of them and whispered, "Are you going to see Marcus soon, Mum?"

She looked at me puzzled.

"Well yes, of course, darling, I'll see him tomorrow at rehearsals. Why on earth are you asking?"

"No reason. I just wondered if he might pop over here at all, and I could ask him about some of his other work, for my, erm, my project in English about Popular Culture."

Mum looked at me sideways and shook her head. "Rosie, you are a funny one, I have no plans to invite Marcus over at the moment. I think we have enough going on, don't you?" She motioned her head over towards Dad, who was sitting at the kitchen table seemingly engrossed in a Horrid Henry cartoon.

I needn't have worried actually. The day passed in a strange fog, between Dad's non-conversation and the darkness that cloaked him, and Mum's scatty forgetfulness punctuated by colours going from greeny-brown to dark plum and seemed to cling to her skin like a fine sheen of rain. It got to 6pm and Mum was just pouring herself and Dad a large gin and tonic, "I'm not really an advocate for alcohol, Rosie, but I think this might perk your Dad up this evening," when the doorbell rang.

It was Marcus.

I actually could have kissed him.

I didn't, though.

"Hi, Marcus," I said with an enthusiasm I usually saved for my best friends. "Come in. Would you like a drink? Mum and Dad are having a gin and tonic actually."

Mum poked her nose out from the kitchen. "Who's that darling?"

"Oh, Marcus!" she exclaimed. Little white sparks began

to pop from around her torso, which wasn't a good sign in my book. "What can we do for you?"

Marcus stepped into our hallway with the confidence of a salesman who had already hit his sales target. "Sorry to disturb your weekend, Rae. I was just passing," (Oh yeah? Brown wisps were coming out of his mouth), "and I thought you might like to take a look at Dicky and Liz doing our play. Maybe not now, maybe once we've opened, but just in case I forget to give it to you."

Mum blushed and took the DVD from him.

"Er, Dicky and Liz?" she questioned, then once she looked at the DVD cover she corrected herself, her cheeks reddening even more. "Oh, Richard Burton and Liz Taylor! Of course, they famously did *Who's Afraid of Virginia Woolf,* didn't they? Thank you, Marcus, that's ever so thoughtful of you."

I had to seize the moment. "So, Marcus, would you like a drink?"

"Well yes, just a very quick one, if that's okay with you, Rae, and your very gracious husband. I really don't want to disturb your evening." (More brown wisps.)

Mum hesitated, glancing at the lounge door. "Come through to the kitchen, Marcus, and I'll do the drinks, then we can go and join John in the lounge."

I dashed into Dad's office and grabbed *Francesca's Finds.* There was an old mug perched on the edge of the desk with the dregs of tea in. I flung it into a neighbouring plant pot and somehow, as my mouth was dry with anxiety, managed to summon up two big pools of saliva, which I deftly spat into the mug. Next, I sauntered nonchalantly into the kitchen and rummaged for the scissors in the drawer whilst keeping half an eye on Mum, who was getting more ice out of the freezer. I grabbed a bulb of garlic, pinched some basil in between my fingers, and reached for the vinegar in the cupboard.

"What on earth are you doing, Rosie?" Mum had clearly spotted me looking sneaky.

"What do you mean, Mum?"

"Why do you need vinegar and is that garlic in your hand?"

"Errr, no, err, I mean yes. Yes, it's good for colds. Didn't you know that, Mum? I'm doing an experiment with making a cold, erm, a coldy, coughy medicine. Lois might try it next time she gets a cough. Or maybe it's good for wind...."

Mum laughed.

"Well, if it's good for wind I'll be very impressed, and I'd say you'd make a fortune. Just don't use too much garlic, and put things back when you've finished with them, please."

She went back to emptying ice in another glass for Marcus. (I noticed she had given him the tall tumbler, whereas the drinks she'd just made for her and Dad were in those funny wine glasses without the stem.) I dashed out the hall to the front door. I just needed rosemary now. I cut a couple of tiny fronds off of the plant and, together with all my other bits and pieces, took them into Dad's office. I dithered about which way was west and took a punt on facing the outside wall, as I'm sure our garden faces south.

I had literally just added everything together with a good glug of vinegar when Miss Nosey Pants, aka Lois, appeared, grinning at me like a Cheshire cat.

"What you doing, Rosie? Can I play, too?"

I groaned inwardly. "Okay, Lois. Quick question. Do you like Marcus?"

"Eughhh, no, he smells funny."

"Never mind how he smells. Do you like him?"

"No. Why?"

"Promise me you won't tell?"

"I promise, I promise," she said gleefully.

"Well, I don't like Marcus either, and I think he might be making Dad sad, so I'm doing a spell to get rid of him, okay? I'm going to put it in his drink in a minute, so you mustn't say a word. Do you understand me?"

"I want to stir it, too."

"Okay, okay, quickly."

"What's in it? It smells yucky."

"Yeah, it is yucky. It's spit and vinegar and some herbs and things."

"Can I put something in it, too? Pleeease?"

I really didn't have time for this.

"Okay, okay, very quickly, just spit in it."

Gosh, I'd almost forgotten my nail clipping! I took the scissors as Lois did an enormous spit into the mug and clipped the tiniest bit of nail into the mixture. It was ready!

"Now, listen to me. We will go into the lounge now. I'll pretend this is my drink, okay? And we will have to try to distract the grown-ups so I can put this into Marcus' drink without him knowing. Got it?"

Lois looked at me solemnly with an excitable glint in her eyes. "Got it."

"Good, because you have got to think of a way to distract them. Do you think you can do that? It's got to be something that gets them out of the room. And I don't mean a big stinky fart."

"Got it."

"Right, come on, partner."

We walked through the hall into the lounge with trepidation but excitement. Mum had already placed the drinks on a tray on the little table, but no one seemed to have touched them yet. This was great!

Mum was sitting on the floor, almost as a go between in the middle. Dad was on her left in the armchair and Marcus on her right on the sofa. Maggie was stretched out on the sofa next to Marcus, with a possessively placed paw on his leg. Every now and then she flexed her claws, and I saw Marcus wince. I flicked a look to Lois by means of "go on, get on with it".

She went back out of the lounge.

"Oh! Where's Lois off to now?" Mum questioned.

"Marcus just dropped by with a DVD, John, of Liz Taylor and Richard Burton doing the play. Do you remember seeing it?"

"No," Dad replied not taking his eyes off his lap.

"It's utterly mesmerising. You'll love it," Marcus gushed. "Don't watch it until after our run, though. I don't want it to put you off, Rae!"

Suddenly there was a bloodcurdling scream from the kitchen.

Mum jumped up. "Oh my god, Lois, what's wrong?" She rushed into the kitchen closely followed by Marcus, and then Dad at the rear, who seemed to take a good few seconds longer to realise what was going on.

I took my chance, and as quickly as I could, emptied the contents into the tall glass that was Marcus'. I gave it a good stir with this cocktail twizzle stick Mum liked to stir drinks with. I crossed my fingers that it wouldn't taste too much of vinegar, or that Marcus would be too polite to say anything.

I then joined the throng in the kitchen.

"For goodness' sake, Lois. You haven't got nits! I checked your hair yesterday. Stop being such a drama queen."

Dad had already turned back, drama averted, to go in the lounge.

"What's happened, Mum?"

"Oh, Lois thought she saw a nit crawling in her hair. Come on, it's bedtime soon. Let's go back and sit down, please. No more histrionics. Sorry, Marcus, you must think this is a mad house."

Mum laughed with embarrassment, and I turned to move back into the lounge. As we all trundled back in Dad, was already firmly on the sofa, Maggie caressing herself against his leg. In his hand, he held a tall tumbler. He lifted it to his mouth and took several generous gulps, followed by an enormous burb.

"John!" my mother berated.

"I think we should stick to Schweppes, Rae. That super-market tonic is gross," Dad mumbled.

I couldn't move. I couldn't speak. Inside my head I was screaming NOOOOOOOOOOOOOOO, for Dad was well over half-way through Marcus' gin and tonic.

The gin and tonic that contained the potion!

THE LETTER

On Monday, I went through school in a daze. My plan had been ruined by my father drinking the potion that was meant for Marcus. Now, all really was lost if my dad was going to be the "Lover" who was disenchanted.

Why, oh why, didn't I just leave the magic to the experts? Mum had only told me the day before to leave magic alone, that it should only be performed as a last resort. I had thought it was a last resort, though. If only I had stayed in the room with the drinks instead of going to see what daft diversion Lois had come up with, then I could have made sure Dad had the right drink.

I ignored all Adi's anxious looks that he was throwing my way. I didn't have the energy to tell him that the plan to get rid of Marcus had backfired spectacularly. Mae and Gloria left me alone at playtime, as I was such a misery. Even Murray and Dan kept a respectful distance, as if I was somehow a fragile ornament to be avoided at all costs.

The only person I noticed in my little haven of solitude was Sarah Jane, who also seemed to be within a world of her own. She, too, had decided to forgo playtime to sit quietly in the classroom reading. I watched her, her head bowed over her book, her legs crossed around themselves, and then I noticed, sitting on her shoulders were two great, heavy rocks precariously balanced. I stopped myself from asking her what they were, as I realised just in time they weren't real, as such. Only I could see them. She really did seem to be carrying a weight on her shoulders.

Maybe my situation wasn't so bad. My mum was okay. My mum hadn't been in hospital for weeks like Sarah Jane's. My dad had a dark cloud and a shadow, but he was still with us, just, I thought grimly. I should be nicer to Sarah Jane. She was always alone and nearly always quiet and withdrawn.

"Hey, Sarah Jane," I began. "How's your mum doing?"

We had been told by Mr Bobbin to try not to quiz Sarah Jane on her mum's illness, in case it upset her. Although my mum always said it was far better to acknowledge sad things when they happened to people, rather than ignore them. So, on this occasion I went with my mum's advice.

Sarah Jane raised her big brown eyes to look at me. They were glistening with the promise of tears. "She's in Cambridge at the moment having some special treatment, but hopefully she'll be home soon."

"You must really miss her."

"Yeah, I do" she paused, as if trying to control herself, but it was too difficult. "Rosemary, I don't know what I'll do if she doesn't come home soon."

The tears that had threatened started to pour down Sarah Jane's face. I felt terrible. Had I done the wrong thing bringing this up?

"Don't think like that. You've got to be positive. It will all be okay. Your mum will be back soon, and she'll be better."

"Do you promise, Rosemary?"

I patted Sarah Jane's arm. "Yes, I promise." I looked at her solemnly, hoping she didn't see the fingers of my left hand were crossed behind my back.

"Thanks, Rosemary," she gave me a wan smile and went back to her book.

It made me feel bad for worrying so much about my situation. At least my mum was here and well, even though she needed to realise that Marcus was a plank. And at least my dad wasn't being pulled completely under by his shadow. I just needed to find a way to help him, if I hadn't blown it completely already. It seemed more and more obvious to me that finding Phyllis would be the key to dealing with both these problems. I decided I wouldn't let last night's setback deter me, nor would allow my dreams about Mal Vine to send me off course. We would find a way to sort all these things. The day after tomorrow, we were going back through the portal, this time with Lois. I would make it a success.

I felt buoyed up and when Lois and I got home after Frances met us from school. A letter was waiting for me on the mat. It looked very official and our address was neatly typed on the front of the envelope:

Miss Rosemary Pellow
21 Arkansas Road
Liverpool
L15 7LY

I tore open the envelope with both trepidation and excitement. It was on beautiful, creamy, expensive-looking paper with a *Dancing Divas* logo and glitter ball at the top of the page and read:

October 26th, 2020

Dear Rosemary,

Thank you for your letter dated 14th September. It's always good to hear from the fans of the show.

Sadly, at this time, we have no plans to proceed with a children's version of **Dancing Divas and Dons***, however we shall keep your details on file in case the situation changes. After all, in show business, anything is possible!*

To alleviate the disappointment this may have caused, we would like to offer your family 4 tickets to come and be a part of our audience on our Film Night Spectacular, which is scheduled to be on Saturday, 10th November.

Please arrive promptly at 5pm, and come to the main reception at BBC Elstree (details enclosed) with your tickets, and you will be shown to your special VIP seats for the start of the show, which goes live at 6:35pm.

We look forward to seeing you.

Yours sincerely,
  Gwyneth Lipp
  Series Producer

OMG! They had actually replied and given us four tickets for the show! It was like a dream come true!

"Lois!" I screamed. "Look what I've got! *Dancing Divas* has given us tickets to go to London and see the show!"

"To see what show?"

"*Dancing Divas and Dons,* you dufus!"

"I'm not a dufus. Can I come?"

"Yes, of course, it's for all of us. We've got four tickets. Oh, hang on a minute," I paused, suddenly realising with a pang of disappointment that Mum would be working.

"Mum will be on stage, so she won't be able to come."

"Ohwaaaaaa," moaned Lois. "Does that mean we can't go?"

"No, it's okay, Dad can take us, and that means we could also take, erm, Adi!" I realised delightedly. Ordinarily I wouldn't have thought that this would be something that Adi would be interested in, but for some reason it seemed really important that he was there that night.

Frances was terribly excited about the letter, too.

"Well, well, well, a night watching the dancing. How lucky you bairns are!" she said touching our heads gently.

I decided not to tell her about what had happened with the potion I had made for Marcus to drink. Sometimes it's best to sort your own mess out. Instead, I hugged the letter to my chest and concentrated on feeling positive for Wednesday night.

Dad hadn't been too happy about the *Dancing Divas* tickets.

"Oh no, I hate that bloody programme," he'd moaned.

"Come on, John" my mum had said gently, like she was talking to Bob after he'd had one of his fits. "The kids love it. This is a big thing for Rosemary, and, unfortunately, I can't go, so you have to take them. It will be a lovely trip out, and it will do you all good."

My dad had sighed, looked down, and said, "Yeah."

His shadow still clung to him, but it was definitely smaller. I wish I had a ruler so I could take its dimensions and compare its size day by day but seeing as I hadn't done this from the first day it appeared, there was no point in starting it now. His cloud was still black, though. I was certain our trip to London would help him. After all, how could anyone watch the Samba and not feel happy?

Wednesday came around all too quickly. Adi said he would be able to sneak out of his house around 10pm and get to our house, throw stones at my bedroom window, which was at the front of the house. I had my fingers crossed that my parents would be in bed.

The night before, I had gone into Lois' bedroom and told her that Adi and I would be going through the portal and that we wanted (needed) her to come, too.

"Remember you saw me and Adi return from the land through the mirror?"

"Is that where the lady sits with the bird on her shoulder?"

"Yes, that's right. Well, we need you to come with us tomorrow night. Do you think you can do that, Lois? If I wake you up in the night when Mum and Dad have gone to bed? You have to keep very quiet about it, though, and promise not to tell Mum or Dad about it."

Lois looked terribly pleased and self-important and sort of raised her chest upwards, pulled her shoulders back, and announced proudly, "I promise. Me and Bea will come with you."

"No, you can't bring Bea, I'm afraid. What if you lose her?"

Lois stuck her lip out. "Then I'm not coming."

"But you have to, Lois. Hecate said we had to bring you. We need you."

"Not without Bea," she stated defiantly.

"Okay, okay," I sighed. "You can bring Bea. Just don't leave her anywhere, otherwise we're going to have a lot of explaining to do."

"I'm a big girl now. I can look after her."

I had to concede. I had no choice. Without Lois, we wouldn't be three, and Hecate said it was important that there were three of us.

On Wednesday, I was in bed reading when I finally heard my mum pad up the stairs. Dad had already gone up to bed not long after he'd got home from work. She poked her head round my door.

"Are you okay, darling? Did you enjoy the trick or treating with Frances?"

"Yeah, it was good. Are you going to bed now, Mum?"

"Yes, I am. I'll be glad once this show opens, then I can collect you both from school again. I've missed not seeing you so much."

"I've missed you, too," I added. "Sarah Jane's Mum is in a place in Cambridge to try to make her better." I don't know what made me say that. I guess I was grateful that even though we weren't seeing much of our mum, at least she was at home with us every night.

"Oh, dear," Mum said looking concerned. "Poor Sarah Jane and Sasha. I'm sure her mum will get better. Perhaps, when she's home, we could make her a binding charm to keep the family all strong and together."

I nodded.

Mum bit her lip. "Dad isn't like that, you know, darling. He's got some special pills now that he's taking, and they are going to make him feel a lot better very soon."

"I thought you said there were no magic potions Daddy could take to make him feel better."

"No, what I said was there was nothing magically we could do. He had to help himself first. And he has. He's seen a doctor, and they have given him some tablets that help restore the missing chemicals in his brain."

"So it's nothing that's happened to make him sad, is it?"

"No, of course not, Rosie! Some people just don't make enough chemicals in their brain to keep them feeling okay, so they need to take a tablet that will help their body to heal, so it can start making the happy chemicals again. It's exactly the same as putting some cream on a graze or a cut." Mum paused. "You love dancing, don't you?"

I nodded.

"Well, dancing will release happy chemicals in your brain, so during and after dancing you feel good. Daddy doesn't have so much of that, so he has to get some from the pills and then hopefully his brain will start to make it itself. Then he needs to find the things that give him joy, like golf or playing the guitar, things that he never allows himself the time to do."

I didn't really want to talk about this anymore, particularly as I felt Dad's cloud had more to do with Phyllis disappearing and possibly Mal Vine meddling than just "chemicals".

"Okay, Mum, you can go now."

Mum smiled. "I see, I'm being dismissed now, am I? Well, night, night, Rosie. Sleep tight, and see you in the morning."

18

AND THEN THERE WERE THREE

I must have drifted off, for I woke suddenly to hear tap, tap, tap at my bedroom window. I nearly banged my head on my bunk bed, as I jumped up out of the bed and rushed to the window. There below, looking absolutely freezing, was poor old Adi! He waved and I waved back.

I pulled on my leggings and school blouse, grabbed a fleece, and crept downstairs with my shoes and the key.

"I thought you'd never let me in, Rosemary," Adi whispered at me. "I'm freezing."

"Shhhhhh, Adi, just wait here while I get Lois up."

I left Adi loitering in our hallway and quickly buckled up my gold Latin-dancing shoes. Again, my feet didn't look like my own once they were on. I nudged Lois gently and whispered in her ear.

"Lois, it's time for our adventure. Do you still want to come with me and Adi?"

She opened her eyes slowly at first, then she jolted herself up. "Is it midnight? Are we having a midnight feast?"

"No, it's not that late. Hopefully you'll be back in bed

fast asleep by midnight. Get those leggings on and your jumper and Bea and let's go."

I helped my little sister dress hurriedly. She clutched Bea in one hand and mine in her other as we stealthily tip-toed downstairs to meet Adi.

We both raised our finger to our lips at Lois as Adi went about dropping a pebble to find the change in gravity. We were becoming a dab hand at this now, as we all three whispered:

"Aradia. Aradia. Aradia."

The lady appeared with Paloma on her shoulder; at least, I assumed it was her, for she had a mask on depicting a skeleton. She raised the mask and laughed, "My leetle Halloween costume," she said. "Come, we are expecting you."

The whooshing sound seemed to engulf the entire house. I was certain it would wake my parents, but before we knew it, we were standing in the polished wooden hallway in front of Aradia's curved reception desk.

I looked down and there, by magic, was my silver penta-gram on my school blouse and Adi's too had appeared once again on his jumper. Aradia came out from behind her desk and placed one on Lois' unicorn jumper and, to her delight, stuck a mini one on Bea's chest. She looked totally incon-gruous wearing a full-body skeleton suit to go with her skeleton mask — with of course the addition of black, very high-heeled shoes. She looked me up and down in the haughty way she had and simply said, "Nice shoes. Good pedicure job."

She sashayed back around her desk and gave Paloma a little kiss on her head. "Go, Paloma," she whispered.

Once again, I was ready, as was Adi, and we opened our legs and arms for Paloma to search us. Poor Lois didn't know what to expect, but with surprising adeptness she jumped her legs open and held Bea aloft, too.

As Paloma deftly flew in and out and round Lois, she was full of giggles. "Rosie, it tickles. She's tickling me."

I think this was probably one of the first times anyone had ever had this reaction, and Paloma seemed to like it. She cawed and spent an awfully long time hovering around Lois and Bea, and then settled on Lois' head, which made her dissolve into even more giggles.

I was worried that the naughty bird was going to do a whoopsie, but no, she gently lifted her feet up and down on top of Lois' head and then suddenly flew off down the corridor. I wasn't sure whether we should take any notice of where Paloma was going to take us or not. She could be a tricky thing, but maybe she wouldn't mess about this time if she knew Hecate was waiting for us.

Lois dashed off down the corridor after her, thinking it was some sort of game. The corridor seemed to go on and, on this time, and I wondered if we were ever going to stop.

Finally, Paloma came to a halt outside a door that was painted gold with loads of small orange and yellow circles on it. She tapped her beak three times, took a tiny piece of Lois' digestive biscuit, and then flew off from whence we had come. The strangest thing happened. The door didn't swing open like a normal door. It laid itself down from its highest point, like a drawbridge.

"Wow!" Lois exclaimed with a mouthful of biscuit.

As the door lowered, we could see a vast garden in front of us. I say garden because the grass was neatly cut, there were two pathways made from pretty stepping-stone paving to the left and right, alongside which were candles on tall sticks showing the way (the kind you might light in the summer to deter mosquitos).

As we walked down the drawbridge on to the grass, I turned and saw behind us was a rambling mansion. It was the size of Buckingham Palace, but at every window, and there were many, were pretty curtains drawn shut, some with lights coming from behind them, some with ornaments and pictures on show.

Once we had landed on the grass, the drawbridge closed and became part of the brickwork of the house. About 200 yards in front of us was a huge bonfire blazing. It was surrounded by a low fence, to keep people safe, I guess.

We could hear the buzz of excited voices ahead of the bonfire and music playing in the distance.

I took Lois' hand and reassuringly said to her, "Are you okay? There's nothing to be scared of. Let's go and find Hecate, shall we?"

"I'm not scared, Rosie, but I think Adi might be."

I glanced at Adi who was just behind us, and he did look a bit awe struck, to be fair.

"Ads, are you okay?"

"Yeah, yeah, don't call me Ads," he muttered, still staring ahead of him. "Come on, let's find out what we need to do and why we are here." With that, Adi strode in front of us and marched ahead, so me and Lois had to do little running steps to catch up with him.

As we reached the bonfire, we could see ahead of us a sort of mini marquee. It was black with glittery moons and stars on the outside of it. It was open with the sides of it tied back to reveal hordes of people sat about on cushions on the floor. Some were dancing and some were chatting and clicking their fingers to the music.

We edged closer. I think we were all feeling trepidation by now, except Lois who was already skipping in tune to the music, which was a kind of jazzy, up-beat number. I could just make out the band on the left, which consisted of fiddle, double bass, saxophone, banjo, and singer. They were very good, I noted.

Then something struck me. The strangeness of it hadn't initially dawned on me. I think, in this peculiar world, we tended to take the bizarre as it came and just accept things. I knew the singer and double bassist had looked familiar, but as I looked again I realised how bonkers this whole place was, for there, singing her heart out, was Maggie, our tortoiseshell cat, with a voice to rival Etta James. And strumming away, looking the coolest cat on the block, was our Bob. He certainly didn't show any signs of seizures here. He had a red neckerchief on and was tapping his white paw to the beat. He even twirled his tail around and tipped it towards me in a sort of wave, when he caught me gawping at him. Maggie blew us a kiss as she finished the number, and the crowds went mad clapping and whooping.

Lois was laughing and taking it all in her stride (whilst rummaging in my bag for another digestive).

"Rosemary," Adi muttered anxiously, punching me quite hard on my arm, "twelve o'clock coming towards us, who is that?"

I moved my attention to directly in front of us and nearly fainted. Striding towards our little group of three was THE STRANGER. I could feel the magnetic power of their gaze, which felt like it was aimed right at me. The rim of their hat was raised slightly, so all I could see was a dark chasm where their face should have been. I felt myself go clammy and my stomach churned. Where on earth was Hecate when you needed her? Or Jonathan for that matter?

I grabbed Lois, who was still jigging about, and Adi, bless him, trying to be the macho protective male I suppose, stood slightly in front of us all. Although I could see his legs were shaking, which sort of made me want to giggle, even though I was scared, too.

THE STRANGER spoke. "We must begin the energy raising without delay. Your sister is the missing link."

THE STRANGER tipped their head towards Lois, which unnerved me. However frightened I was, nothing, absolutely nothing, bad was going to happen to my little sister. I would make sure of that. I looked down at my grown-up looking feet in the gold dancing shoes and gathered strength.

"We're here to see Hecate, please. Lois is not going anywhere without me or Adi. Also, she gets very tired and needs food frequently, so we really can't be here for too long. We've all got school tomorrow."

It was not a pleasant experience having a conversation with someone whose eyes were hidden. Even though the huge white hat had been pulled down once more to mask the shadow where their face should have been, you could still feel their eyes penetrating into your very soul. I had to keep focused.

There was silence. I swallowed nervously. Adi cleared his throat. Lois farted loudly.

THE STRANGER at last spoke quietly and very slowly.

"Give me your hands, all three of you. Let me show you something."

The hypnotic timbre of their voice was like a call to prayer. Each one of us offered THE STRANGER one of our hands. Our hands were placed on top of each other and then THE STRANGER placed one hand above and one hand below ours.

All our eyes were on the wide-brimmed hat, which lifted slowly to reveal a swirling ocean of blackness. I could not react. I felt shocked and scared, and, yet, as if I had been drugged. It was the same feeling you get when you are really sleepy and you wake up but cannot quite gather any energy to haul yourself out of bed.

The dark ocean disappeared and was replaced with a flowing river with a young beautiful woman swimming in it. She was doing what looked like back stroke and had long, blonde hair, piercing blue eyes, and creamy white skin. She waved from her horizontal position and then brought herself upright to tread water. She looked very much like Hecate. In fact, I'm sure it was.

She went back to her swimming, and as she swam, she seemed to change before our very eyes. He body became more rotund and swollen. As she lifted herself on to her back you could see a huge, pregnant belly. Again she waved, brought herself upright and shouted, "Flow with the river."

Once more, she swam forward and then disappeared from sight under the water. I felt anxious but not enough to cry out or be overly concerned. It was just an observation of a feeling, rather than an actual feeling. I knew somehow that she was going to resurface, and resurface she did. She appeared, treading water, a shadow of her former self. It was the face of the old crone that had scared Adi and I last time. It was the last face of Hecate. I remembered Jonathan telling us that Hecate was a transformer. She embodied the three faces of woman: the Virgin, the Mother, and the Crone. In the swirling abyss of THE STRANGER's face, we had been shown the three faces of the Goddess Hecate.

The wizened old Crone version of her pointed her finger at me (it looked like it was at me, but later Adi and Lois both said she'd pointed to them) and said, "Fear not. You would not be given this challenge if you did not have the power to meet it."

With that, the images faded into blackness again. THE STRANGER bowed their head so we were faced once again with the white brim of the hat and could no longer see the black hole where their face should have been.

"Now do you understand?" THE STRANGER said.

"Y-y-yes," I stuttered. "You are Hecate."

19

ENERGY RAISING

"Oh my God, of course!" Adi exclaimed happily. "That all makes sense now. So is this you in your everyday getup?"

I glared at Adi. What a thing to say to someone who was "the boss" here! "I think what Adi means is…"

"I think it must be quite tiring, changing from a young person to an old person, so it must be quite nice to just be a bit invisible, like when I don't really know what to wear, so I put my onesie on," added Lois with a sort of wisdom that certainly seemed to make sense to Hecate.

"Exactly, Lois," she replied.

"Now you are no longer afraid of me, we can get on with what we are here for: the energy raising."

She started to head off, back toward the bonfire, where a crowd had begun to gather with various musical instruments.

"What is energy raising and how on earth are we equipped to find Phyllis?"

Hecate stopped suddenly, causing a little pile up of me,

followed by Adi, followed by Lois and Bea. She turned to face us, and her voice was serious.

"You are not obliged to find Phyllis. This will be something, if you take the challenge, that you have CHOSEN to do. Now, energy raising is something we do regularly in our meetings; it's a way of sending out light into the world, of channelling our hopes and dreams, and creating such a buzz, such a ball of energy, that it eventually explodes, and those wishes we have concentrated on then manifest themselves."

"Come on, Rosie," Lois took my hand. "Come on, Adi. Let's go and have some fun!" And we followed Hecate, running to keep up with her.

We pushed our way through a throng of people who were gathered around the bonfire, which had died down somewhat, so that one could see right across from one side of it to the other. There was a small podium by a low gate which led right up to the fire itself. Hecate stepped up on to it and beckoned us to join her.

The crowds were about a few feet deep, full of people dressed in all sorts of Halloween costumes. There were cats and ghosts and vampires and zombies, witches and wizards, and even a few pumpkins. Most people were carrying percussion instruments, anything from small drums to recorders, that could be banged together to make a noise. The hum of the crowd gradually subsided as Hecate raised her hands and lowered her palms down in a silencing gesture.

Adi and I glanced at each other, then down to Lois, who was whispering something into Bea's ear, seemingly not perturbed at all by standing in front of a crowd in a strange land with a faceless person.

"Merry meet," Hecate began, to which the crowd responded back, "merry meet."

"Before we call the deities in, let me just quickly brief you on what we are energy raising for today. We need to send our light into the world to allow our dear Phyllis to return to us. We need to show her the way, and likewise, we need to be shown where she is, so that our three witches here can secure her freedom and allow events to unfold that will put an end to the No-Law's tyranny of misery."

There was much cheering and clashing of tambourines.

She shushed the throng once again and began a kind of chant:

"I call upon the earth gods of the North. I call upon the southern gods of fire. I call upon the eastern gods of air. I call upon the watery gods of the West. Bring us your strengths. Bring us your power. Let us bathe in your healing rivers and fly on your wings. Let us warm by your fire and feel the earth at our feet. I call upon Hecate, Virgin, Mother, and Crone to bless our journey and show us our path."

She then started turning briskly in a circle whilst muttering something over and over again which sounded like, "Fly from the fire and sing from the earth, wet from the oceans and joyous born mirth."

Suddenly, Hecate's white suit and wide-brimmed hat just fell to the ground in a heap, as if her body had completely evaporated from her clothes. Adi and I gasped in shock. Even Lois was silent and wide eyed. Then we looked up and hovering over the bonfire was Hecate in her three forms: the beautiful young lady with long, blond hair and blue eyes; the pregnant lady with the baby in her arms; and the old wizened lady. They looked a bit like holograms, sort of real and yet not, if you know what I mean.

"Wow!" Lois exclaimed. "I hope she shows me how to do that."

The crowd then went mad, drumming and banging instruments together. We heard the cat band start up once again, and this time they were playing "Don't Stop Me Now" by Queen.

The music was transforming and electric. The crowds were singing along — it was infectious. One or two people suddenly appeared in the sky, swooping up and down and around on their broomsticks.

"Look, Adi. Look, Lois." I pointed to the sky.

"I know," Lois replied, taking it all in her stride. "I've already waved at Frances, and she's waved back."

"What?" I shouted above the din. "Did you say Frances is here?"

"Yes," Lois replied impatiently. "She's up there on one of the broomsticks."

Adi and I exchanged a look of shock, horror, and wonder as we gazed up. One of the broomstick trio was wearing a witch's outfit with unmistakeable flesh-coloured pop socks, one of which was already half-mast.

Frances waved an excited hand at Adi and me. I didn't know whether to be overjoyed she was here or embarrassed. Plus, it meant that if *she* was here, so were Uncle Vic and Mr Foggerty. They all knew by now that we had found the entrance to the portal and been brought on board by Hecate to help locate Phyllis. My guess was that none of them would be cross about that, not if Hecate, their boss, had arranged it.

I looked back down at my little sister. She was dancing with Bea quite happily, shrieking and giggling and being picked up by all sorts of strange looking people who would share a few beats of the music with her and then pop her back down on the podium. Adi, in contrast, was in his own little world. He had been given a drum and was drumming along to the beat with his eyes closed, in a solitary yet blissful state, with a smile on his lips that was utterly serene. I, on the other hand, was worrying about who knew we were here. I was worried about needing to relax, which made it doubly difficult then to relax!

I glanced at the floating figures of the three faces of Hecate. The Mother figure, who had reminded me of my mum the first time we had met her, had fixed her gaze on me and seemed to be saying, "It's okay, Rosie. Relax, let go, let the music wash over you, float with the beat, close your eyes, and dream a dream, my darling."

Her lips weren't moving, but I could hear her voice. She held her hands out to me. They were just like the hands of my mum. Hands that worked hard, but that had also stroked my hair when I was sad, mopped my brow when I was sick, and cuddled me when I needed to feel her comfort. Almost involuntarily, I held my hands out to hers, wishing at that moment that Mum was here, too, and not busy "working", or should I say "pretending" to be slippery Marcus' wife in the play they were doing. She would love all this, particularly the chance to actually fly on her broomstick. I felt a warm glow as our hands made contact. Hecate squeezed mine gently, and I was lifted towards her.

I didn't feel my feet leaving the ground. I was just in the moment of imagining being with my mum. I closed my eyes and allowed my body to swoop upwards, still holding both her hands. In my mind Mum was laughing and singing along to the music as she swirled me round and round.

I could feel the wind in my hair, the warmth of the fire below us, and a feeling of pure joy as the song filled my lungs, filled my body, and allowed my soul to soar.

"Rosie." I imagined Mum's voice whispering in my ear as the guitar solo started. "Keep this feeling in your hands. Hold on to it like a ball of energy."

I felt my feet touch the podium once more. I opened my eyes and looked up. The three faces of Hecate were still floating like holograms, shimmering in and out of focus. The imagined image of my mum had gone. It didn't matter. I was holding on to the feeling and clasped both Adi's and Lois' hands, and we danced the last few lines of the song in a little group, singing and giggling and whooping like we were completely carefree, not about to embark upon an impossibly scary, grown-up mission.

The band stopped playing amidst a huge roar of clapping and cheering, and then pure-white candles started to fall from the air. We all grabbed one, as pretty much everyone else in the crowd was doing the same thing. Adi looked up.

"Hey! It's Jonathan dropping the candles." We all looked to the sky.

"Who's Jonathan?" Lois asked.

"He's Hecate's assistant, an owl, and he's lovely."

"I like his outfit," Lois said.

Jonathan was wearing a large, floppy chef's hat and a purple-full apron, which went over his head and then tied at the back, with the printed words: *My Other Bird's a Pigeon.*

"What does that mean on his apron?"

"Precisely," Adi interjected

Lois opened her mouth, thought for a minute, and quickly shut it.

"What do you think we should be doing with these candles?" I asked Adi.

Before he could answer, Jonathan hovered above us and hooted down. "In a moment, when Hecate gives the green light, you will concentrate all that energy you've just raised into a ball and throw it into your individual candles. Whatever you were focussing on during our energy raising will be manifested in your candle. When you need that wish to come true, simply burn your candle and your spell will materialise."

I was slightly worried. I hadn't really been thinking about Phyllis at all during our energy raising. I'd been thinking about my family, and how I wished Mum and Dad would be happy together again. I wanted Dad to get better. I hadn't been wondering where Phyllis was, or hoping we could get a sign to her, or vice versa. I felt horribly guilty.

I turned to Adi.

"What were you thinking about, Adi?"

Adi nervously pushed his glasses back up on to his nose. "Erm..."

"Tell the truth, please."

"Shall I tell you what I was thinking about?" Lois butted in.

I sighed, wondering what on earth a five-year-old with lethal wind would wish for.

"Go on then."

"I was wishing that I could have a go on a broomstick, too, like Frances. So was Bea."

Great.

"Come on, Adi," I continued. "Fill us in."

"I was wishing that I was able to go to India and see my grandparents and my cousin Selma again."

"You know, guys, we were meant to be wishing to find Phyllis, or for her to show herself to us. This is a disaster."

No sooner had the words left my mouth, then Hecate began reforming herself as THE STRANGER very slowly, like a huge balloon being pumped up. She raised her hands above her head, turned her back on the crowds, and faced the bonfire.

"Throw your energy into your candles everyone. Concentrate, and arghhhhhhhhhhhhhhhhhhhh," she commanded.

Hecate exhaled and seemed to go into a deep trance-like state. The noise coming from deep within her sounded a bit like a meditation chant, and it went on and on as we all threw our energy into our candles. I wasn't sure how to do it, so I just mimed holding a ball and pretended to throw it into the candle, and Adi and Lois watched and copied me. It was freaky as everyone's candle lit up in an orangey colour, even ours, which surprised me, as I had felt we had cheated by not concentrating on finding Phyllis. Almost simultaneously, the bonfire suddenly blew up flames of about ten-foot high, as if it had been re-ignited.

"She's alive. She's still alive!" came a voice from the other side of the bonfire.

"I've just seen her in the flames. She's still alive!"

We all cast our gaze over to where the voice had come from.

A small man with a long, grey moustache was jumping up and down excitedly. It was difficult to take him seriously, as he was dressed as a mouse. He had on a pointed green hat from which two furry grey ears protruded, a belted green tunic, and was holding a long grey tail that must have been attached to the back of his costume. I couldn't think for the life of me what the link would be to Halloween.

"Tell me what you saw, Solomon," Hecate said to him as she floated effortlessly over to the other side of the bonfire.

"I saw Phyllis, in the flames, sitting in a dark room against a door. Her knees were bunched up, and she had her arms around them, but she was singing." Solomon could barely get his words out, he was so excited.

"What was she singing?" Hecate asked calmly.

"'Show Me the Way to Go Home'." And Solomon started singing.

"Thank you, Solomon," Hecate cut him off quickly and floated swiftly back to us on the podium. She addressed the crowds: "Well this is wonderful news, everyone. We have proof that Phyllis is still with us. She is still alive, blessed be!"

The crowds whooped and repeated, "Blessed be!"

"This is not the time to celebrate prematurely, though. Although we now know she is alive, we still do not know her whereabouts or how to reach her and bring her back safely. However, I am confident that after our energy raising this evening we are closer than ever, and our three friends here will know what to do and when to act."

I could see Lois was starting to flag. She had sat down and was cuddling Bea. I bent down to check on her.

"Lois, are you okay?"

"Rosie, I'm sooo sleepy," she replied. "And I want my doe."

"Okay, don't worry. We will be home in a jiffy," I said more confidently than I felt. To be honest, I had no idea how we were going to get home. I was hoping Jonathan might offer to take us as before. I whispered to Adi, "Lois is exhausted. We need to go before she gets really emotional and starts booing."

"Rosie, I need a wee, too, desperately," Lois said.

Sometimes my sister's timing was terrible! "Okay, I'll find you a loo, don't panic."

I looked up to try to speak to Hecate, but she already floated back over to Solomon and was speaking to him at length. I knew we had to find a toilet for Lois or there would be trouble.

I grabbed Adi. "Come on, Adi, we need to find Lois a loo before we can go home, otherwise she will have an accident."

Adi, thankfully, took charge of the situation and said he was sure he had seen a facilities tent back over near the Cat Band enclosure. We half-carried, half-dragged Lois over in that direction, battling our way through the crowds, which by now were beginning to disperse. At last, we saw a small blue tent about 200 yards behind the marquee where the band had played, and we made our way over.

Once Lois had done her business, we came back outside. But something felt different. It was so quiet for a start, as if we had been in the toilet for hours rather than just a matter of minutes.

"Rosie, I'm really, really sleepy now. I want to go home," Lois said wearily, and I could tell she was about to fall asleep on the spot.

I looked at Adi, slightly nervous now, as it was one thing just the two of us finding the way home, but a whole different ball game with a sleepy sister.

"Come on, Lois, I'll carry you," Adi offered, and to my surprise, Lois, who never likes being carried unless it's by Mum or Dad, gratefully lifted her hands up to him and sank her head against his shoulder.

They looked very funny, as Lois is quite tall for five, and Adi still quite short. I did have to stifle a giggle, seeing him trying to look all macho but struggling to see over the top of Lois' body.

We walked towards the direction of the Cat Band marquee, which we must have got wrong, as after a few moments I said to Adi, "I can't see the marquee at all, can you? Have we gone the wrong way?"

Adi shook his head. "No, it was definitely right in front of the blue tent, about 200 yards, that's all."

I started to get that sick feeling in my tummy again. "Stay here, Adi. Let me just look in the other direction."

I ran back towards the blue tent and round the other side of it. Again there was nothing, just grass and darkness. I went through the flaps of the tent to find the blue plastic door, but it had disappeared. There was no door. It was ridiculous. How could that have gone? We were only in it a few moments ago!

It was starting to freak me out. I headed back to where Adi and Lois were still patiently waiting for me.

"Adi, the toilet has gone, and I can't see any other signs of life at all." My voice was shaking.

Adi was practically keeling over from holding on to the dead weight that was my sleeping sister. He was remarkably calm. "Okay, don't panic, Rosemary. There has to be a way out of here. Let's head straight on toward where the big house was, and we are bound to come across someone."

"Okay, good idea," I agreed. "But let me take Lois now, give you a rest."

Adi readily handed Lois over, and we carried on walking as fast as we could towards the direction of the house. By then, my feet were beginning to throb in the gold dancing shoes, and I was longing to just collapse into bed.

Think, Rosemary, I said to myself in my head. *How do we get out of this place? How do we get home?* I glanced down at my aching feet and cried out.

"Adi, it's not my feet that are throbbing. It's the shoes! Look, I can see them vibrating." I pointed to them. "Maybe I need to ask them to take us home?"

Adi looked very sceptical. He let his breath out and puffed his cheeks out. "Worth a try, I suppose."

I looked at him nervously, licked my lips, gave my little sister a kiss on her soft blonde hair, and said confidently: "Shoes, take us home. Please, to 21 Arkansas Road, Liverpool L15 7LY." Nothing happened. We stood waiting for some sort of miracle — a gust of wind to sweep us up into the air, Jonathan to appear, a magic fairy to wave her wand to send us home. I squeezed my eyes shut tight, waited for five seconds, and then re-opened them, hoping that maybe I would find myself back in my bed having had a funny dream. No, we were still standing in a dark field. There was absolutely no sign of life. *Nada. Rien.*

Adi patted my shoulder sombrely and said, "Let's just keep walking then, Rosemary, for a bit more and see what happens."

I felt like crying, as I was so tired myself and thirsty and just totally fed up with all of this nonsense, when I heard Adi stumble and fall in front of me.

"Adi, are you okay?" I asked anxiously.

"Yeah, I'm fine. I've just tripped. Be careful, it goes from grass to some sort of wood."

I reached the area where he had tripped and gently placed Lois down on the grass. It was so dark, we could barely see anything in front of us. I was scared and tired and just wanted to be in my own bed.

How could Hecate have let this happen? I was furious that we had been asked to come to this great energy raising evening, which was supposed to be a fun party, and then be abandoned like this.

Adi was on his hands and knees, examining what had tripped him up, when he gave an excited shout.

"Rosemary, it's a door knocker."

"Eh?"

"Come and feel. I tripped over a door knocker, and I can feel below it is a keyhole."

He guided my hand to where he was crouched and, *yes!*, I could feel wood. Then my hands came across a solid metal knocker, below which was unmistakably a keyhole.

"Oh my God, Adi, the key! I have the key we got from Hecate. She told me to bring it! Shall we try it?"

"Yes, quickly, let's see if it fits."

I reached into my pockets and brought out the large black key and, feeling my way, inserted it into the keyhole. It fitted! Before I turned it, I suddenly thought of Lois. "Adi, hold Lois so we are all together. Make sure she's got Bea, too, or we'll never hear the end of it."

Adi cradled Lois, and thank goodness he had, for as soon as I turned the key, the door opened into the ground like a trapdoor flinging us downwards. We landed in a heap, Adi still holding my sister protectively, bang slap in the middle of my hall.

Home sweet home.

Adi and I clung to each other, almost sobbing with relief that we were back. We whispered our goodbyes once he had helped me take Lois upstairs and place her in her bed. I kissed her cheek flushed with sleep. Her long eyelashes seemed to flicker in repose, and she reached out automatically for her doe. I placed it on her sheet and watched as her fingers made contact with it, and she popped it in her mouth and began to furiously suck on it.

I undressed and slid into bed, glancing at the clock in my room: 2:45 am, the witching hour. I barely remember, as sleep tugged at my eyelids, hearing the urgent scream outside of distant sirens.

20

PINS, PALOMA AND PLANS

I was woken abruptly the next morning by my mother gently shaking my arm. "Rosie, wake up. It's ten past eight, darling. It's very late. Go and get yourself washed and dressed, and hurry up."

The memories of the night before came flooding back to me: the energy raising, the dancing, the realisation that Hecate was THE STRANGER, the disappearance of everyone whilst we were in the toilet, and the panic about how we would get home. That part of the night was not something I wanted to dwell on. It felt like a chapter from a nightmare. How lucky were we to have found that door in the ground? But then, maybe, I thought, as I dragged myself into the bathroom, there was no such thing as luck. Perhaps, I made it happen by trusting that the shoes would lead us back home.

One thing I knew for sure. I certainly was not in a hurry to go back to the other dimension. No way.

The kitchen was empty when I got downstairs, no evidence that my dad had been there, apart from his empty coffee cup and the fact that BBC news was blaring out from the TV. He must have gone to work already. I was about to switch over to a kid's channel, when I recognised South Parkway train station on the screen with the caption:

Breaking News: Railway Disruption Over Entire North West

The newscaster went on to say:

"Network rail over the entire North West of England, including Merseyrail, TransPennine Express, and Arriva are all suspended indefinitely due to a suspected attack. Police were called out in the early hours of this morning to what appeared to be several broken-down trains in the Merseyside area. The late running 23:11 train from Manchester Oxford Road to Liverpool Parkway Station became stuck between Warrington and Liverpool, with power lines down all over the North West. Several other trains were also run aground. Hundreds of thousands of metal pins had been scattered all across the lines, culminating in large mounds in various places blocking the lines and forcing train travel to be suspended. There were reports of large numbers of people in fancy dress costumes which led police to initially believe this was a Halloween prank, however the sheer volume of pins that have been deposited have ruled this out. Eyewitnesses say the Halloween partygoers boarded the stationary trains, which had been plunged into darkness, and were seen giving out candles to passengers trapped on the trains before disembarking. A costume mouse tail and a pointed satin red slipper were retrieved; however no clear forensic evidence has been able to be obtained from these items, which have baffled the experts."

As the newscaster droned on about the various locations of the pins around the North West, the TV went grey and fuzzy. It spluttered and then a picture came back into view, rather like a grainy home video. There stood Mal Vine beside an enormous pile of pins.

"What do you think, Rosie?" he said grimacing as he gestured towards the pins. "Just a little reminder of the past for your witch friends? Last chance now, girl. Let me help you find Phyl. Time's running out, and you need me." His expression grew hard, and I felt myself backing away from the screen as his face filled it. "You don't know how awful it is to grow up without your mum and dad. I don't want to have to put you through that, but I might have no choice." He spat the last sentence out to me, and I swear I could feel droplets of his spittle hit my cheeks and top lip. He saluted me once again, his mouth set into a line, his brown eyes like flints.

The TV went fuzzy as before and the picture reverted back to the news announcer saying that the pins were identified as being handmade from around the 1600s. My heart felt like it was jumping outside of my chest, and my mind was racing. What did he mean that he might have no choice? Was he threatening my family if I continued to look for Phyllis without him? And why was *he* so keen to find Phyllis? I swallowed nervously, unable to get his menacing presence out of my head.

I vaguely remembered the pins that Alizon Device had been trying to buy back in 1612 from John Law. Mal Vine had pretty much admitted responsibility for placing all these pins in order to cause disruption. Had everyone at the energy raising event disappeared in order to give out candles to the passengers stranded on the trains? I wondered if my dad knew, or whether he had been turned back from the station and would shortly be coming through the front door again.

Mum swiftly arrived in the kitchen, looking harassed, with a sulky-faced Lois who had been wrestled into her uniform by the looks of things.

"Now listen, girls," Mum said quite seriously. "Daddy can't go to work today because there's been trouble on the train lines, so he's going to take a few days off while they sort things out. He's gone back to bed as he's not feeling great, I don't think, but he will get you from school later, okay?"

"I just saw something on the news about pins being put on all the train lines," I interrupted.

"Pins?" Mum questioned looking puzzled.

"Yes, they found piles of pins from years and years ago, apparently, and they've blocked up the train lines, and it's going to take days to move them. They also found some fancy-dress costumes, too."

"Fancy-dress costumes?" Mum repeated.

"Yes. Probably from the people who got on the trains and gave out candles to passengers."

Mum sighed and muttered something about needing to be kept in the loop.

I didn't have the energy to challenge her further. I was mindful of Mal Vine's veiled threat, and it all just confirmed to me that this most certainly did have something to do with the Pendle Witches. How on earth were we going to find out what was going on if Dad was at home? If he was here, we wouldn't see Frances or Uncle Vic or Mr Foggerty, nor would I know how safe it was to carry on with our task to find Phyllis.

There was only one way to get an answer: to go back through the portal again. My heart sank.

I purposely sat alone on the bench on the other side of

the playground at lunchtime, in hope that Adi would come and join me, so we could discuss our next move. He did.

"You're right, Rosemary," Adi agreed. "We have no choice but to go back through the portal to find out why they deserted us last night and how we go about trying to complete the mission to get Phyllis back. Plus, you've got to tell someone about what Mal Vine was threatening."

"But, Adi, don't you see? They don't know how we're going to get Phyllis back, do they? Otherwise, if they knew, why didn't they tell us instead of doing all this crazy energy raising stuff?" I groaned with frustration. "And what if Mal knows how to get to her? I don't trust him, but he seems keen enough to find Phyllis."

Adi sighed. I followed suit, and we watched our friends and classmates playing in the cold winter sun.

Skipping was in full flow, Gloria and Mae were "performing" on the makeshift stage, and Dan and Murray were chasing girls with a puffed-up paper bag (probably which had just been farted in by Murray).

Sarah Jane was the only one inside. I could see her forlorn face staring out at the lively throng of children who were living another life to the one she was experiencing. I felt a pang of sadness for her. It was tough when you could see everyone else being different to you and not quite ever being able to fit in.

I felt like an outsider, too, at times. No one except Adi knew about our family set up, and I liked having those secrets, but, luckily, I was also good at pretending, so that no one knew how I really felt inside.

Maybe Mum was pretending to like Marcus so much, then? I took a moment to ponder this and then dismissed it. No, she really did like Marcus, I could tell. Oh God. The spell. Not only had we disenchanted our dad, who was probably ill because of that awful spell he'd drunk that had been meant for Marcus, but we still had so much to do in terms of finding Phyllis. I felt suddenly exhausted by the magnitude of it all.

"Walking slowly, even the donkey will reach Lhasa."

"What did you say, Adi?" I asked, relieved he had broken my thoughts.

"I said, walking slowly, even the donkey will reach Lhasa."

I looked at him questioningly.

"It means we need to move forward. We need to do something and not sit still. It's an old Indian proverb. So, I will come over later, and we will go through the portal and find out what we need to do next."

"Okay," I agreed. "But it's going to be tricky, as my dad is off now for a few days so it's not going to be that easy to do our own thing."

How wrong could I be?

The man that met Lois and I from school was not our father. This man was a shadow of my dad. Literally, actually. All I saw was Lois holding the hand of a dark shadow that was almost entirely wrapped around my father. His cloud was completely eclipsed by the creeping wisps of blackness that shrouded him, clasping him to their bosom like a precious offspring that they were reluctant to relinquish.

As I took his hand, his skin felt clammy and waxy at the same time.

I felt like my dad was disappearing into his own cloud, and the despair that seemed to surround him only buoyed me up further to get on with solving the mystery of Phyllis and trying to right all the wrongs.

We shuffled home in silence, apart from the periodic munching of Lois on her crisps.

"I need you to help me and Adi with something," I whispered to her. We watched Dad stumble up the stairs, and I gave Lois a biscuit and some milk whilst we waited for Adi to arrive.

"I don't want to go back there," she moaned between mouthfuls. "I'll go another day, Rosie."

"Lois, listen to me," I begged in whispered tones. "We have to go back. We need to find out when and how to find Phyllis. I think Daddy's health depends on it. Plus, remember he drank the potion we made for Marcus? Well, I think it's working on him, and we don't want that. We'll be there fifteen minutes max." I had my fingers crossed, once again, behind my back.

I could hear a "tap, tap" on the front door — it must be Adi! Distracted by this, Lois reluctantly agreed to do what I asked. I think part of her felt flattered that she was being considered a "big girl", old enough to do things with me and my friend who were four years older than her.

We let Adi in quietly, and I hurriedly retrieved my school blouse from the bottom of my wardrobe and Lois' unicorn jumper. We stood in a line facing the mirror and repeated those words:

"Aradia. Aradia. Aradia."

This time, the whooshing sound was very quiet indeed. In fact, I wondered if anything was happening at all, when suddenly we were there in front of Aradia's corner desk. But where was Aradia? The desk was very high, too high, to be able to peek over to see if she was crouching down. We stood quietly, all slightly apprehensive, until Lois broke the ice, or should I say broke the wind, so to speak.

"Lois!" I berated. "Do you have to do that, honestly? I just hope as it was so loud it won't be a smelly one."

"It wasn't me," she said.

I raised my eyebrows and glanced at Adi who looked slightly embarrassed. I suppose he thought girls didn't do that kind of thing. Until he met my sister, that is.

"It was her," Lois pointed giggling.

We looked back to the desk and there, perched on top of it, was my favourite bird of all time (not), Paloma.

Paloma cawed several times, as if she had got the joke, then she swooped in and out of our arms and legs, finally perching on Lois' shoulder. She nibbled delicately on Lois' ear, which sent her into fits of giggles. She let Lois stroke her head gently, all the while cawing into her ear. After a few minutes of allowing Lois her indulgences, I said to Adi, "Right, come on. We need to try to find someone like Frances or Hecate or anyone who can tell us what the next step is. Come on, Lois, let Paloma do her thing."

"There's no one here, Rosemary," Lois stated confidently.

"And how do you know that?"

"Paloma says Aradia is on anal leave."

"I think you mean annual leave," Adi corrected.

Lois looked up.

"It means on holiday," I added.

"Oh, right," she continued, "and everyone else is busy."

"Eh?" I was beginning to feel a bit confused and anxious. "How do you know this?" I said impatiently.

"Paloma is telling me, stupid!" Lois rolled her eyes at the bird who continued to caw into her ear.

"Right, let me get this straight. You're telling us that Paloma is talking to you?"

"Yes."

I raised my eyebrows, knowing even if I didn't believe this, I had to humour the pair of them.

"Tell Paloma we really need to speak to someone to find out what to do next."

Lois huffed and puffed, obviously feeling quite important in her new role as Dr Dolittle. "She knows that. She said there's no one here except Jonathan, and he's busy making," she stopped mid-sentence to make a long, noisy fart sound with her mouth, "jam."

"What did you just do?" I said, distracted by the noise she'd just made.

"I blew a raspberry."

"And what's that got to do with anything?" I asked.

"Rosemary, what is wrong with you?" Lois rolled her eyes. "He's making raspberry jam." (She whispered the word "raspberry".)

"Why didn't you just say 'raspberry' then?"

"Ssshhhhhh! Because they don't say that word here," she continued, talking to me as if I was the biggest idiot who had ever walked the planet. "They just make the sound here. They never say the word, okay?"

I stared incredulously.

Thank God for Adi. Very calmly, but very seriously, he spoke up.

"Lois, please will you tell Paloma we need to speak with Jonathan very urgently. She needs to go and get him NOW."

He did raise his voice at the end of the sentence, just to show them he was serious. At last, Paloma flew off and the three of us were left feeling slightly anxious, knowing that all was not what it seemed. Aradia on holiday? That in itself sounded odd. The fact that no one seemed to be here was also a concern.

Where was everyone?

After what seemed like an age, we saw Paloma flying back down the corridor towards us from a distance away, followed by another bird, which we assumed must have been Jonathan. Paloma landed rather gracefully on to Lois' shoulder, and they continued to share a little mutual appreciation for each other. The owl that was following Paloma swooped down behind Aradia's desk, and a moment later the full-sized feathery head of Jonathan appeared. He waddled round to where the three of us were standing.

"My, my, how wonderful to see you all. Looking good after our antics last night!" He winked.

He was wearing a dark blue apron this time with white writing on which said: *We're Jammin'. Hope You Like Jammin', Too*

He caught me staring at the words and raised his wing to scratch his nose. "Ah yes, it's the ********* variety," he said cheerfully (********* = blows raspberry).

Adi sniggered.

"Would you like a pot, young man, when it's finished?"

"Erm, no thanks, Jonathan. But thank you for asking."

"Oh." Jonathan looked crestfallen.

"We love ********* jam, don't we Rosie," Lois chimed.

"Yes, we do, Jonathan, if you can spare any?"

Jonathan smiled proudly. "I'm sure I can find a spare pot or two, chums." Why were we discussing rasp.... whoops, ********* jam? I couldn't believe it. Everything was falling apart, and we were blowing raspberries at each other like it was going out of fashion. I took a deep breath.

"Jonathan, we're only here briefly. We really needed to find Frances to ask her about our dad. He's really poorly, and we think it's our fault, as he accidentally drank the disenchanting potion that was meant for Marcus, this man my mum's working with, who is trying to take her away from our dad. Plus, we need to find Phyllis. We don't know where to start. Oh, and Mal Vine appeared on the TV this morning and told me if I didn't let him help me find Phyllis he..." I hesitated. "I think he might hurt my parents. And everyone just disappeared last night. We couldn't find our way home. It was awful."

"I fell asleep, I was soooooo tired," Lois interjected.

"I had to carry her. She was blimen heavy," Adi added.

Lois glared at him.

"Whoa, whoa, whoa," Jonathan waved his painted talons in the air dramatically. "Let's all slow down."

He pointed to some cushions that had miraculously appeared on the floor. "I find it much easier to concentrate with a little drinkiepoo and some sustenance. Don't you agree, Lois?"

"Oh, yes," replied my sister smugly, as if she and Jonathan had planned this entire meeting between them.

He motioned us to sit, and there in the middle of the cushions was a tray with a big jug of delicious-looking pink lemonade and a plate of mouth-watering cookies. We sat at once. I glanced at Adi, who looked positively worried.

"I'm not allowed fizzy drinks," he said reluctantly, gazing with a sad expression at the appetising jug of lemonade.

"Nonsense," scoffed Jonathan.

"Anyway, this isn't a fizzy drink. This is Jonathan's medicine, and Jonathan prescribes a glass of pink lemonade for us all."

So infectious was his speech, that we were all giggling at the end of it. We raised our glasses full of pink lemonade and did a "cheers" to each other.

I felt the juice slide into every corner of my body, like a

silky caress, massaging away all my fear, my worries, and my anxiety.

Jonathan passed the biscuits around next. I couldn't really tell you what flavour they were, but my, when you bit into them, it was like being transported to the best party ever! My sides ached as if I had been laughing for hours. I had a lovely, happy feeling in my tummy, and most of all, I felt as if I was enveloped in the biggest hug ever.

I looked around at Adi and Lois. Both seemed to be feeling what I was experiencing. Lois, still with Paloma on her shoulder, was giggling and chattering away to her. Adi was smiling so much I could see two dimples appearing on his cheeks, which I'm sure he'd never had before.

"So," Jonathan piped up, his mouth full of biscuit, "let's start with your dad. Did you intend for him to take the disenchantment potion?"

"No, of course not, we meant it for Marcus."

"Well, that's alright then. If you made the spell with Marcus in mind, it doesn't matter who drank it. It's not going to work on anyone else except the person you intended it for. Which means any illness your dad is experiencing is nothing to do with the magic, I promise you."

The relief was indescribable. Although it did, of course, mean we still had to find out how to make him better.

"Frances and the others are not here, but I can tell you the reason everyone had left rather abruptly last night was because of our sworn enemies, the No-Laws. This group of low lives are led by a rather unscrupulous fellow called Mal Vine, who, my dear, you are now sadly familiar with. He is of course a descendant of John Law, the pedlar. John Law and Roger Nowell, the local magistrate, were both responsible for so many innocent witches being hung in 1612. Last night they struck again, this time conjuring up hundreds of thousands of pins to disrupt the train lines in the North West. Are you aware of the Pendle Witches story?"

I nodded my head.

"Yes, I think so."

"Well, to recap for young Adi and Lois here: in 1612, a young lady called Alizon Device stopped John Law, a pedlar, to ask to buy some pins that were used for divination, for love magic, and were particularly good for getting rid of warts. Law refused to sell her the pins and a bit of an argument ensued. As he left, he stumbled and soon after had a stroke. He accused Alizon and her family of putting a witch's curse on him, so Roger Nowell, the local magistrate, looked into this and other accusations made on many local people who were actually healers. He decided that the recent deaths within the community were caused by witchcraft — black magic, to be precise — which was all nonsense."

Lois gasped. "Were they bad witches?"

"No, my dear, they were simple people using traditional healing methods. A bit like your mother does, but communities called them 'witches' and were terrified of them. There was of course nothing to fear, but the highly religious folk of the town thought they were evil and wanted them dead. And so it was, that ten of them were hung later that year, for crimes they didn't commit."

"That's awful," Adi remarked, wiping a lemonade moustache from his top lip.

"You are right to trust your instincts about Mal Vine. He has been searching for Phyllis since he was released from The Tunnel of Eternal Darkness, a kind of prison. He knew that if his group, the No-Laws started to cause disruption, Phyllis, being part of BUTBUM (AW), would come out of hiding to try to prevent the attacks. Once this happened he could take further pleasure out of targeting your family, whom Phyllis loves. And we all know destroying love is what he thrives on. Luckily for Phyllis, she got stuck in a wormhole before he could get to her, so he is trying to use you to reach her."

I opened my mouth to ask him whether making Dad ill was one of the ways he was targeting my family and why he had such a vendetta against Phyllis, but he raised his feathery wing and continued:

"Where was I? Ah yes, your houseguests are descendants of the Pendle Witches who were hung. So, in many ways, it's history repeating itself all over again, only this time the Pendle Witch descendants must defeat the No-Laws. All you need to worry about, my chums, is finding Phyllis. Remember, Mal Vine has no power to carry out his threats to you unless you start to doubt yourself. Once Phyllis is back, everything will take care of itself. You will see."

Jonathan smiled and shoved another biscuit into his beak and chomped loudly.

We all took a moment to think, and I was busy wondering why Jonathan still hadn't told us where to start looking for Phyllis, when Lois interrupted my thoughts by whispering very loudly, "Are we going to go home in a minute please, Rosie? I'm bored."

I glared at her. Adi was still smiling benignly. I felt strangely relaxed, even though I was wondering how we were going to proceed.

It was as if Jonathan had read my mind. "You'll know when to start the mission. You'll be shown. Everything will happen as it is meant to."

"Follow the river and you will get to the sea," Adi piped up.

"Precisely, young man," agreed Jonathan, wiping the last of the biscuit crumbs from his beak.

"Okay," I smiled, deciding to do as both Jonathan and Adi had suggested, i.e., go with the flow. I was beginning to enjoy his Indian proverbs, even though I didn't always understand them.

"Now, I haven't time to drop you back as my *********s need bringing to the boil. So, come on, all three of you stand over there." Jonathan pointed to the panelled walls. We got up hastily. Paloma squawked and returned to the desk. We stood facing the wall, holding hands.

"Close your eyes and repeat after me: AIDARA. AIDARA. AIDARA."

I kept my eyes closed whilst we followed his instructions. "Now what should we do, Jonathan?" I asked gingerly.

There was no reply. I squinted open one eye cautiously, then fully opened both in a start. We were standing in our hallway with our back to the mirror.

"We're back, guys," I whispered.

"I'm desperate for a wee," Lois added, making for the stairs. She turned her head as she ascended. "Make sure you've got your shoes and the candles and the key for Saturday when we go to *Dancing Divas*, cos that's when we go to find Phyllis."

She grinned at me and Adi's shocked faces.

"Paloma told me," she added as she flicked her hair over her shoulder and continued up the stairs.

21

DANCING DIVAS AND DONS

We spent the following week in a blur of nerves and excitement, worsened of course by the fact that Mum was now in her Tech Week, where she was doing crazy hours, going into work at ten in the morning and not coming home till ten at night. The house felt dead without the jollity of Frances, Mr Foggerty, and Uncle Vic, not to mention dear Phyllis, who was goodness knows where.

Dad was still not back at work. He loped and lounged like a sleepy cat, pouring his body from bed into an armchair and then back to bed. To be fair, his shadow did seem to have reduced somewhat. It didn't cling in such a possessive way. It didn't curl around his shoulders and legs. It just lingered behind him. I could see his raincloud again. It was still black but less dark, greyer in places, which should have been encouraging.

The problem was, as Dad wasn't at work, partly due to the clean up on the tracks, but also down to him finding it so difficult to even get out of bed, I was getting more worried about how on earth we were going to get to London on

Saturday for the *Dancing Divas and Dons* show that we had been sent tickets for. I broached the subject with my very jittery mum on Friday morning, the day of her first show.

Mum was already downstairs drinking coffee and muttering to herself when I got up on Friday morning. She looked exhausted. Her skin was tight and grey looking. She had swirls of orange and yellow with dark-blue fizzes around her, but the closest colour to her body was a greeny brown, which gave me a slight feeling of unease. It looked as if something unsavoury was clinging to her: something Marcus-like, I shouldn't wonder. She was fingering a silver necklace with her initial on. The "R" was sparkly and caught the lights from the kitchen ceiling. They bounced around, as if unleashed and ready to create havoc.

"That's nice, Mum. Is it new?"

I think I must have known what her answer was going to be.

She had the grace to blush slightly and looked down at it, as if surprised she had been unconsciously fiddling with it.

"Yes, actually. Marcus gave it to me yesterday as a good luck present. It's gorgeous, isn't it?"

"Mmmmm, if you like that sort of thing," I replied nonchalantly.

She eyed me curiously.

"It's only a necklace, darling. Marcus hasn't bought me a private yacht! Do you think Daddy might be jealous then?"

I sighed heavily.

"I don't think Daddy is anything right now. And tomorrow he is supposed to be taking us to *Dancing Divas*. How's he going to do that when he can hardly get out of bed?"

Mum took hold of my face between both her hands. "Now listen to me, Rosie. Your father WILL be taking you, Lois, and Adi to *Dancing Divas* tomorrow, if it's the last thing he does. He made a promise, and he will be doing it. Leave it with me."

She swept off upstairs. I was partly relieved that Mum was going to sort it, but partly annoyed that I had allowed her to divert my attention away from the necklace that lecherous Marcus had given her.

I munched my croissant thoughtfully, not paying much attention to the raised voice of my mum upstairs. I'm not sure that shouting at my dad was really going to make much difference.

A few minutes later, though, Dad duly appeared in his Darth Vader dressing gown, looking unshaven and a bit smelly. Lois trailed behind him with Bea, anxious to be near him. He silently made himself a coffee and some toast for Lois and sat at the kitchen table sipping his drink. At least he was out of bed, I thought rather optimistically.

Mum re-entered the kitchen and slammed an envelope containing our tickets for *Dancing Divas* on the table.

"Got to go, girls. I will see you in the morning before your trip. Wish me luck, or should I say tell me to 'break a leg'?"

"Mummy, why would I want you to break a leg?" Lois piped up. "So, don't 'break a leg', please."

Mum laughed and bent down to give Lois a big kiss on the cheek. I handed her a card that we had made rather hastily last night. It had a big red heart on the front that I had outlined and Lois had coloured in, then, standing next to it, were figurative drawings of Mum, Dad, me, and Lois.

It had a big "Good Luck!" in glittery writing on the front and inside it said:

Dear Mum,

    We know you will be amazing as Martha! We hope you remember your lines, and if you forget them just don't say "Baaaa!"

    Love from Rosemary and Lois

    xxxx

Mum looked a bit teary. "That's lovely, thank you, girls. I will put that in my dressing room in the most special place of all, and I will touch it for good luck before I go on tonight."

Mum looked challengingly at Dad huddled on his chair sipping coffee. "Well, darling, I don't think I can carry that huge bouquet you've given me as good luck."

Dad didn't rise to it (he clearly hadn't got her any flowers), though he did rummage in his dressing gown pocket and produce a postcard.

"You'll be great tonight, love," he whispered, handing Mum a *Charlie and Lola* postcard with the words "I've Seen Big Ben" emblazoned on them.

Mum read the card and popped it in her bag.

"Thank you, John." She dropped a kiss on top of his head, hugged me and Lois, and fled out the door.

I don't know what the postcard said, but I guess it must have been sort of okay, otherwise she wouldn't have kissed Dad — she would have thumped him. It didn't, however, go unnoticed by me that the postcard was one he had clearly torn out of Lois' *Charlie and Lola Go to London* book, which at the back had two postcards you could tear off and fill out. We had never done this, so I didn't mind betting that if I went to look at the book right now, it would be missing one postcard. I just hoped Lois hadn't noticed.

The day at school seemed to drag, but at last the bell rang, and I literally grabbed all my stuff and dashed out of the classroom.

I waited impatiently for my dad to show up, wishing instead that one of our houseguests were collecting us. I'd be so happy to see dear Phyllis right now, with her gangly legs and earnest desire to help you, which usually resulting in causing an accident of some sort. But hopefully we would see her tomorrow — fingers crossed. I was really missing all four of them.

I saw my dad's dark form coming towards us with Lois clinging on to him like a limpet. His shadow had gone from his shoulders, and I could just make out the remnants of it clutching his lower legs and ankles in a desperate bid to cling on to him somehow. I just longed for my dad to kick out his legs and free himself from this black mass that seemed to have devoured him slowly. I suppose it wasn't that easy.

I noticed he had shaved, which was good, and he'd put proper clothes on to meet us. I knew the trains had been back to normal for a day or so, and I wondered whether Dad would make it back to work next week. I said a little prayer to God, hoping Dad would go back at work. Then he might feel better, and then we would see Frances, Uncle Vic, and Mr Foggerty again.

Finally, the day had arrived. I jumped out of bed, crept down to the kitchen, and heated up a chocolate croissant for myself in the microwave. Soon after, Lois joined me and, realising we weren't sure how to turn the oven on, I galloped up the stairs to gently wake Mum.

I crept into my parents' bedroom. It was 7:30 by now, and my dad stirred, rubbing his eyes. Mum's side of the bed was completely empty, not even a ruffled cover or pillow indentation. She hadn't slept here last night. She hadn't come home. I felt butterflies quicken in my tummy, whizzing like popping candy, but not in a good way.

"Where's Mum?"

Dad roused himself and grabbed a pillow from the floor to put behind him as he sat up.

"What time is it, Rosie?" He sounded hoarse and sleepy.

I ignored his question.

"Dad, where is Mum?"

"It's okay, Rosie. She sent a message last night to say she was staying over at the B and B next door to the theatre. She was so exhausted, and she wanted a drink after the first night. She'll be home tonight, and then she's got a day off tomorrow, so you can ask her all about it then."

I stomped out the room and, as I pulled the bedroom door closed, I said, with venom, over my shoulder, "It's 7:30 and we need you to put the oven on please, DAD."

I was suddenly furious. We had all been trying to look after my dad; we cuddled him, we checked he was okay, and we put up with his dark moods and his silences. Basically, we tip-toed around, trying to make things better for him, sacrificing our own happiness at times, and now my mum obviously didn't want to come home. I was sure it was because of him. I was certain it was his fault that this was happening, that she would rather be with someone like Marcus, who wore dress shoes with jeans, than us.

I threw myself on my bed and sobbed. How were we going to get out of this mess? What if Mum truly didn't want to come home again? What if Dad never got better? Was all this being orchestrated by Mal Vine in an attempt to take my family away from me? What if we never saw our witch family again? Suddenly going to *Dancing Divas* just seemed trivial in the light of my family falling apart around me. I just wanted my mum and dad to be normal again with each other — to smile, to laugh, to spend time with us.

I was crying so hard and snotting into my pillow, that I barely noticed my dad crouch next to me. My head was face down on the pillow, and he put his arms around me and whispered close to my ear, "Come on, love, what's wrong? Tell me what's wrong? We're going to London today. Don't you want to go?"

I raised a blotchy, red face, my nose dripping, my lips trembling. It wasn't my best look.

"Of course I want to go. But how are you going to take us if you can hardly get dressed? What if Mummy doesn't come home tonight? What if she goes off with Marcus and never comes back? You need to get better, Daddy. We need you."

I couldn't speak anymore. I was crying so hard my voice had gone all wobbly and staccato. I felt like a limp rag.

Dad just held me tight and stroked my hair and made shushing noises. Finally, after I'd deposited half a ton of snot on to his Darth Vader dressing gown, he took my face in his hands and said, "Come on now, you're reading things into all this. Mum will be back tonight. She'll be desperate to hear all about our trip to London. I'm more than capable of taking three reprobates on the train to some daft dancing programme. I might even have a Big Mac if I fancy it. I might even tap along to the dances. I might even wear some-thing that isn't black."

I giggled in spite of myself and sniffed away until Daddy passed me a grey-looking hanky.

"No, s'alright, Dad. I'll get a tissue."

"Are you okay now, love? I'll go and put the oven on for some croissants, and we'll get ourselves all ready for Adi's arrival, okay?"

"Okay," I paused. "Dad?"

"Mmmmm?"

"I think you might need to put Darth Vader in the wash." I pointed to his damp shoulder.

And so it was that three excited kids, plus one slightly more animated parent than I've seen in ages, boarded the 13:47 train from Liverpool Lime Street to London Euston. I had crammed together my gold shoes, the key, and our candles into my backpack, along with a few other emergency "essentials". True to his word about not wearing black, Dad wore a navy-blue shirt, blue jeans, and socks with Bart Simpson on.

Once we arrived in London, Dad grabbed us all a Maccy D, as he said we would have to have it on the train. We had to get the tube to St Pancras Station and then another Overground train to Elstree & Borehamwood Station. It was on this train that we were allowed to eat our food. It was packed full of people. Lots of them were dressed up to the nines, and so I wondered if they, too, were heading for an evening of *Dancing Divas and Dons*.

We were giddy with excitement. Even Bea (whom Lois had insisted on bringing) was dancing up and down on her lap, occasionally jabbing her paw into Lois' "barmeque" sauce.

I hadn't been to London very often, but it didn't look much different from Liverpool, really. Just a bit bigger, I guess. Oh, and Mum said usually the weather was better. If today was anything to go by, then that was a fit, fat fib, as it was FREEZING as we walked up the high street towards the Elstree Studios.

We followed the signs to "Audience Check-In", and Dad handed our tickets to a miserable-looking, dark-haired woman who spoke in a completely monotone voice and sounded as if she was having trouble getting her breath.

"Right, follow the yellow signs to the left. You've got second row, special VIP tickets. Toilets are up the corridor on the right. Enjoy the show."

For the "enjoy the show" part, just imagine she was saying, "stick your head up a dead bear's bum". That's how miserable she was.

We followed the yellow signs, which led us into a corridor, and we were then shepherded by a very familiar looking man to the studio. Lois' face lit up. "Mr Fogg—" I clamped my hand over her mouth as quickly as I could and glanced at my dad, who was busy studying the seat numbers on the tickets.

"Shhh," I whispered to her. "Don't give the game away."

I was shocked to see him, but also it was as if it was not out of the ordinary. I suppose I had been warned by Lois that today was the day for our mission, so nothing should have surprised me.

Lois continued to grin like a lunatic at Mr Foggerty, who didn't look very happy to be there. Usually it was only "believers" that could see our houseguests, but today was one of those occasions whereby they had allowed themselves to be visible to all. He surreptitiously put his finger to his lips and ushered us to our seats. His hair looked as mad as ever, but he was wearing what looked to be a new suit.

I kept glancing at Dad to see if he had noticed Mr

Foggerty, but Dad was clearly more interested in the lighting states to take much notice of who was guiding us to our seats and kept saying to himself, "Christ this must cost a fortune to put on."

Meanwhile, Adi jabbed me in the ribs and loudly whispered, "Flippin' 'eck, Rosie, that's your Uncle Vic, isn't it?"

Over to the stage area, a large, round man was waddling out in a brown-check suit with a bottle-green tie. He looked clean and tidy and would have been unrecognisable for this fact, if it hadn't been for his crossed eyes, which were his most distinguishing feature, I suppose. He held a big microphone and spoke into it with relish.

"Good evening, ladies and gentlemen, I'm Vic. I'm your warm-up man for this evening. Welcome to our movie night extravaganza! Just a little bit of housekeeping before we get you all warmed up and ready for the main event. Should anything untoward occur, like the fire alarms going off, or Aunty Beryl's pacemaker," (the crowd laughed), "then the emergency exits are to my left, to my right, and one directly in front of me. Can you tell I were cabin crew once upon a time?" (more laughter), "Failing that, follow the band! Oh no, they'll be heading for the bar," (even more laughter). "If you do need the little boys' room during the show…"

"Eh?" I questioned, frowning.

"The toilets," Adi whispered to me and to Lois, who was quite disinterested.

"…then please just sneak out to the ones directly behind, and we will pop one of our lovely supporting artists in your seat, so it doesn't look like we have any gaps. So, when you pop back, don't have a go at them for being in your seat. They don't get paid much, love 'em."

I slid my eyes back to my father, who was still engrossed in the changing lighting states.

All of sudden, after what seemed an age, the opening music started!

Bess and Babs, who hosted the show, tottered on to the stage amidst rapturous applause and introduced the pro dancers who then started to perform a fantastic group dance to "It's A Kind of Magic" by Queen. I might have known Frances would turn up. Every time a Queen record featured, there she was. She must have been their biggest fan.

I whispered to Adi, "Can you see Frances dancing like a lunatic out there, or is it just me?"

"Yeah, I can see her," Adi whispered back.

"Me too," giggled Lois. "She's funny."

As the show continued, Bess would introduce a dance and then the couple would go upstairs to be interviewed by Babs and we would get told to clap and cheer loads.

We were all having a great time. Even Adi, who wasn't a fan of dancing, was grinning away as the music and atmosphere was so infectious.

The time flew and, before we knew it, the show was over, and Uncle Vic was back on the stage telling people which exit to use and that ushers would show them out safely.

We pulled on our coats and followed Exit B, as we had been told. We were all desperate for a wee by now, so we broke away from the crowd and hot-footed it around to the toilets, which were signposted.

Dad said he and Adi would meet me and Lois right outside in a few minutes and not to wander off anywhere. We did our business and, after washing our hands, came back outside. The corridor had become very quiet. I guess people must have exited the building extremely quickly.

Dad looked a bit brighter than he had been recently. His shadow was still lingering, but it was right by his feet, like an unwelcome stray dog weaving in and out of his ankles. His cloud was now pale grey. A dark shade of white, you could even call it. It looked like rain could be imminent or, equally, it could pass over. These were all encouraging signs, and I wondered if it meant we were close to finding Phyllis. Dad was keen for us to find our way out immediately and head for home.

"Right, which way did we come?" Dad questioned, looking puzzled. Both ends of the corridor looked exactly the same.

"It was definitely this way," Adi said, pointing to his right.

"Yeah, I think so, too," I added.

We continued to walk down the corridor, hoping for a sign or to see one of the ushers. There was nothing. Just stark, bright light that came from the overhead strip lighting and millions of photographs up either side of the wall of big stars.

We carried on down the corridor and were about to think about turning round and going the other way, when we reached the toilets again, the ones we had just been into...

"Hey," Lois said, "we've just been in these toilets, Dad."

"Are you sure, Lois? There's probably more than one set of toilets here."

"Daddy it is the same ones. Look, there's the girls' door, there's the boys', here's the bin where I put my empty water bottle." She shoved her hand unceremoniously into the bin, which luckily was quite full so she didn't have to dig too far into it, and pulled out her distinctive blackcurrant-flavoured water. "See?" she gloated.

Dad looked a bit confused. "Well, this is strange. We seem to have just walked round in a circle. Ah, hang on, there's another door here. Perhaps we missed this before. Do any of you remember us coming through a door to get to this corridor?"

We all shook our heads silently.

"Come on, let's try it."

We looked at Dad with serious faces. We were experts by now at going through strange doors. We knew it was going to take us somewhere unexpected, but the question was, would Dad be able to be a part of all this?

I didn't have to wait long. Dad took the bull by the horns and pushed down on the handle of the very ordinary-looking, cream door. We followed him through to a dark expanse of space. The door closed behind us and immediately faded into the distance. We were without an exit. There, about five feet in front of us, was my mum standing with Marcus, talking earnestly.

Dad turned around to face the three of us, looking pale. He rubbed his eyes and put his head in his hands. "Oh God, what's going on? Please let me feel normal. I'm going to count to five and breathe."

I couldn't bear my dad to think that this vision was part of his illness.

I had to convince him it was real.

"Dad, it's okay. We can see this, too."

"What?" he whispered, uncovering his face.

"We can see Mum and Marcus, too. Don't be scared."

Adi had walked away from us now and was scouring the area for clues. Mum and Marcus didn't seem to be aware of us — they were deep in conversation.

Dad turned back to where Mum was standing, in her full costume by the looks of things, with smarmy Marcus, his hair slicked back so his nose looked even more ginormous. Mum was wearing a bit of padding underneath her clothes, so she looked chubby and voluptuous. She had a black wig on and her dress had bat-wing sleeves, which swished as she moved her arms. She didn't look like herself at all, and it made me feel uncomfortable.

"Rae," Dad called. "Can you hear me?"

Silence.

"Rae?" Dad shouted even louder. "For God's sake, will someone tell me what the bloody hell's going on?"

"Mr Pellow..." Adi interjected.

"John, call me John, for goodness' sake, Adi."

"Er, John, I would say we are below stage at the Theatre Royal, St Helens, where Rosie's mum is performing. There are stairs just over there behind Marcus, which lead up to the main stage. Stage right, I'd say. Your wife and Marcus cannot hear us, because we have entered their world as trespassers. We have come forward to the future and are just voyeurs on the events which are yet to happen."

At that moment, Marcus grabbed my mum and thrust his face on to hers in a big smackerooni. Mum pushed him away in horror. "Marcus, that's enough. Please get off me."

"Come on, Rae. You know you want to."

Again, he pushed his face on to hers, and his arms were like spider's legs grappling with her waist and trying to stop her from pushing him off.

Suddenly, Mum's arms went limp, as if she had accepted defeat and surrendered to his advances.

We were all aghast. Dad raced over to the spectacle and threw himself on Marcus, but to no avail. It was as if they were just mirages, and Dad's hands went straight through him.

Suddenly there was a loud bang, and the room seemed

to vibrate in its aftermath. Lois, Adi and I were flung backwards, landing on top of a huge chest that gave way as we plummeted on to it. We sank like jelly babies being thrown into melted ice cream. All I remember as we were sucked down, was hearing Dad's cries reverberating around.

"Noooooooooo."

22

INSIDE THE WORMHOLE

We landed very quickly, so thankfully, this time, our fall was not like the epic drop that we experienced when we went through door Number 3 on our first journey through the portal. This experience was more like unbalancing and falling into the chest, which gave way to yet more darkness. I didn't feel scared, just very confused, and slightly anxious that my dad had been left behind with Mum and Marcus, who couldn't see him anyway. I was wondering whether Dad would be looking for us or if he'd panic. I think Adi might have read my thoughts.

"Don't worry about your dad, Rosemary. I'm pretty sure we've fallen into a wormhole, which links the present with the future. That is to say, the present is where we were at the studios watching *Dancing Divas*, and the future is where we've just been with your dad watching your mum being accosted by Marcus. So, I think we are in a time tunnel really. Thus, by the time we get back to your dad, no time will have gone by at all. It will be just like we've fallen into the chest and then got straight up again. And by the time we do get back to the corridor at *Dancing Divas*, no time will have passed there either, so we will still get our train home. See?"

Adi had been using his hands in an intricate way, drawing pictures in the air (which I could barely see anyway), and he pushed his glasses back up on his nose with a flourish. I was pretty confused.

Lois was holding on to my hand tightly. "Are we in the future or the present now?"

"We are in neither, Lois. We are in the fold of a piece of paper, really, the space of nothing. And the space of everything." He paused, clearly realising that Lois' comprehension of this would be limited.

"Does this mean we can go home now?" she whined.

"I think it means we can go home as soon as we've found Phyllis," Adi continued.

"But I'm quite sleepy," Lois moaned.

I felt in my pocket and by some miracle managed to find a digestive biscuit wrapped in cling film. It must have been one from a few that she'd given to me to save for later.

"Here, have this." I passed it to her, unwrapping the clingfilm and making sure she had it in her little paw as the light was so limited.

"I know!" a delighted Adi said. "Let's light one of our candles! Then we'll be able to see where we are going!"

"Great idea, Adi," I replied. "Going back to this wormhole thing, though, how the hell are we going to find Phyllis? I mean, is it massive? Are we going to be searching for ages for her?"

"I don't know. But what I do know is that wormholes are prone to collapsing, so we need to be quick."

Suddenly, Adi put his fingers in his ears and did his funny, throaty "uhhhhhhhhhhhh" noise loudly.

"What's the matter?" I shook him to try to bring him out

of it. He only ever did this when someone told him something he didn't want to hear, so I couldn't work out what was going on, as he had been the one speaking!

"How can we light the candles when we've got no lighter?" he moaned in a squeaky, high-pitched voice that made it sound like he had given up.

Luckily, I was planner.

"Adi, don't panic. I brought some matches from the kitchen drawer. I didn't think there was much point bringing the candles if we didn't have a means of lighting them."

"Hurray!" Lois cheered.

Adi exhaled slowly and loudly.

"Well done, Rosemary."

After a few attempts, I finally managed to light the match, and I smiled to myself with quiet triumph on seeing the illuminated eager faces of Adi and Lois (whose mouth was covered in biscuit crumbs) in the yellow glow of candlelight.

We were in a very cramped space, about four foot by four foot, and as I looked up, the ceiling was only about an inch above my head. The entire area was painted black. There was not a light to be seen. I began to feel a bit sick and breathless. Was this what it felt like to have claustrophobia? All at once, the relief flooded me that in front of us I could see within the black wall a keyhole.

My breath was coming in pants now, and I wanted to point out to Adi and Lois that I had seen a way out, but I couldn't speak. My shaky hands held the candle and I gazed into it to try to gather some calm so that I could speak. Adi was looking at me wide eyed through his glasses, with obvious concern. Lois was flicking her eyes around the tiny area, clutching Bea to her chest for comfort. Their faces became more and more blurred, and I felt as if I was moving away from them rapidly, even though my feet hadn't left the ground. It was eerily silent, and although I wanted to speak, no sound could come out of my mouth.

The candle flame was mesmerising, and I was moving without moving, if that makes sense. I could see their faces becoming further and further away until they were just tiny pin pricks in the distance.

Suddenly my candle went out.

Darkness once again.

I caught my breath in a gasp, as if I had been under water and thrust back out of it into the fresh air. I gulped in the oxygen that my body clearly needed and felt my breathing and my rapid heartbeat going back to normal. I reached into my pocket for the matches and once again lit my candle.

I was back under the Theatre Royal, St Helens, where Mum was performing. I turned to Adi and Lois, when I realised I was alone. There was no sign of either of them. Not even a lingering fart smell. My attention was caught by the sound of voices, and there, over to my left, were Mum and Marcus.

"Mum?" I shouted. "Mum, it's me. I'm here. Can you see me?"

I ran over to be closer to her. There was no acknowledgement from her whatsoever that she had heard me calling. I was as invisible to her as my dad had been, and the sense of loss and longing was immense. I was almost crying with anguish and frustration that she couldn't see or hear me. I was totally helpless and confused. Why on earth had I found myself back here?

It's no point being scared, I told myself sternly. *Concen-*

trate on the present. What can you see, what can you hear, what can you feel, what can you smell?

Fortunately, I couldn't smell anything. I *could* feel my own body. I pinched my arm. Yes, that hurt. What could I see? Well, I could see my mum talking to Marcus as before when we were here. Then a chill ran through me. Although it was clearly "Marcus" in costume, his face had morphed into that of Mal Vine. I took a deep breath and listened to them.

"Remember, when I wink at you take your pause, then Donna will have to go stage left and hopefully stop bloody well upstaging me, little cow."

"Oh, Marcus, wouldn't it better to speak to Nikolai about this, or Donna? She might not realise she's doing it."

"Sweet girl, she knows exactly what she's doing. I've been on the case for a while now. I've been watching your back, darling. Look where that's got me."

"Oh dear, don't do anything on my account. You think about yourself and your performance, please. I'd feel terrible."

"My darling girl, that's what I love about you, always thinking of others. But yes, you're right, I really must now concentrate on myself. I'm far too selfless. What can I say, I'm a gent."

To Mum he must have still looked like Marcus. I blinked. He still had Mal Vine's face to me. He paused and very gently pushed a little piece of my mum's hair behind her ear. As he did so, his fingers cleverly slid down to her neck and fingered her necklace.

"I'm so glad you liked your little pressie, darling."

"I love it, thank you, Marcus," Mum went to move, but Marcus stopped her with his hand.

"Please, don't go yet, dear Rae. I'm feeling so nervous tonight. I need one of your pep talks." He laughed.

"Marcus, I need to get back up there. John's coming tonight."

Marcus placed his fingers over his mouth and tapped them a few times, as if he were trying to stop himself from speaking, but then on further contemplation realised he simply had to say it.

"I'm worried about you, darling. I know things are a strain at home. I know how much you adore your husband but, darling, and I hate saying this, you really deserve so much better than him. I'm only telling you this because I care about you deeply... and I really feel that it's time..."

Well, thankfully, I never got to hear what it was time for, as at that moment, as if by magic, my father appeared, trundling down the stairs just behind them.

"Rae?" he called. "Are you down here? Jane said you were taking five minutes below stage. Oh, hello, Marcus."

Dad shot Marcus a contemptuous look followed by a tight smile. Marcus' face, which on my dad's arrival had morphed back into his own, was a picture. He looked like he'd just stepped in the biggest dog poo you'd ever seen.

"John," he replied tersely. "Lovely to see you." (Huge amounts of brown smoke came out of his mouth.) "Well, I'd better leave you to it. I have a regime to follow before I can get out there on the green. Rae, see you out there." He nodded to my mum and brushed past my dad rudely.

"Break a leg, Marcus," Dad called after him, which was a bit naughty really. I know this is what you say to people instead of "good luck" in the theatre, but on this occasion, I really do think Dad meant it quite literally.

"Sorry to interrupt, Rae." Dad paused. "Was I interrupting something?" he asked somewhat more seriously.

Mum threw herself on him in a hug. "Absolutely not. In fact, I dread to think what he was going to say or do if you hadn't come down."

"Have you finally seen the light, love?"

"There's no light to see, John. I just think Marcus is little too fond of me, and it's not reciprocated," Mum replied a little defensively.

Dad nodded.

"Thank you for coming," Mum whispered. "I didn't know that you would…" She trailed off.

"Of course I was going to come. I know it's been hard for you these last few weeks, but I feel I'm getting there now. I couldn't do any of it without you, Rae. I really couldn't. I know I never say things like this, but I'm nothing without you, nothing."

I saw Mum wipe a tear from her eye.

"You do pick your moments, don't you?" she sniffed between tears. "I've got to go on stage in a minute, and you're being all daft and romantic. Couldn't you wait till we were in the bar after the show?"

"I don't like to be predictable," replied Dad, grinning. "I'll see you after, love. You'll be great." He planted a slow kiss on her lips and turned to go back up the stairs.

I noticed Dad's colours had changed. No longer were they brown and black and grey, but there was a purply colour trying to break through, with some pink shimmer to it around the edges. It looked very pretty and new and glittery. I rather liked it. I hadn't noticed his rain cloud, so maybe the sun was beginning to push through, at last?

Mum watched him ascend the stairs and whispered to herself. "Please let John be alright now, and please let me be great tonight. And please keep my family safe."

She then took a deep breath and made her way up the stairs.

I felt warm inside watching this exchange take place. Was this the future? I know Dad was planning to go to her press night, which was on Tuesday. So had I jumped in time to witness what was going to happen between them on Tuesday? If so, how? And why had it happened without Lois and Adi? All I knew was I felt that this would bring our family back together again, which was all I longed for.

Suddenly I remembered what Jonathan had said to us during the energy raising,

"Whatever you were focussing on during our energy raising will be manifested in your candle. When you need that wish to come true, simply burn your candle, and your spell will be out there, ready to materialise."

We had all completely forgotten about this! It all made sense now. It was *my* candle that we had lit, therefore it was *my* wish to bring my family back together that had manifested. This had to be proof that it was going to happen! I looked down at my candle, which had burnt down about half-way now. How was I going to get back to the others? This time travel malarkey was all well and good, but only if you were confident with the outcome. I needn't have worried, as I heard the Tannoy at the top of the stairs boom out, "Beginners please, may I have beginners, please."

The voice seemed to slow down, so it was more like, "Beeeeeeginnnnnnnnnnerrrrrs, pleeeeeeeeease."

My candle blew out as a gust of air swept across it from the top of the stairs.

I nearly screamed, as I felt a hand on my arm.

"Rosemary, are you okay?" came the concerned voice of Adi.

I could feel my little sister bring her arms around me and hug me close, her little head nestling under my armpit.

"Yeah, I'm fine. Just a weird thing happened. After I'd lit my candle, I went back to the sub-stage area where Mum and Marcus were. But it was the future, as Dad was there, but he was in their time zone, if you know what I mean?"

"Your Dad was talking to them, was he?" Adi questioned.

"Yes. Marcus was being slimy and all over Mum, and he looked like Mal Vine. Then all of a sudden, Dad appeared and his face went back to normal. Dad got rid of Marcus and then he and Mum sort of made up and had a kiss."

"Does that mean we can go home now?" came the muffled voice of Lois, who was practically glued to me now.

"No, not yet, Lois. We just need to find Phyllis first, but I think it means we have to be careful with our candles. Remember at the energy raising, we put a kind of wish on them each? Remember, Adi, that you said you wanted to go to India to see your grandparents and cousin? And remember, Lois, you wanted to fly on France's broomstick? Well, my wish was to see our family happy and back together again, so I was taken to a place to witness it actually happening. So, if we light Adi's candle we could end up in India, if we're not careful!"

"Woah!" Adi exclaimed breathlessly. "I am so lighting my candle when I get home."

"Just be careful, Adi," I warned. "You know it has to be the right time for these things."

"I thought we were given the candles to find Phyllis?" Lois questioned.

I felt a bit uncomfortable. "We were, Lois, but I'm afraid we all put our energy of other thoughts into them, not finding Phyllis. We didn't mean to, it just happened." I frowned. "Maybe it was meant to happen that way. And maybe they are linked... If Mal Vine wants to destroy love then surely the fact that I've just seen Mum and Dad happy together again means we are close to defeating him and therefore on the right path to finding Phyllis."

"Great, let's re-light your candle and then see if your key fits the door we saw in here. One thing's for sure, we've got to get out of this cramped space, it already feels like it's got smaller," Adi said.

"No, we can't risk lighting my candle again, Adi," I added emphatically. "Just in case I end up back at Mum's theatre. We'll just have to find the keyhole with our hands."

How right Adi was. When we felt around the walls there was no denying it. The room was shrinking. It felt like the ceiling was coming in on us. Then I remembered what Adi had said about the danger of wormholes collapsing.

"Oh my God, Adi, we need to act fast. This wormhole is starting to collapse on us."

I fumbled in my bag for the key and, with sweaty hands, tried to fit it into the lock. It worked!

I glanced at Lois and Adi, seeking both their support and encouragement. I turned the key in the lock and, *bingo!*

The door opened.

As the ceiling was getting increasingly lower, we ended up having to crawl through the door on our hands and knees. The door closed behind us, and we found ourselves negotiating a dimly lit tunnel.

The tunnel was smooth with black walls and seemed to go on for an eternity. "Rosie, I can't go any further," Lois wailed behind me. I was leading the way whilst Adi was bringing up the rear.

"Please, Lois, I'm sure it won't be much further."

No sooner had I said that, the tunnel ended. I say

ended, but what actually happened was there was no more tunnel. I was presented with just a black, circular wall, which was somewhat disconcerting. *Oh bums*, I thought, trying to remain calm. I pushed against it, which seemed the sensible thing to do, and thankfully it gave way very easily, and I found myself sitting with my feet dangling out of the tunnel.

I suppose the tunnel opening was about a foot from the ground and as I looked around, the walls of the room in front of me appeared to be made of white flimsy-looking paper. I jumped down on to the floor and noticed the whole room swayed slightly with the addition of my weight, which made me nervous that it wasn't going to hold me, let alone the three of us. The ceiling, too, was paper, which hung down quite low. The only remarkable item in the room was a rope ladder, which extended from the paper ceiling down to the floor. I guessed we had no choice but to go up the ladder.

I waited for Lois and Adi to come to the end of the tunnel and carefully helped my little sister out of the hole, holding my breath in case the floor gave way. But thankfully, apart from a small shudder, it held. She looked fairly unimpressed.

"Well, where's Phyllis?" she said with a sigh.

"Hopefully we will find her soon," I placated, but I too was beginning to give up hope.

Adi took the lead with climbing the rope ladder, which was only short, as the ceiling hung low. I was still at the foot of the ladder, ready to follow Lois up, as well as make sure I was there to catch her in case she fell.

"Okay, this is freaky," came Adi's voice from above. I could no longer see him, as he had reached the top of the ladder. But as I looked up, I noticed, with surprise, that I could see the bottom of his feet clearly imprinted on the ceiling above us!

"Adi, where are you?" I shouted in disbelief. "I can see the soles of your feet as if you're standing on the other side of the ceiling!"

"I am!" he replied jubilantly. "Hurry up, girls, and I'll show you."

I half-pushed Lois up the ladder until we reached the end of it, where there was no choice but to turn right and stand on top of the flimsy-looking paper ceiling. Adi assured us we could step on to it and it would safely hold us. It was very odd seeing the floor of the room we were just in beneath us through the transparent paper. It felt like we were in some weird origami experiment. Suddenly I gave a shriek and clung on to Adi and Lois, for the paper floor we were standing on started to move, as if we were going down in an elevator.

"Don't panic, everyone," Adi shouted confidently. "We'll stop in a minute."

And we did.

"What on earth was that?" I asked shakily, noting how the rope ladder had completely disappeared and the floor we were standing on had joined the floor of the room we had started our climb from.

"Can't you see, girls?" Adi asked excitedly. "Remember I said a wormhole is like a piece of paper folded, so it allows you to get from A to B in a shortcut? Well, it's given us exactly that, how I've always described it. We started in the paper room looking up at the rope ladder. We climbed the ladder, i.e., we made a journey, and now our starting point and our destination have merged to become one point — exactly as would happen if you folded a piece of paper!" He sounded so full of jubilation and started to demonstrate his theory with a candy wrapper, showing how if you start at one end and want to travel to the other side, folding it over means the two points are on top of each other.

I didn't really like to burst his bubble, but I had to, seeing as all these technical explanations were quite frankly getting us nowhere, apart from encouraging Lois to create more filthy wind in the process.

"Yeah, okay, Adi, great and all that, but where is Phyllis? Lois can't go on for much longer, and goodness knows how we'll ever manage to get back out again the way we came."

"Shhhhhh," Lois held up Bea.

"What's wrong?" I asked her.

"Bea says she can hear something."

The three of us stood together in silence, our eyes surveying the area around us, searching for clues. Suddenly, very faintly, we heard singing.

The voice sounded wan and lost, not full of happiness; but one thing we were certain of: it had to be Phyllis. Now we just had to find exactly where it was coming from.

"Paloma said to tear a hole in the paper."

"Eh?" Adi and I looked at each other questioningly.

"Paloma isn't here, Lois. What are you on about?" I sighed, exasperated with my sister.

"Just because we can't see Paloma, doesn't mean she's not here, or I can't hear her. Just do as I say, or she'll poop on your shoulder again, Rosie." Lois looked very smug relaying that piece of information, and I remembered back to that horrible bird and her runny poo. I thought we'd better just humour her, so I got down on my knees and started frantically tearing a hole in the paper floor. Adi joined in, rolling his eyes at me, whilst Lois and Bea were performing a little celebration dance and not helping at all. I was about to complain that we were getting nowhere, for the paper seemed to be awfully difficult to rip, when, all of a sudden, the tiny hole I'd made expanded and we found ourselves dropping again, just a short distance, before we landed in a heap on the floor.

The room we found ourselves in was large, with every wall except for one covered in newspaper clippings. There were pictures of famous people from history and snippets of local information from Bedford to Bangkok. Adi even pointed out a story from Agra (in India) about a man-eating spider. The fourth wall was just black and there, sitting in the corner between the black wall and a headline that read "Hottest Summer Since 1904", was Phyllis.

Her lanky frame was bunched over, as she had her arms clasped around her knees, hugging herself. Her skin looked grey and pinched. Her large blue-framed glasses had one lens smashed, and she was missing a shoe. Her grey curly hair, which was usually shampooed and set once a week, was hanging drearily in wisps around her ears and neck.

But, as Phyllis looked up to see the three of us, she broke into the biggest smile I have ever seen, opened her arms wide and said:

"Welcome to the Room of Free Will."

23

THE ROOM OF FREE WILL

"I have never been so pleased to see three children in my life," Phyllis stated, pausing momentarily to think and then continuing. "Yes, that is an absolute truth."

Lois and I ran and hugged her whilst she was still sitting. I got the impression she would find it difficult to stand up quickly. I felt quite overwhelmed with emotion that we had finally found her and had to swallow back a lump in my throat before I could speak again.

"Goodness me, girls, you have grown, haven't you?" She paused and turned her gaze to Adi, who was shyly looking round the room, not knowing how involved to be in our reunion.

"And who is this handsome young man?"

Adi nervously pushed his glasses back up on to his nose and looked slightly embarrassed.

"It's Adi, my friend from school, and he's a maths genius and he helped us get through the portal in the first place by setting Aradia a riddle and guessing her age and shoe size."

"Mmmm." Phyllis raised her eyebrows. "I shouldn't

think you were popular with her after that. She is very touchy about her age."

"You weren't singing a very jolly song, Phyllis," Lois added, and placed Bea in Phyllis' arms, whether she liked it or not.

"No, dear, I wasn't, was I? I don't know what has happened to me, but since I've found myself in this room, I feel so terribly sad, and it's not just because I've been trapped here. I'm usually quite a resourceful person."

"How did you come to be in this place, Phyllis?" I asked as I scanned the walls.

"Well," Phyllis continued looking worried, "I was trying to go forward in time to the night of your mother's press night. I knew that she was going to get this job and I had a feeling Mal Vine would use this occasion to plan something big." She paused. "Have Frances or Uncle Vic told you about the No-Laws and their leader?"

"Yes, they have," I continued. "Roger Nowell and John Law, the judge and the pedlar who thought Alizon Device caused John Law to have a stroke..."

"That's right, dear. Alizon wanted to buy pins from John Law to make herself a love spell, and John wouldn't sell her any. She got very upset with him, as she was desperately in love with this chap in her village, Michael Todd. He was no good, but anyway, young love. She pleaded with John Law, as for some reason she felt that Michael was her soul mate, though Michael was already engaged to be married to John Law's niece, as it happened. Poor Alizon didn't realise this. Alizon was so angry that John refused to sell her the pins, that as John walked away the silly girl shouted to him, "I hope you lose your loved one to another, like you are forcing upon me, you selfish man!"

Phyllis looked wistful.

"What Alizon didn't know, was that John Law's wife had just died in childbirth, alongside his new-born daughter, who was stillborn. So he had only recently lost both the love of his life and his only child. Her words brought back all his grief and devastation, which is probably what brought on his stroke — not a curse of any kind, which is what people like to believe." Phyllis sighed and continued. "After this occurred, John was so heartbroken and shaken by Alizon's words, that when Roger Nowell arrived in the village with his mission to discover and wipe out any witchcraft, the first name on John Law's lips was Alizon Device and her family, all of whom were known healers who used herbal medicine to help draw out illnesses and ward away evil spirits. Alizon's grandmother was a midwife who had recently delivered a number of stillborn babies, and this, of course, was more ammunition for Roger, who then found it much easier to arrest her for murder."

"What's stillborn?" I asked tentatively.

"It's when a baby is born dead, my dear, which happened a lot in those days, not from witchcraft or the devil's work, but because sanitation was so poor, you see. People's diets weren't as good and, of course, there wasn't the medical knowledge that there is today. Since that day in 1612, when the Pendle witches, as they became known, were hung, John Law made it his mission to destroy love in the world."

"So why have they been trying to disrupt ordinary people's lives, and why did they pick Mum's press night?"

"Since Mal Vine was released from The Tunnel of Eternal Darkness, he has reformed the No-Laws with a view to causing chaos, so that BUTBUM (AW) would intervene to protect the people of Britain. In doing so, it allowed him to find our whereabouts, who he wants to destroy, as well as an opportunity to meddle with the happiness of your family, who the four of us adore. I knew he would choose your mother's press night, as it would be a highly dramatic event to cause disruption at."

I frowned, taking in the enormity of what Phyllis was saying.

"Also, I had an inkling that your parents might resolve their differences and rekindle their love for one another that night, which of course is something Mal and his followers would hate. Where love is strong and beautiful, they want to bring hate. John Law never came to terms with his own losses, and his bitterness has been passed down through the ages in a need to destroy love wherever it is found."

"Phyllis," I asked quietly, still taking in all the information she had given me, "how do you know all this about John Law in so much detail?"

"Because, dear, John Law was my great Great-great-great-great-great-great-great-great-great uncle."

Adi spun round in shock, and we all gazed at Phyllis with surprise. Even Lois, who was still snuggled up to her, pulled away slightly, knowing that this information was pretty big, even if she didn't know its significance.

"So, if you are related," Adi asked, "how come you can't put a stop to their actions, and how come you are on the other side?"

"Yes," I joined in, "surely you more than anyone can stop this, Phyllis, as they are from your family?"

"I wish it were that simple, dear. I was brought up in the late-nineteenth century, having been born in 1865, so during the reign of Queen Victoria."

I was trying quickly to do sums in my head, as I could see Adi was, and ascertained that if Phyllis had been born in

1865 then she was well over 100 years old now. I felt my mouth fall open with surprise.

"Is that the lady at Victoria Underground Station, on the wall?" Lois piped up.

"Yes, that's right dear."

"Carry on, Phyllis. You were telling us about why you are not able to put a stop to all this," Adi interjected impatiently.

"Ah, yes," continued Phyllis. "Where was I? All my family would tell the story of John Law and how he had been cursed by Alizon and her family of witches, which I obviously believed with all my heart. I was fascinated with the story as I'd always felt very different from my parents. As a little girl, whenever my family went to church every Sunday, I would sneak out of the service and play in the graveyard, where I met my dear friend Beowulf. He would always run away when my family came out of the church, and one day, I asked him why he would never show himself to my parents. He told me that his family and mine were arch enemies because of the legend of John Law and his Great-great-great-great-great-great-great-great-great Aunt Alizon. I couldn't understand how I was supposed to hate this boy who I played with, who was the one person I could really talk to. And of course what I didn't realise straight away is that the reason I felt different is because I had been bestowed with magical powers myself. Some people inherit their witchcraft ability, as in the case of Beowulf, and others like myself are simply gifted it."

"And did your family find out about your friendship with him?" Adi and I were both transfixed, but I could see Lois was fidgeting now.

"Sadly, yes, I'd just turned 18, and my parents caught Beowulf waiting for me one morning behind the church.

They forbade me from seeing him again, telling me I was consorting with witches and wizards, and that I, too, would be cursed if I spent time with him. The thing was, Wolfie made my heart sing. That's how I started singing. I couldn't bear the thought of life without him, so I ran away to be with him. Consequently, my family cursed me and swore that there would forever be war between us, for I had flouted the rules of loyalty by befriending him. You see, I simply couldn't live without dear Wolfie, and so we were banished from our families." Phyllis sighed sadly. "Instead of love bringing us together, my darlings, it has ripped us all apart. But we felt it was a price we had to pay, in order to be with each other."

"But surely so much time has gone by, Phyllis, that all this shouldn't matter anymore. Shouldn't everyone just move on?" I added.

"Yeah, move on," Lois chimed in.

"Sometimes people are afraid to move on," Adi piped up very wisely. "We have a saying in India that my mum uses all the time, "You do not stumble over a mountain, but you do over a stone."

Phyllis looked blank.

"It means we need to put this into perspective. It is but a stone in your past, not a mountain. See it for what it is, and do not let that stumble make you falter on your path towards happiness," Adi finished.

I was open mouthed at his wisdom. Sometimes he did surprise me.

"You, young man," Phyllis said, smiling wanly, "are terribly clever and wise. I shall take your advice."

"So," I interrupted impatiently, "how did you find yourself here, Phyllis, and not at Mum's press night?"

"Oh yes, I was talking about that, wasn't I? I made one mistake, children. I forgot about free will."

"Isn't that the film about the whale?" Lois asked with her head cocked to one side in thoughtful repose.

"No, stupid, that's *Free Willy*."

"Don't call me stupid, Rosie." Lois glared at me.

"Okay, let's just get on with the story, please," Adi pleaded at us both.

Lois, having sneakily swiped Bea back from Phyllis, turned away from me with her nose in the air.

"Free will. We have all sorts of possibilities in front of us. You could take one route home from school and trip over a paving slab, or if you took the other route home you would avoid the paving slab."

She looked at our expectant faces.

"What I mean to say, children, is that there would be no need for me to interfere in trying to mend the paving slab to stop you tripping over it, if you chose to go the other route."

"So, how is this relevant to this situation?" I asked, puzzled.

"Well, you see, I knew that Marcus was going to try to throw himself on to your mother. What I didn't take into account was the fact that she would rebuff him, or that your father would intervene at the right moment. I'm rather ashamed to say I thought she might welcome his advances." Phyllis looked embarrassed and glum.

"But it's okay, Phyllis, she didn't. We saw, didn't we?" I urged the others to back me up.

Lois to my surprise piped up. "Mummy tried to push Marcus away, but he was so strong, she got tired. She's just tired all the time at the moment, and she lost her strength, and then there was a big bang, and we ended up in that small dark room."

Phyllis looked thoughtful.

"Ah, so as soon as Rae stopped fighting, the explosion was able to happen. Tell me what else you saw, children."

Adi looked to me. "Go on, Rosemary, tell Phyllis what you saw when you went back the second time."

"The second time I got taken back there, when we lit my candle from the energy raising event," Phyllis went to open her mouth to question me, but I continued, desperate to get the information out, "Marcus was trying to wheedle his way into Mum's good books, and Dad suddenly appeared, so Marcus went off in a huff, and Mum and Dad made up, and there was no explosion."

"Do you see what I'm saying, children?" Phyllis continued excitedly. "Our actions all have consequences, and we have the ability to change things all the time, so sometimes travelling into the future to try to intervene is futile, as well as downright insulting to ourselves. We have to trust that we will all make the right decisions in life, don't we?"

"Are you saying that you should never have gone into the future to stop the No-Laws then?" Adi asked slowly, as if trying to process all the information.

"No, dear, what I'm saying is we have to choose our fights. Wolfie and I have been very careful about which attacks we have intervened in. On this occasion, I was playing at God, and I was foolish. I should have known and trusted that the love your parents have for each other would outwit the No-laws."

"What about the future, though?" I asked anxiously. "How can we stop them from doing any other horrid attacks. How can we defeat them? How do we know there won't be other times and places they will strike at?"

"Children," Phyllis took our hands in hers, "this is the

point. We don't really know. But what we do know, is that it is down to each and every one of us to continue this fight in our own little lives. We do this by living each day with love and kindness and compassion. We must never give into petty hate and fear. Where there is light, we can always defeat the darkness. If your parents can resolve their differences and reignite their love for one another, then Mal Vine and his followers will be rendered powerless, for they feed off of unhappiness and hate. I know press night hasn't happened yet, so we can't be certain as yet of the outcome, but this is one of those occasions when we have to trust in our family, to allow them to find their own way. Let me show you something."

Phyllis turned her attention to the black wall where she was sitting. "See this wall? This is the untold future. This is where we make our decisions, where those things that cannot be predicted happen. All around us in this room, on the other walls, are news stories, some of which have happened, some of which might have happened, and some which did not happen. See this one here?"

She pointed to a large headline which read:

Hilary Clinton Becomes USA's Latest President

(This might have happened but didn't.)
Followed by:

Donald Duck Becomes USA's Latest President

(This did not happen.)
Followed by:

Donald Trump Becomes USA's Latest President

(This did happen.)

"Now watch this carefully." Phyllis tapped the black wall three times with her knuckle. Slowly the darkness shrank from the outside in, like it was being burnt away by light filling the screen. As more light appeared, I could see a busy car park and my dad driving into it in our familiar blue car.

"That's our car, and Daddy's driving it," Lois shouted excitedly.

I raised my eyebrows. Duh! It was like watching home-video footage. Dad drove around the car park. Every now and then, there was a close up on his face, looking more and more fed up. Finally, we watched Dad give in to his frustration and drive away, back to the motorway towards home. The film then cut to the back of the Theatre Royal, St Helens and a beaten-up orange Mini pulled up where some cones were placed just outside of the stage door. We saw a tall hooded person, completely in black, get out of the car, furtively carrying a black bag. Outside the stage door, a dark-haired woman was stubbing a cigarette out, and as she went back into the theatre, the hooded person just managed to grab the closing door and slip inside. As he did so, his hood slipped down, revealing his face as he looked around. It was Mal Vine himself. I gasped.

"That's Mal Vine." I pointed at the screen.

There was a moment where Phyllis inhaled deeply. "Yes, Rosie, that is the No-Law's leader, the rarely seen Mal Vine. How did you know it was him?"

"I've seen him several times in my dreams, and once he appeared on the TV screen. He wanted to help me find you, said I couldn't do it without him, and that if I rejected his offer he would take my family away from me." I swallowed back my emotion as Phyllis took my hand gently. "I also saw his face appear on to Marcus' when I went forward in time to Mum's press night."

"No one is going to take your family away from you, dear girl," Phyllis said. "Sadly, when my family cursed me for choosing Wolfie, they didn't realise that that the very thing they thought they were fighting — black magic — was the thing they were getting themselves involved in. In true witchcraft, there is only one type of magic: white. If one dabbles on the dark side, it comes back threefold on you. So, by my parents cursing me, they inadvertently brought about their own downfall and that of Mal, who, tragically, is my brother."

There was silence, each of us unsure what to say about this revelation, until at last Phyllis spoke once more.

"Mal and I were incredibly close when we were young. Some would say he idolised me. When my family banished me, he was devastated and never really forgave me for leaving him. Shortly after I left, the reverberations of what my parents had done started. They both died suddenly within days of each other, so poor Mal was left an orphan. In those days the plight of a poor orphan was often the workhouse, I'm afraid."

"What's the workhouse?" Adi enquired curiously.

"It was a dreadful place, where the poor or orphaned would be sent to work for their food and lodgings, often in cruel, dirty, miserable surroundings. I was too far away by then to know what my brother's plight had been, but clearly it left a mark on him, in more ways than just the scratches on his cheeks. Let's just say, Mal's sadness at losing both me and our parents sent him to the dark side. Since his release from The Tunnel of Eternal Darkness, he has been searching for me. He wants to punish me, and anyone I am close to." Phyllis gravely resumed the video. "Let us continue to watch." A few minutes later, there was a bang and the screen went black. The three of us looked on, horrified, each of us not knowing what to say.

She eyed us all silently and then spoke. "This, however, is scenario two." Once again, she knocked her knuckles on to the black wall, and again the light appeared and, as before, we could see our dad driving round the car park looking for a space that wasn't there. This time, we became verbal in our frustrations.

"Come on, Dad, don't give up. Find a space," I shouted at the screen.

"Don't go home, Daddy," Lois added.

Adi, meanwhile, was standing with his eyes screwed tightly shut, his fingers in his ears, doing a much paled-down version of his "uhhhhhhhhhhhh".

I touched his arm. "Adi, it's okay. It's okay to watch. It's going to be alright." I said this with more fervency than I actually felt.

He reluctantly removed his fingers from his ears and watched with one eye open, the other eye closed.

We saw my dad start to drive away.

"Noooooooo!" Lois screamed, fighting back the tears.

"Just watch, Lois," I pleaded, praying Dad would find an alternative parking space. The film then cut to Dad's car pulling up outside the back of the theatre. We all cheered.

He got out of the car, and we laughed and whooped when he moved the cones to block the area behind his car. We then watched Dad nod to the dark-haired girl smoking outside stage door. She keyed in a code for him, and we saw him enter the theatre. Literally a minute later, we saw the orange Mini pull up outside and pause. The girl stubbed her cigarette out on the ground and re-entered the building just before Mal Vine got out of the car. As the stage door clicked shut, white sparks flew out of the top of the theatre like a pretty firework display, whizzing and whooshing, whilst, simultaneously, the orange Mini vanished into thin air. We all cheered victoriously. All of us, that is, except Phyllis.

"What is it, Phyllis?" I asked. "Why aren't you cheering?"

"These are possibilities, my dear. Any of these could happen. There may be other outcomes that we haven't seen yet. It's totally down to your dad, your mum, Marcus, and even the girl smoking outside the theatre."

"But Dad's already seen what might happen, so I'm sure he'll do everything to get to that theatre to stop creepy Marcus from pawing our mum," I added positively.

Phyllis still looked glum. In fact, everything about her was grey, so to speak. Her usually bright eyes looked dull and cloudy. It wasn't helped, of course, by the fact that her glasses were broken and she was missing a shoe.

Lois, ever sensitive and sweet, in spite of her sour bottom, placed her arms around Phyllis.

"Come on, Phyllis, please smile. Why are you so sad?"

Phyllis shakily replied, "It's a shock, my dear. Discovering that Mal has been threatening your sister. I feel so glum. As glum as a plum in a sour man's tum. As dark as the night in an owl's place of flight. As silent as the grave and a drowning man who can't be saved. As lost as ..."

"We need to get out of here now, Phyllis," Adi interrupted.

Thank god, I thought. Phyllis was off on one, but this time, instead of her usual jolly singing, she had turned into a dark, miserable poet.

"Dear boy, I have no idea how we return to the land of

the living. How we can bloom like the rockets that zoom away from the gloom and the dark, dark tomb. I have no plan for us to flee, you and me, you see."

Adi and I stared at each other, each of us clueless how to proceed.

Lois, thankfully, had a plan, and now I knew why I had brought my daft, smelly little sister with us.

"Phyllis," Lois shouted at her whilst she was reciting all this nonsensical rhyming gloom, "how do we get out of here, please?"

There was no answer, but Phyllis was silenced by Lois' voice. I thought I was imagining things when I heard a gentle caw from above. I looked to Adi, who had clearly also heard it, for his gaze went firstly to me in trepidation, then to Lois. We looked up simultaneously, and I must admit I felt a mixture of relief and dread.

It was Paloma.

"Paloma!" Lois shrieked with abandoned glee. "I've missed you so much."

She allowed the bird to flutter all round her face and then settle on her shoulder. The two of them looked totally engrossed in deep conversation, if you could call it that. By this time, Phyllis had once again sunk to the floor with her knees up and her arms wrapped around them. Her head was down, and she looked like a toy that had just run out of batteries.

"Right," Lois said with authority, "Paloma says Phyllis is ill."

"You don't say," Adi chimed.

"Adi, Paloma doesn't like starcasms, so I'd keep quiet, if I were you." Lois looked very pleased with herself at having gained such authority.

"Paloma says we need to give Phyllis medicine."

Lois stroked Paloma gently on the head and kissed her before the bird flew upwards to the ceiling and seemed to disappear into nothing.

I had given up with working out how all these things happened.

"That's a great observation, Lois, but the thing is, where can we get medicine from? We don't even know what medicine she needs."

"She needs the best medi," Lois stated as if we were idiots.

"Well of course she needs the best medi," I replied, "but what medicine is the best for her?"

"Laughter," stated Adi with faint surprise in his voice.

24

NOBODY EVER DIED OF LAUGHTER

"Laughter?" I repeated after Adi incredulously. "That's not a medicine."

"Yes, it is!" Lois contradicted. "Paloma said laughter is the best medicine, so we need to make Phyllis laugh, and then she will feel better and get some of her powers back."

I surveyed the room, which, apart from the three walls covered in newspaper cuttings, was pretty stark.

I contemplated the three of us trying to find funny stories amongst those on all the walls but decided it would a) take too long and b) I couldn't cope with Lois constantly asking me what certain words were.

"What's a footballer's favourite meal?" Adi suddenly piped up.

We both looked at him blankly. Phyllis was still sitting with her head bowed down on her knees.

"What are you talking about, Adi?" I sighed.

"I'm telling a joke, which hopefully will make you laugh. So, come on, what's a footballer's favourite meal?"

"Chicken nuggets," Lois piped up seriously.

I gave her a look.

"Beans on post!" Adi sniggered.

"Ha ha, very good." I smiled. "Okay, if we're telling jokes, it's my turn. Why does a football pitch become a triangle?"

"I don't know, Rosemary. Why does a football pitch become a triangle?" Adi asked, smiling.

"Because somebody took a corner!" I laughed. Adi groaned, Lois giggled, and Phyllis was silent.

"My turn, my turn!" Lois shrieked, eager to join in. "Ermmmmm... I've got one. I've got a really good one! What do you call a chair without a window?"

"I don't know, Lois. What do you call a chair without a window?"

"A lekanor," Lois stated, smiling gleefully.

"A what? That doesn't make any sense!" I sniggered, rolling my eyes at her craziness.

"Okay, let's do some knock-knock ones," Lois said excitedly. "Me first. Knock knock."

"Who's there?" Adi and I piped up together.

"Barnacle Bill."

"Barnacle Bill who?"

"Barnacle Bill who shows his butt...."

Adi and I stared at Lois incredulously, then at each other, and we both started to laugh helplessly.

"Your jokes are total nonsense!" I giggled, ruffling my little sister's hair.

"No they're not," she faux pouted. "Your turn, Adi."

Adi pushed his glasses back on to his nose and looked thoughtful. "I'm not so good at jokes."

"I've got one," I said eagerly.

"No, wait," Adi raised his hand. "I've got one, I think. What does Dracula have for breakfast?"

We both looked at him expectantly.

"Don't know..."

"Ready neck!"

Adi and I creased up whilst Lois looked bemused.

"What's ready neck?" she asked.

"Never mind Lois," I replied. "Now my turn. What did the vampire Dr say to his patients? Necks please!"

And so it went on:

Knock knock
Who's there?
Dunnop
Dunnop who?
Oh no, you did a poo?!

Hysterical laughter.

Why did the sun leave university?
Because it had too many degrees.

Why are the crickets playing football in the saucer?
They are practising for the cup.

What do you call a priest on a motorcycle?
Rev.

Knock knock!
Who's there?
The interrupting sheep
The interrupt—
Baaaaaaa!

By now, the three of us were totally in fits of laughter, especially at Lois' jokes, which she clearly made up and hadn't yet seem to have grasped the concept of a punch line or a witticism, which made them funnier, really, as they were so ridiculous. She was on a roll:

What do you call a glass that can't find its light?
A book

What do you call an iPad that can't even charge?
A Wi-Fi

What do you call a person who forgets to bring a suitcase?
A cup.

We were so busy rolling around entertaining ourselves, that we had momentarily forgotten about Phyllis and the whole reason behind the joke telling. I was just about to launch into my washing machine set of jokes, when Adi nudged me and motioned his head towards where Phyllis was seated.

I looked round at her whilst telling my joke:

"What's this?" I waved my arms about in a circular motion. "A jumper in a washing machine."

To my delight, she had raised her head up from her knees, but when I looked at her face, I could see she had tears pouring down it. Oh no! Had we made things worse?

"Phyllis, what's wrong? Are you okay?" I asked anxiously.

"My dear child, I'm fine," she finally said whilst wiping the tears that had been rolling down her cheeks. "I'm crying with laughter, children. I've never heard such utter ridiculous nonsense in my life, and it's tickled me pink. Tell me some more!"

So we did.

. . .

We continued for a good few minutes, telling ridiculous jokes, Adi and I trying to outdo each other with our knock-knock jokes, and Phyllis and Lois trying to out-nonsense each other, I think.

At last, our well of mirth had run dry.

Phyllis wiped her eyes again, which were wet from yet more laughter and declared, "Well, there's nothing like a good old laugh, is there, folks? Did you know, a day without laughter is a day wasted? I think we've spent enough time shilly-shallying around here, don't you? I think it's time we got out of this room. Quite frankly, I'm sick of looking at these same four walls."

"Hear, hear!" Adi applauded gently. "I'm sick of it, too."

"Me too!" I smiled with relief at Phyllis' apparent recovery.

"Me too. I'm sick of it. We're sick of it, aren't we, Bea?" Lois stroked her bunny and kissed its worn-away, once-pink nose.

"So, how are we going to get out, Phyllis?" I added, searching round the room with my eyes for an exit.

"That's a very good question, my child. For a start, I'm like Blind Pew. I can only see out of one lens, and I've lost a shoe, which really is terribly annoying. I won't get very far like this." She pointed to her shoeless foot which, though it was housed in a tennis sock, was black with filth and a mixture of blood, where Phyllis must have either cut it or got terrible blisters.

"You could borrow my shoes, Phyllis," Lois piped up earnestly.

"Don't be daft, Lois, then what would you wear?" I scolded.

"Hey!" Adi suddenly pointed at me excitedly. "You could lend Phyllis your trainers, Rosemary. You've got your gold dancing shoes with you. Put those on instead!"

The penny dropped big time for me. "Adi, you're right, and how could I not have thought before to put them on? They will take us wherever we need to go, which is out of this room and back to the *Dancing Divas* place, because we've got to get Dad and get the train back home. We can't just bypass all of that and go straight back to Liverpool, especially now that Dad's involved."

"Yes, you're right," Adi agreed. "We can't leave your dad. For all we know, he's still in that sub-stage, replaying that possible scenario with Marcus and your mum. I can only hope time has frozen."

"Don't worry, children, you will be able to get to your Dad and get home. Time isn't always linear, and our brain can play tricks on us as to how much time has passed."

"What's linear?" I quickly asked.

"It means time doesn't always go in a straight line. Sometimes it goes from 5 to 7 back to 2. We need to get you back, so that time hasn't really passed at all. And I expect you could do with a little sustenance, too. I know a little girl who's normally always hungry." Phyllis eyed Lois and gave Adi and me a wink.

"I'm hungry, too, as well as that other little girl you know, Phyllis. In fact really need food right now." This was all we needed.

"Okay, Lois, we will get you food as soon as we get back to Dad. He's bound to have something in his bag that you haven't eaten already," I said with my fingers crossed.

I started to take my shoes off to give to Phyllis while I reached into the bag we had brought for my gold dancing shoes. "Will these fit you Phyllis?" I asked, handing them over to her. "I'm only a size two."

"Dear girl, you'd be surprised what an old witch can get her feet into." I watched her wiggle and push her feet into my trainers. They seemed to exude a small sigh and then stretched slightly to accommodate her much longer feet.

"There," she exclaimed, "perfect."

I had taken my socks off and done up my gold shoes, and once again it looked like I had someone else's painted toes.

I surveyed our little group. We looked bedraggled and worn out, especially Phyllis, who, in spite of her messy attire, looked much happier and more like her sparky self.

"Now, I won't interfere, dear. Frances always tells me I get things wrong by being too effusive with my suggestions, so this time I will leave it to you. You somehow managed to get here and find me, so I know you will know what to do. I'll just quietly hum a tune, if it's all the same to you."

Adi looked up above his head. I saw him glance to Phyllis and then he whispered, "Rosemary, what the hell is she singing. What's she done?"

I, too, looked up and could see the ceiling very slowly starting to move downwards toward us. It was so slow, you could almost be fooled into thinking that nothing was happening. "Phyllis," I shouted, "stop singing. You're making the ceiling move down. It's going to crush us."

But Phyllis had seemed not to hear me. She was in her own little world, her high-pitched, reedy voice killing the tune, yet we could clearly see the joy on her face. I turned to Adi, my anxiety rising.

"Scour the room. There will be a way out. We will find it, trust me."

25

A BELCH IN TIME

Phyllis was now singing her heart out, a catchy number that we all knew. Lois was singing along, too, and dancing with Bea. Meanwhile, Adi and I were on opposite sides of the room, frantically feeling our way over every inch of the wall to find a way out

I gave the ceiling a glance every few seconds, watching with nervous agitation at it inching towards us. Then I remembered Phyllis saying earlier about sometimes having to trust people or situations that they will all turn out for the best. After all, wasn't it just what I'd said to Adi? How could I expect him to trust me if I didn't trust myself?

I will have faith, I thought. *I will, I will, I will.*

I was whispering this mantra under my breath, when out of the corner of my eye, I noticed what looked like a door handle on the left-hand side wall. It was difficult to be sure, as the newspaper cuttings were masking it fully. I headed in that direction and there, in the middle of the wall, slightly obscured by the headline "Handel's Undiscovered Genius: The Prequel to the Water Music", I could plainly see a round, black doorknob.

"Hey, everyone!" I shouted excitedly. "I think I've found a way out. There's a doorknob here. Gather round, so we can quickly get through it together if it opens the door."

Lois didn't need asking twice. She literally sprang over to the area I was standing. "Rosie, let me open the door. Please, can I do it?"

"Yes, but only when I say go, okay?"

She nodded, pleased she was allowed this momentous responsibility.

Once we had all gathered, intrepid and quiet, I gave the command:

"Go, Lois!"

She put her grubby little hand on to the doorknob and twisted. There was a creaky noise followed by a long, loud fart noise.

"Lois!"

"It wasn't me," she said crossly. "It was the door."

"Actually, it really was the door. I'm pretty sure of that," Adi said seriously.

"Come on then, push the door open."

Lois pushed and then stepped back slightly for me to take the lead, which I wasn't that thrilled about. It's always nerve-wracking going first, though I was kind of getting used to not having any expectations. It was always better that way, to expect the unexpected.

As usual, when going through strange doors that seem to magically appear, we found ourselves in darkness. I heard the click of the door shutting behind me.

"Are we all through?" I called behind me.

"Yes," came the unified responses of Adi, Lois, and Phyllis.

"It's terribly dark in here, children, isn't it?" Phyllis said, stating the obvious.

SAMANTHA GILES

I really hate the dark, but it was incredibly empowering to realise that, despite this fear, I was able to still function and be brave — much braver than I ever thought possible before this adventure began. "Fortune favours the brave" was another one of my mum's favourite sayings, and I can sort of see why now. Nobody ever won a prize by sitting on their backside, did they? We were in a dark place right now, and I wasn't sure what to do except move forward.

So I did.

"Owwwwww!" I exclaimed. "That really hurt."

"What is it, Rosemary?" Adi asked. I could hear the worry mixed with anxiety in his voice.

"Are you okay, Rosie?" came Lois' voice.

"Have we encountered an impasse?" Phyllis queried.

"I'm okay, but it really hurt my nose and head. I've bumped into something, but it's pitch black, so I'm having to feel my way."

Adi made his way to the side of me and grabbed my arm, using his other to do as I was doing, feeling in front of us.

"It feels like a wall," he whispered to me. "Let's not panic the others until we've found a way out of here."

"Not easy in the dark," I whispered back.

"We could always light one of the other—"

"No," I interrupted him, "we can't keep wasting time like that. We'll end up in India. I thought we agreed you would wait to use that when the time was right."

"Yeah, I know, but Rosemary, if we can't find a way out of here, then we'll be forced to use one of the candles."

I really didn't want to think of that. Instead, I concentrated on feeling in front of me for anything that might lead us out of this black hole. All I could feel was smooth wall; there were no lumps, bumps or any kind of change in its surface that might give us a clue how to get out. I was starting to feel more than a bit panicky.

I tried to calm my breathing. After all, we had been in awful scrapes before, like after the energy raising when everyone and everything had disappeared. I had to trust that the shoes had brought us through one door and would take us out eventually.

All at once, the worst smell in the world accosted my nose. It was literally like someone's bottom had exploded. "That smells worse than a rabbit's hutch," my dad would say.

I pulled my shirt over my nose and, as loudly as I could, said, "Lois, is that you?"

"No, it was Bea," came her usual reply.

"Good lord!" Phyllis exclaimed. "I've been to many places in my lifetime, but I've never encountered a smell as bad as that. That really is a Get Out of Jail Free card, young lady."

As soon as Phyllis had uttered those words, the strangest thing happened.

We were thrown out of our black space and into the corridor of the London TV studios. I can only describe it as being belched out. As we all heard a long, loud guttural sound, we were simultaneously catapulted through the air by a warm breeze, followed by the smell of cheesy crisps, and we landed on our feet unharmed.

"Well, I've never been so insulted in my life," Phyllis remarked, brushing down her clothes. "What a way to ask guests to leave!"

"Phyllis, we're out of whatever that was. This is a good thing, isn't it? Well done, Lois, you actually farted at the right time there. I think it was so lethal that wherever we were trapped didn't want to accommodate us any further."

"I really must ask Wolfie about this. I've never come across anything quite so strange before. I can only think it must have been a throat hole. Perhaps one has to go to a throat hole once you've left the worm hole. Who knows?" She shrugged. "Now, I must leave you shortly."

"Phyllis, no," Lois pleaded, "How are we going to find Daddy? And we've only just found you. Don't go yet."

"My dear child, I'd love to stay, but I need to get my glasses fixed and buy some new pumps. I want to look my best when I make my grand entrance and surprise Wolfie, Frances, and Uncle Vic."

I could see Lois was about to dissolve into tears, when suddenly I saw my dad coming towards us, waving. He broke into a jog.

"Daddy!" I ran towards him.

I could hear Lois following me at a run, also shouting. "Daddy, where have you been? I've missed you!"

We leapt into each other's arms. Never had I been so delighted to see my dad, who was at last without his shadow! There was no sign of it clinging to his feet anymore. Had finding Phyllis made it disappear? His rain-cloud was still above his head, though, dark grey and threatening, but the colours around him were definitely brighter, and the pink hue remained. Dad looked very tired, as though being out for the day and all our adventures had just about finished him off.

"Are you okay, Dad?" I asked tentatively, as Lois was already fumbling around in his pockets to see if she could find any food.

"Yes, I'm okay, Rosie. Are you all okay? We were in the theatre just now watching Mum with Marcus and then there was a bang, and I lost you all. Tell me I didn't dream that, did I?"

"No, Dad we were all there. We slipped into a chest and got a bit a lost, but we're back now." I patted his arm.

"It was most strange. I really can't explain it, Rosie. I literally heard a bang and then next thing, I opened my eyes, and I was back here in the corridor. I tried to find the door we initially went through, but then I heard your voices and walked round and here you all are, so you can't have been lost for long. Maybe we both came out different exits."

"Dad, you've got to go on Tuesday to Mum's press night. You've got to stop Marcus from kissing her, please!" I blurted out, worrying that my dad might put the events down to his imagination or a dream or something.

"I have every intention of going to see Mum's play, don't worry about that. And I will deal with that little prat if necessary, too," Dad said stiffly. "Now, Lois, are you pleased to see me or are you just hoping for some food?"

"Some food please, Daddy." Slight pause. "I mean both!"

Dad smiled and pulled out a squashed sausage roll from his inside pocket and handed it to Lois, who fell on it as if she hadn't seen food for days.

"Right, come on, troops. Time to get out of here and get our train."

I turned back to Adi and Phyllis, and, of course, I should have guessed.

Phyllis had gone.

26

WHAT IF?

I remember very little about our train journey home. I just about remember falling into bed and feeling sleep envelope me like a warm hug on a cold day. My dreams were thankfully unremarkable, and I woke on Sunday not knowing where I was, what day it was, or even what my own name was.

I crept quietly into my parents' room and was relieved to see my mum's familiar red hair splayed out on her pillow, and my dad's great bulk hidden almost entirely underneath the covers like a giant mole. The fact that we had completed our mission to find Phyllis felt like a huge anti-climax. Where was the welcome home committee? Where was the big box of chocolates waiting to be opened and hungrily devoured?

It felt like a very ordinary Sunday morning.

I went downstairs.

I fed the cats.

Lois appeared.

She farted and hogged the armchair.

Mum came down, doing lots of yawning.

Dad stayed in bed.

I had to keep pinching myself that we weren't in some peculiar time loop again. Was something extraordinary about to happen? Had yesterday really occurred, or was it all a very bizarre dream?

"How was *Dancing Divas* girls?" Mum asked as she made herself a cup of coffee.

So that bit was real then.

"It was amazing," I replied.

"Well, that's great. So why the long faces today? You look like you've lost a pound and found a penny."

I wanted to tell her we'd found Phyllis, but to be honest I wasn't sure whether the whole thing had been a dream. And if she knew *we'd* found Phyllis, then she'd be cross because she'd know we'd been through the wall.

"Just a bit tired that's all, Mum."

Mum studied my face with her serious expression.

"And how was Dad? Was he okay with you all?"

"Dad was actually really cool," Lois piped up, her eyes not leaving the TV screen.

"Well, that's wonderful," Mum continued. I could hear the surprise in her voice.

"I think it might have worn him out, though. We got a bit lost leaving the TV studios last night," I added mysteriously, looking sideways at my mum.

"Well, that doesn't surprise me. If the exit signs point left, your father will always go right. I'm amazed, to be honest, you all got home in one piece. Did you have food and everything? Did Dad make sure Adi got home safely?" She clearly didn't know about Phyllis.

"Yeah, yeah," I replied sullenly. "Why isn't Dad up?"

"He's shattered, Rosie. I think the tablets he's on make him tired, and though he is getting better, it's slow, and days like yesterday tend to knock you back a bit. He might be in bed for a few days, darling."

"No!" I shrieked. "He's got to go back to work tomorrow, and then he's got to go to your press night on Tuesday. He can't miss that," I said with urgency, my eyes filling up with tears at the thought of Dad not being there to intercept Marcus.

"Hey, Rosie, what's wrong? It doesn't matter if Dad misses Tuesday night. He can come any other night. We are running for three weeks. I'd rather he came when he felt up to it." Mum was stroking my arm. I tugged it away petulantly.

"Well, he IS up to it. He was fine yesterday. And anyway, where were you on Friday night? You should have been here, Mum. You weren't here. If you weren't doing this stupid play, you'd have been here. I hate this play. I hate it. And I hate Marcus for taking you away from us, and I hate you!"

I ran out of the kitchen and up the stairs to my room. I shut the door and flung myself on my bed and cried as quietly as I could. Why did I feel so miserable today? I just wanted everything to be good and everyone to be happy, and there was Dad, in bed, unable to get up. I just couldn't understand how he could have been okay yesterday and then not today. It didn't seem fair. We achieved something amazing yesterday, didn't we?

Then I remembered the scenarios that Phyllis had shown us in The Room of Free Will that were in the future, waiting to happen. Until Mum and Dad re-affirmed their love for each other, Mal Vine and the No-Laws would continue to have power. Phyllis said they thrived on sadness and hate, so love would diminish them. We were relying on Dad going on Tuesday and making things right between him and Mum before the No-Laws would finally be defeated. We just had to wait.

There was a faint knock at my door.

"Rosie, it's Mum. Can I come in, please?"

"Mmmm," I replied noncommittally.

Mum crept in and closed the door behind her. I turned away from her on my bed and hoped she wouldn't see that I had been crying.

"Darling, I'm sorry I wasn't here the other night. I should have phoned earlier, so I could speak to you both. It's very tiring doing your technical rehearsals and then having an audience in for the first time. Nerves use up lots of energy. But you must never think I've abandoned you all! Marcus hasn't taken me away. It's the play. It's only work, but we all have to work. You've been such a lucky girl because Mummy hasn't really had much work, so I've always been around at home whenever you need me. But darling, I *need* to work too, sometimes. It makes me feel alive."

I chewed my lip.

"You're a creative person, too, so when you get older, you will understand that need that you have to fulfil. If you're not allowed to be creative, it feels like a little part of you is dying inside. This job has made me come alive again, so even though I've hated not being able to be here as much for you all, I think it's helped to make me a better Mummy. Do you understand what I mean, darling?"

"Sort of."

"We have to be patient with Daddy. When you're poorly like him, it can take a while to be back to normal. I know it's hard to be patient when someone is ill in their mind. It's not like a broken leg, which you can see."

"I *can* see his illness." It had come out of my mouth before I had really thought what I was saying.

"What do you mean?"

"No, nothing. I just mean I can see when he's poorly."

Mum stroked my hair gently. "You can tell me, Rosie. I might understand, you know."

I paused, wondering anxiously whether telling a grown up might make it go away. But this was *my mum*, not just any adult. I took a deep breath. "I see colours around people, and they change according to how they are feeling, and Dad has a raincloud above his head when he's feeling poorly."

"I wondered if you had inherited that gift," Mum whispered.

I looked up, startled. "What do you mean?"

Mum smiled at me conspiratorially. "When I was a little girl, Rosie, I could see colours around people, too."

"Really?"

She nodded.

"What about now?" I asked.

She shook her head sadly. "It all stopped around the time I became a teenager. I can't pinpoint the exact moment it went away, just one day I realised I wasn't seeing colours anymore." She squeezed my arm. "Don't see it as a burden, darling. It's a wonderful gift to have, and it's part of what makes you unique."

I smiled at my mum, grateful for her understanding, as well as appreciating the fact I could quietly enjoy watching swirls of pink vibrating out from around her body.

We sat there for a few moments in silence, her arms around me, me taking in the comforting smell of her: Chanel Number 19 mixed with her body lotion, which is slightly woody and lemony.

"Let's have a really lazy day today and make pizzas and popcorn and watch a film. After Tuesday, I will only have to go into work in the evenings, so I will be able to pick you up from school."

I looked my mum in the eye. "I don't hate you, Mum. Sorry."

"No harm done," she replied as she stood up from the bed and left the room.

Dad didn't go to work the next day, so there were no Aunts, no Uncle Vic, and no Mr Foggerty again. I was beginning to think they had deserted us, and the lonely empty feeling in my tummy remained.

To make matters worse, Adi wasn't in school either on Monday, which was so unusual for him. Mae and Gloria kept questioning me about why I was so quiet and if I wanted to meet up later online. It was hard to be enthusiastic about anything. Then I noticed Sarah Jane wasn't in either, and I felt guilty again for feeling so morose myself.

I started to feel that if Sarah Jane's mum was okay, then my family would be okay, too. One depended on the other. I was so caught up in my thoughts and anxiety, I had barely noticed my dad.

"Are you alright, Rosie? You're very quiet."

I looked at Dad properly for the first time since Sunday morning when he'd been huddled up in bed. His shadow had gone, and his cloud was just grey. At least that was something. The colours around his legs were muddy but got brighter as you went up his body. Around his chest was a pink hue. I didn't really know what that meant, but it felt okay. It didn't feel bad.

"I'm fine, Dad," I sighed.

"That's a big sigh from a little girl. Do you want a piggyback?"

"Dad!" I said half embarrassed. "I'm too big for piggybacks."

"I'm not! I'm not!" came the voice from below.

"Can I have a piggyback please, Daddy?" Lois simpered.

"Come on then, madam. But no farting on my back, thank you."

Lois giggled.

This was definitely better, but things still didn't feel quite right.

I woke up the next day missing Frances and Phyllis even more and wondering what had become of Hecate. There was nothing to stop me going back through the wall myself, was there? The thought of seeing all my friends again on the other side seemed to buoy me up, and I got ready for school feeling much more positive.

Dad was also up and dressed and ready to get his train to work — AND he was going to Mum's press night tonight!

I was so thrilled about this, I didn't even mind that Lois hogged the rocking chair and had the remote control at breakfast. I was hoping this would mean Frances might be collecting us from school, so we would see them all, at last.

As we arrived at the school gates, my mood was further enhanced. There in the playground, kissing Sarah Jane and Sasha goodbye, was their mum. She looked thin and had very big eyes, but she was draped in a silvery-blue light, which shimmered off her shoulders and moved around her like a living thing. It had little tongues that flickered like a snake's towards people if they stood too close to her or if someone else's energy colour field was dark and muddy.

I approached Sarah Jane.

"Hey, your mum's back!" I exclaimed.

"Yes," she answered quietly, but with a smile that seemed to reach her boots.

I brushed her arm with my hand.

"I'm really glad, Sarah Jane."

I then saw Adi running down the slope towards the playground, just before the gate was locked. He was out of breath, his hair flying everywhere, his glasses bouncing about on his nose ready to plunge on to the ground at any moment. I grinned to myself and walked towards him. He looked happy and carefree.

"Adi, where were you yesterday?"

He took a long pause, on purpose I think, before he answered me. Then he raised himself up, puffed out his chest a little, moved his glasses back up his nose in one quick gesture, and said nonchalantly, "Mumbai."

"Mumbai, India?" I asked him, flabbergasted.

"Yup," he smirked.

I grabbed him by the arm impatiently.

"Well come on, tell me everything! Obviously, you burned the candle then?"

"I certainly did."

"Adi, stop acting like a smooth TV cop and tell me about it!"

"Okay," he grinned, back to the Adi of old, "I'll tell you all later. Let's just say, I was there for Diwali and, freaky as it may sound, my parents are planning to take us there next year to celebrate, so I reckon I was seeing the future."

I smiled to myself and hoped that maybe tonight one of the Aunts would be picking us up from school.

They didn't.

As the bell rung, I stood outside in the playground waiting for someone to collect us. I couldn't play that old trick to Mr Bobbin of saying I could see our Aunt, as I was one of the last to head out of the classroom, because stupid Dan had put my coat in his locker for a laugh. Lois' teacher led her up towards me and Mr Bobbin, who took charge immediately, as if it was the most exciting thing that had happened to him all day.

"Right, young ladies, let's pop along to the office and ring your mum, shall we?"

"Mum's at work at the theatre, and Dad's working in Manchester," I told him with a sigh. It wasn't worth suggesting he call our house. We hadn't seen any of our houseguests for days.

We reached the office. Lois was whispering to me constantly,

"Where are we going, Rosie? I'm hungry. Are we going to Mr Bobbin's house?"

I glared at her. "The office, oh dear, and no."

I suppose I was being a bit harsh on her, so I held her hand and gave it a squeeze.

"Mum's forgotten to arrange anyone to pick us up, so Mr Bobbin is taking us to the office to phone someone," I explained.

"Ohhhhhh," she replied.

Mrs Sykes was peering over her huge glasses at us as we approached.

"Ah, Mr Bobbin, I thought it might be you with the two Pellow girls. Mum's just phoned to say Jonathan and Paloma will meet you both at home, if Mr Bobbin would be so kind as to drop you off. Is that okay, Mr Bobbin?"

"Yes, no problem, Mrs Sykes." Mr Bobbin motioned for

us to wait in reception while he gathered his things up and then would take us to his car.

"Paloma and Jonathan?" Lois whispered loudly. "Oh goody!"

I was shocked that Mum had asked them to meet us at home. She must know about us having gone through the wall, otherwise how would she know that we knew them? Mrs Sykes eyed us sympathetically, as if we were Orphan Annies.

"I love Paloma," came the next words of wisdom out of Lois' mouth.

"Good," I said through gritted teeth. I was anxious to get home to find out what was going on.

At last, we followed a spritely Mr Bobbin through the car park to his car, and we both sedately placed ourselves in the back of his Fiat 500.

The journey was silent, apart from some interesting "holding my breath" faces due to the inevitable odours that filled the car courtesy of my sister. I watched Mr Bobbin try to open his window and gasp at the fresh (cold) air that blew into the car whilst simultaneously trying to look nonchalant.

"Is it this one, girls?" he asked, pointing to our house.

"Yep," I replied, as he missed the break and accelerated up on to the kerb, narrowly missing the lamppost.

"Right, off you go, and I'll just sit here and check there's someone at home to let you in."

I tentatively ding-donged, wondering what on earth Mr Bobbin would do at the sight of a giant owl opening the front door. I turned, smiled at him, and waved a sort of "it's okay, you can go now" wave.

He didn't move. He wasn't going anywhere until he was certain a grown-up was there at our house.

I turned back to the door, wondering what we would do next.

All of a sudden, the door opened widely. I turned to look at Mr Bobbin. He was looking ahead of me and above me, as if his eyes were fixed on someone taller than me. He gave the thumbs up and waved at this someone and drove off. I turned back to our house. There was no one there. Who had Mr Bobbin given his thumbs up to?

Lois and I went into the house and shut the door.

"In here, girls," came the familiar voice from the kitchen.

There was Jonathan, holding a tray of delicious-smelling cookies with a fabulous new looking apron on that said:

I Don't Give a Hoot.

27

A NEW BROOM SWEEPS CLEAN

"Jonathan!"

"Paloma!"

We both shouted in unison. Jonathan dropped the cookies on the hob and engulfed me in his feathery arms, whilst Lois seemed to be air kissing a chirruping Paloma, who was hovering directly in front of her face, receiving the air kisses with delight.

"So, did Mum really ask you to be here for us today?" I asked whilst snuggling into Jonathan's downy chest.

"She absolutely did. I think you'll find your mother has been fully briefed on all events now." He winked at me. "Now hurry up and get changed, we've got a party to go to!"

"A party?" Lois interrupted, suddenly looking rather pleased with herself. "Can I come? Can Bea?"

"You can bring whomever you like, my dears. As soon as Adi is here, we will go."

"Is Phyllis back now then, for definite? When Dad reappeared at the TV studios, she disappeared again, and we haven't seen anybody since. I've really missed you all."

"Yes, Phyllis is back, trying to organise the world as

247

usual, and Hecate has ordered that tonight we have a grand celebration to welcome her back and to thank you all for your wonderful work."

"Does this mean the No-Laws have been stopped now? They won't be trying to cause any more harm, will they?" I asked nervously.

Jonathan went to open his beak and then tapped the side of it with his freshly painted talons (they were pale orange this time). "All in good time. Let's wait and see what Hecate has to say, shall we? Now, pop off upstairs, and get yourselves in party clothes."

"One more thing, Jonathan," I added.

"Mmmmm?" he answered, pausing from flicking out still-warm, delicious-looking cookies on to a plate.

"Don't ever say 'pop off' when Lois is around," I giggled, running out of the kitchen.

We emerged five minutes later in our party clothes.

"Now, you two girls have a cookie, and Paloma and I will see you on the other side! Don't be long." Jonathan was already untying his apron as he strode out of the kitchen with Paloma fluttering all around him.

"When should we come, then?" I called anxiously after him.

"When Adi arrives," came the reply. "I must change my apron," were the last faded words I heard before the house became empty once more.

Moments later, the doorbell rang, and I rushed to let Adi in.

"How did you know to come over, Adi?" I still couldn't quite believe he was here.

Adi faltered. "I have no idea. I just felt really strongly that I ought to. Have I done the right thing?" he asked anxiously.

"Did you bring your school jumper with the pentagram on it?"

"Obvs." Adi unzipped his anorak and showed me he was wearing his jumper.

"Then you've absolutely done the right thing! Come on, we've got a party to go to." I grinned, taking him and Lois by the arm.

We were all very silent as Adi used a pebble to find the point where gravity changed. I don't know if the quiet was out of nerves, or excitement, or maybe an underlying premonition that this might be the last time we visited this other world. As the pebble hovered, we all said in unison:

"Aradia. Aradia. Aradia."

The familiar whooshing sound overwhelmed us. Lois put her hands over her ears, as it was so loud. I wondered if something had gone wrong and closed my eyes, yet when I opened them, we were standing in the same familiar foyer with its polished, wooden walls and high reception desk. Aradia was dressed in a very smart, scarlet woollen coat. She wore dark glasses and had a fascinator in her long dark hair. There were suitcases stacked in front of the desk.

"Well, I see the three of you are still elllive. You surprise me." She still had that contemptuous attitude when she spoke to us.

She swiped her little scanning machine over the area of our chests where our pentagrams had been placed, and Paloma miraculously appeared from a corner in the ceiling and did her usual swooping around us and between our legs. With a squawk, Paloma started to head off down the long corridor once again.

As we followed her, half-running to keep up, Lois said rather loudly, "Paloma said Aradia's been sacked. She was moonlighting."

"Eh?" Adi questioned, looking at Lois.

"It means working in the moonlight, I think," Lois replied haughtily. "Mind you, I thought that's when all witches worked."

While we followed Paloma down the corridor, I cast my thoughts to who we were going to see at this party. I was getting excited about seeing the Aunts and Uncle Vic and Mr Foggerty — Wolfie, as Phyllis affectionately called him. I wondered whether Hecate would be there and, if so, in what form? At last, we reached the gold door with all the orange and yellow circles on it, incongruous amongst all the muted shades now. I remembered it from the energy raising, so I knew it would lead out into the strange garden.

Paloma tapped her beak three times on the door, then, not before taking a large piece of biscuit from Lois and exchanging "kisses", she flew off. The door opened downwards like a drawbridge, as before, and we stepped into the garden beyond.

There was a collective buzz amongst us, as we could see the lights ahead and hear the noise of a funfair. How exciting! I absolutely loved fairs. They were always best at night, and yet we were never allowed to stay up late enough to go and enjoy them.

"Come on, everyone, let's explore," I said to the others.

They didn't need any encouragement. The three of us started to run towards the lights, desperate to see what was available. We could already see a huge Ferris wheel turning slowly against the black night sky. As we got closer to the fair, the crowds increased.

There were people of all ages, and they eyed us strangely, as if we were trespassing on their territory. As we approached the fair, we could see stalls of all varieties: a coconut shy, Hook-A-Duck, and some old-fashioned, shooting-type ones, where you shot at the moving target and won prizes if you hit them.

There was a massive carousel which, instead of having horses to ride, had gigantic cats, ranging from domestic to all manner of big cats: lions, tigers, leopards, jaguars. There was a Wurlitzer that looked like it would make you throw up, gauging by all the screams coming from those riding on it. There was this hilarious strength-test machine, which featured a picture of a man in shorts flexing his huge muscles. You had to hit the buzzer on the floor with a mallet, and if you hit it hard enough, it rang a bell. However, with this machine, if you managed to ring the bell, the man on the picture behind came alive and picked you up in the air with his hands, threw you up far into the sky, and then caught you before placing you gently back on the floor.

We headed over to the refreshment tent, which had different areas for different tastes. There was a pink area for "ladies who like pink gin", a blue area for "drowning your sorrows", a red area for "need an energy pick me up drink", and a purple area with smiley faces on it for "giggles". Instinctively, I felt drawn to that area. It was full of groups of witches. I could tell they were witches because most of them were carrying broomsticks or had cats zig-zagging in between their feet. There weren't any pointy hats or warts or green faces — they weren't *that* kind of witches. These witches just looked like you or me. The only give away was the broomsticks and the familiars.

I heard our lot before I saw them, the unmistakeable sound of Frances laughing at something, with her hooty, infectious laugh. Then I remembered!

What do you call a gaggle of witches?

A giggle.

Phyllis' "joke" — that's why I'd felt inclined to go to this area of the tent. Frances and Phyllis had linked arms and looked rather strange with their opposing statures. Mr Foggerty was looking the most animated I had ever seen him, with neat hair and trimmed beard. Uncle Vic was holding a huge pint glass up to his face and winning, by the look of things. His face was red with exertion, and his head shiny, as he sank the last of his drink and smacked his lips in appreciation.

"Oh my! Oh my! It's ma wee bairns!" Frances shrieked spotting us. "Come 'ere hen, give me a squeeze." She grabbed me with both hands and flung me to her bosom. "I've missed you two girls so much," she whispered to the top of my head.

I looked up at her kind face, which was brimming with tears that threatened to fall.

"We've missed you too, Frances. It's not been the same without you at home."

"Come here, wee Lois. Come and give your Aunty a big smacker."

"You want me to smack you, Frances?" Lois asked innocently.

"No, yer daftie! A smacker on the lips, girl. And mind you, wipe your mouth first. I do not want a wet one, lady!"

Lois giggled and gave Frances one of her best kisses.

Adi was hanging back, slightly awkward.

"Ah, young man," Uncle Vic interjected, having put his pint glass down. "I'm so very happy to see you, too." He shook Adi's hand vigorously and then turned to us all.

"We are all terribly proud of what you three achieved. Aren't we, Foggy? Phyllis?"

Phyllis looked at us all fondly. Her glasses had been fixed, her hair was neatly styled into her usual waves, slightly austere, and she looked calmer and back to the Phyllis of old.

"I wouldn't be here without them, Vic, that's a fact. I think that experience in the wormhole, and then subsequently in the Room of Free Will, almost sent me doo lally."

"What do you mean 'almost?'" Mr Foggerty joked, gently squeezing her shoulder. I'd never seen him make an affectionate gesture before. It was really bizarre, but then I guess we'd never known that he and Phyllis were an item.

Suddenly, we were silenced by the sight of Hecate. She appeared in the sky above the hospitality tent, sitting perfectly still on a broomstick. She was dressed as THE STRANGER once again, in white suit and large brimmed fedora, so her face was not visible. As she spoke, the throng of party goers were silenced, even Lois, who had been chattering away to Frances, went quiet.

"Merry meet!" Hecate cried.

"Merry meet!" came the unified response of the crowd.

"We have welcomed our dear Phyllis back into our fold. We thank our intrepid adventurers, the Pellow sisters and Mr Adjani, for their determination in completing their mission successfully."

I smiled proudly at Adi.

"As I speak, the threat of the No-Laws hangs by a mere thread. In order to fully suspend their actions, Mr Vine must be thrice thwarted. So far, he has been once rebuffed by Miss Pellow, once by Phyllis being found, and if Mr Pellow is successful in impeding his plans, we shall be victorious."

I swallowed nervously. Mr Pellow. Our dad. He was at the press night. Was he going to be able to foil Marcus' seedy plans to throw himself at our mum and therefore repair relations between them? Would love literally conquer all and banish the threat of Mal Vine and his crew? I felt a rush of nerves as Hecate finished her speech.

"We must continue to spread our light. My work here is done for now. I am needed elsewhere. BIWIT is dissolved, as the mission is complete. I bid you farewell, fellow spell weavers. Remember: spread your light. It's the only way to eradicate the darkness. Keep shining. Keep the faith."

With that, she sped off on her broomstick, leaving a trail of white sparkly mist behind her. As she disappeared into the distance, we could see something white floating back down through the air towards us. It was her hat!

Instinctively, we ran toward the clearing where the hat seemed to have landed. Lois got there first.

"It's sand!" she exclaimed.

"What do you mean?"

I put my hand down to touch the brim, and as I did, it disintegrated into the earth like gravy granules.

"She's gone," I said flatly. "It's over. We'll probably never see her again." Adi patted my shoulder as I turned away sadly and started to make my way back to the Aunts.

"Rosemary!" Adi called me back. "Come and look at this."

As the hat had disintegrated, the grains that remained had formed words on the grass:

> You may not see me,
> but I am all around you.
> Live with the shadows behind you
> and the light in front to lead your way.

I couldn't move. I wanted to stay looking at her words. Frances broke the silence.

"Now, come on, folks," she said. "This is a wee celebration. Let's go out and celebrate! There's so many rides to go on, and I've been waiting for my three favourite little people to take me on the big wheel!"

How could I celebrate when we still didn't know whether Dad had managed to make things right between him and Mum?

"Yay!" Lois cheered, oblivious to my anxiety, and we all made our way out of the tent and towards the big wheel. "Can we go on the carousel first, pleeeease?" Lois begged.

"We can go on whatever you want, darlin'," Frances replied, skipping along holding Lois' hand.

"Oh, dear," Phyllis remarked to Mr Foggerty. "I do hope she's careful on that. Do you think Frances should tell them to choose the cats that aren't scratching?"

"I'm sure they'll be fine, dear."

I didn't know what they were talking about until we were merrily going round, and I suddenly felt something bite me on my arm. I looked down and to my horror saw these huge creatures the size of boiled eggs crawling all over the neck of my cat. They were fleas!

"Urghhhh! Get off!" I shouted, smacking the creatures off of my skin whilst still trying to hold on.

Luckily for us all, the ride came to a stop, and me and Uncle Vic leapt off of our cats. My arms had come up in red welts that were incredibly itchy. Phyllis rummaged in her bag and found some soothing balm, which she rubbed on to our bites, making them immediately feel better.

Finally, we all did the big wheel, which was magnificent. Me, Adi, Phyllis, and Mr Foggerty were in one car, and Frances, Lois, and Uncle Vic in another. As we reached the top of the wheel, the view was simply stunning. Although it was night, there were so many stars lighting up the sky and, somehow, they seemed like beacons of hope amidst the darkness.

The moon was full, so it was big and yellow and looked as if it was watching over us and guarding us all. Suddenly, a shadow cast itself over the moon's face. It passed slowly over its surface, like someone drawing a curtain over it. As the blackness passed over, everything went quiet.

It was as if we were all holding our breath.

The air seemed to chill. The lights seemed to dim. There was silence.

We were all awestruck, watching this blackness pass across the moon.

After a few minutes, the moon was completely eclipsed in darkness. It was eerie, particularly as our car was swaying gently at the top of the big wheel. I wondered what was going to happen next.

I was half aware that Adi had taken my hand, and I felt glad of the comfort. As much as this place was full of fun and excitement, it was equally uncomfortable, too. I clearly felt my insignificance, my vulnerability, and I longed to be home in bed knowing my parents were next door and my sister in her room.

There was a collective exhale as the shadow passed and the moon was bright once again. The atmosphere went back to normal. I could hear music, and the wheel began to turn again. I felt a peculiar sense of calm.

"What happened?" I asked Phyllis breathlessly.

Her eyes were glistening, but she looked relieved.

"It was a total lunar eclipse, dear." She took my hand. "It's over. Mal Vine and his mob have been vanquished."

"How do you know?" I whispered, hoping that I would never have to see that man saluting me again.

"Momentarily, we were in darkness, Rosie, as Mal Vine

made his last attempt to destroy love. But as he was finally defeated, the shadow passed by, and we can once again bask in the light of the moon," she replied, glancing at Mr Foggerty with a smile.

Perhaps she was right. The party certainly seemed to take on a new lease of life. Frances dragged us back over to the hospitality tents after we got off the wheel.

"Come on, wee bairns, let's go and get something to eat. You must be starving."

It was like a paradise to Lois. We saw areas marked "teeny bit hungry", "hungry", "stomach thinks throat's been cut", "sweet tooth", and "eyes bigger than belly".

I didn't feel like eating. I was still thinking about Hecate's parting words to us. If we all concentrate on the light to lead our way, we will not get lost in the darkness. I suddenly had this overwhelming urge to get home. I needed to see my parents. I needed confirmation that things really were sorted between them.

I moved out of the hospitality tent and closer towards the house. There was a figure looking out of the window — a woman. She wasn't particularly looking at us, just caught up in her own thoughts.

I strained my eyes to get more detail. There was something familiar about the way she held herself, the way she moved her hair behind her ears, her smile as she turned back to look at something or someone behind her.

Mum.

It was our mum looking out of the window!

I turned back to the tent, running now.

"Lois!" I screamed. "Adi! We have to go home now. Mum's home."

The words were out of my mouth before I had even considered them. Was she home or was she here?

I needed to trust my instinct.

I fumbled in my bag to grab my dancing shoes. These would guide us home.

"Not necessary tonight, my dear girl," came the comforting voice of Jonathan.

I looked up and saw that he had indeed changed his apron.

It was now gold and silver with cerise-pink rockets on it and said: *Party Animal*

"I can take you all home. It's no bother."

"Would you please, Jonathan? Thank you so much, for everything." I hugged him.

He seemed surprised by my outburst of emotion and stroked my hair briefly with his feathery wing.

"Dear girl. Let's gather our things, everyone, and hop aboard."

"Come on, Lois, it's time to go," Adi said, gently pulling Lois away from the sausage rolls and mini cheese chunks that she was devouring like a fiend.

The Aunts and Mr Foggerty and Uncle Vic looked on quietly.

Frances came forward. "Come along, wee one. Let's get you home and to your bed. It's been a busy time."

We hugged Phyllis and gave Mr Foggerty a very quick peck on his hairy cheek.

"I'm so glad you're back, Phyllis," I whispered in her ear.

"No one more than I, my dear. No one more than I." She winked and pushed me toward Uncle Vic to say my goodbyes.

He, too, like Mr Foggerty, was slightly embarrassed by all the kissing and hugging that was going on. We were buoyed up with tiredness and emotion.

"No need for fuss now, Rosie, Lois. Hurry along now," he added.

Adi shook hands with everyone whilst Lois was embroiled in Frances' arms.

"I don't want to go," Lois sobbed. "When will we see you again, Frances?"

"Soon, my darlin'." She wiped a tear.

Lois gave a watery smile, and we helped her climb on to Jonathan's back first. Then it was my turn, with Adi bringing up the rear.

He took off as gently as he could. The night air was warm on our faces, in spite of the fact it was mid-November. We flew up over the top of the mansion, over lakes and mountains, until the land became barren and flat.

"Get ready now, folks," Jonathan warned us.

"Lois, hold my hand tight," I said to her, clutching Adi's with my left hand. Jonathan took a sharp dive to the right. As he did so, we were swept off of his back and into that strange whirling plughole, like being in the eye of a hurricane. We swirled about in a fast circle. I thought I was going to be sick, until, all of a sudden, we landed gently in my bedroom.

"Are you okay, Lois?" I asked her gently.

"Yes," she nodded sleepily.

I tucked her up in bed and then went downstairs with Adi to let him out. "Hope you don't get into trouble, Adi. It's 11:30!" I couldn't believe where the time had gone.

"It's okay," he grinned. "I put a bolster in my bed, so Mum will think I'm already fast asleep."

"Sleep well." I grinned at him, marvelling at his ingenuity and feeling so grateful that he had shared this adventure with us. "See you tomorrow."

I crept back up the stairs and sneaked a look into my

parents' room. There was a trail of clothes on the floor. I recognised my mum's shoes and my dad's jeans. Mum was fast asleep, her red hair splayed out on to the pillow, her arm flung over my dad, who was sleeping peacefully with a slight smile on his face.

I rubbed my eyes and looked again. Just above his head was a shining light. The sun was out! It was the dead of night and velvety-dark outside, but inside here, in this dark room, the sun was shining above my dad's head. His cloud had gone. At that moment, I knew it didn't matter how long it had gone for, or even whether it would return, we would deal with that as and when, but for now the sun was shining and the storm had passed.

EPILOGUE

M um never really spoke to us about our adventures through the portal and how we found Phyllis. The day after the party, she just gave me a massive hug and said, "I'm so proud of you, Rosie. But please remember not all adventures are good ones. I'd never forgive myself if I'd put you in danger." She'd looked away quickly, as if she were going to cry.

The sun continued to shine above Dad's head. Mum finished her play and got great reviews, and they both seemed much more at peace with each other.

We didn't see the Aunts or Mr Foggerty or Uncle Vic again. But a week later, we received this postcard from Egypt and hope filled my heart once more:

Darling girls,

Fabulous place for a holiday — surprising how many believers there are over here! Our North West branch is closed temporarily. It turned out Aradia was working as a spy for none other than Mal Vine! Missing you all madly.

We are waiting to see where we are posted next, but never fear, we will be seeing you soon.

Much love,
    Frances, Phyllis, and co
    xxxx

ACKNOWLEDGEMENTS

Writing this book has been a hugely personal journey, and one which I could not have undertaken without the love and support from my friends and family, particularly my wonderful parents, Ann and Robin, who have always done nothing but encourage and champion me. My husband Sean and my girls were the inspiration behind the original idea which grew and grew. I only ever wanted to write a magical story as something to leave behind of myself for my children to keep, so finding firstly a literary agent (thank you for help with this Stephen Gittins) and then a publisher, who both believed in my story has been a dream come true. Silvia, you have been such a source of help and support and I thank you for taking such a punt on me, as well as never giving up on me. Thank you to Sam and Peyton at Agora for making the journey of publication so much fun! Thanks also to Melanie and Amanda for all your hard work and help in terms of PR for this book. Huge thanks to Milly Johnson for her support and encouragement, to my sister Suzanne, for helping out with the kids, to my pretendy sister Nicola, who read an early draft and finally to Sean, whose ear I bent on many an evening out, relaying what my characters were up to next....! I hope you're going to read it now it's in print!

LOVE AGORA BOOKS?

JOIN OUR BOOK CLUB

If you sign up today, you'll get:

1. A free novel from Agora Books
2. Exclusive insights into our books and authors, and the chance to get copies in advance of publication, and
3. The chance to win exclusive prizes in regular competitions

Interested? It takes less than a minute to sign up. You can get your novel and your first newsletter by signing up at www.agorabooks.co

facebook.com/AgoraBooksLDN

twitter.com/agorabooksldn

instagram.com/agorabooksldn

Printed in Great Britain
by Amazon

45597976R00161